familiar

familiar

AN OCCULT MISADVENTURE

CARA NOX

STELLA CHARTA PRESS

FAMILIAR

ISBN 978-1-960379-13-9 (hardcover)
ISBN 978-1-960379-12-2 (paperback)
ISBN 978-1-960379-11-5 (e-book)

For more information on the publisher, including upcoming releases, preorder bonuses, giveaways, and more, visit stellachartapress.com. For more details on the author and their works, visit caranox.com.

For those who are a bit of a mess.

CONTENT WARNINGS

I've attempted to compile a list of prominent warning keywords to the best of my ability. However, since I'm only human, it's very possible I've glossed over something that could be sensitive to you. Please use your own discretion when reading and only continue if you feel safe to do so.

This story contains: Alcohol, anxiety, blood, death, depression, implication of discrimination, mention of drug use, emotional abuse, gore, grief, homophobia (including biphobia), kidnapping, loss, manipulation, murder, parental neglect, physical abuse, mention of suicide, violence, and mention of vomiting.

familiar

1 SPIKED HOT CHOCOLATE

Every night I would go on a coffee run. There's a little place four blocks away that I like—it's got the good shit, especially the hot chocolate when autumn hits and you don't want that bitter garbage from one of those big chains. And honestly, that didn't sound half-bad on a night like tonight.

I shivered as the cold slosh of stagnant rainwater lapped over the soles of my canvas sneakers and seeped into the fabric, threatening to go for my socks next. The waxing moon's reflection warped and jittered in the puddles as I bounced around the mostly dry splotches of pavement. A sneeze tickled my nose, adding insult to the numbing chill that tended to blow up into a fever for me like clockwork every October. That usually turned into a marathon of being told to man up and chug cough medicine while still looking like death warmed over.

Fortunately, the cure to stave off that cold was just up ahead: the red neon sign with a simple steaming cup over the word OPEN in all caps. The decorative wood exterior was painted a deep ruby to match, but it'd clearly been a while, seeing how flecks of the original blue peeked through the chipped parts.

Apartment balconies across the street touted little jack-o-lanterns and strings of light-up ghosts. Paper bats were pasted in windows and sliding doors. In contrast, the couple stories above the coffee shop stood bare, all the glass blacked out with blinds and curtains. The only piece of décor I could make out was the single potted plant in the protruding bay window: a limp, sad, browning little thing sharing its soil with a printed out smiley face mounted on an ice-pop stick.

The door to *The Crown Café* jingled as I pulled it open and pushed back my hood. Soft white bulbs glowed in the pendant lights over each table, tossing shadows through the room whenever a soul moved, so I jolted when one halted next to me. The girl's liquid-caramel irises twinkled with joy as she adjusted her maroon apron. "Welcome back, Jules."

"Hey, Allie," I said, not even needing to check the name tag on her chest, which was covered in chubby cat stickers above a pin with 'SHE/HER' stamped onto it. I'd probably seen them a hundred times by now, but I'd always managed to catch a new addition. I smirked and tapped the little black cat with an arched back. "You're going to run out of room for your name soon."

She rolled her eyes and nudged up her tortoiseshell glasses. "I've still got plenty of space before I get my new one next week." She folded her arms over her chest, beaming. "I'm a manager now."

"Seriously? Congrats! That's awesome!" I grinned and tucked my hands into my hoodie pockets, rocking back on my heels. I'll be real, I was a little disappointed that my favorite barista just got an upgrade and now I'd have to go through the trouble of saying something other than, 'I'll have the usual' on most nights. "So… who's your replacement?"

Maybe I shouldn't have dared to steal a glance over at the counter before she said anything. Because the second I did, my heart did that horrible thing where it felt like I was headed straight for a panic attack.

"That would be Saint," she chimed in. I couldn't tell whether she realized I was trying to keep myself upright over the clean-cut, black-haired twenty-something taking inventory of the pastry case. "He's been training for the past couple of weeks with me and Tyler."

I'd already figured that out during the last several visits when Mr. Dashing in his long-sleeved black tee-shirt had been shadowing the other nightshift worker. I'd been quietly admiring him at a comfortable distance during that time, hoping that I'd get to talk to him and that I'd also never have to. Fuck me, of course I didn't have the choice now but to go make a fool of myself by riding that line of workplace harassment and embarrassing myself to the point of finding a new caffeine dealer.

"O-oh," I forced out, praying she didn't hear me trying to clear my throat.

"Don't worry," she said, patting my shoulder. "He came from another café up north. He knows what he's doing. I normally wouldn't drop new hires into the fire, but it's also the night shift." She shrugged and smirked. "A nice insomniac haven. Judging by your habits, you'd fit right in with the rest of us if you ever wanted to apply."

"Er, yeah. I'll think about it," I finally answered, my mind clearly on other things.

Okay, it was on Saint. Sue me.

I instinctively reached for my mess of wavy chestnut locks and shook it out with a nervous laugh. God, I wished I had a mirror then to make sure Saint didn't see me looking like I'd rolled out of bed at noon. I mean, I *had*, but I didn't want *him* to know that. I probably needed it cut again since it was starting to cover the tops of my ears.

"I should probably get my order in," I said, jabbing a thumb in Saint's direction as I shot Allie one final, pained smile. "You'll still be around, right?"

"Yep! Just doing a lot more backroom and stock counting stuff unless it miraculously gets super busy one night."

"Great. Thanks, Allie."

"Mm-hm!" She started through the tables, half-pointing at each one and mouthing words I couldn't quite catch before she pushed the door open to the back.

Which left me alone. In the coffee shop. With Saint.

I forced myself to step forward, taking it one glittery, black diamond-angled tile at a time. Saint glanced up when I was about a yard away from the counter, and I almost turned on my heel and ran. Admittedly, my gay-dar is horrible. And seeing how this guy was drop-dead gorgeous in a light-goth sort of way gave me the tiniest glimmer of hope, but that could also simply be from the fact that he has a sense of style. Unlike me with my seam-ripped sweatshirt, dirty shoelaces, and jeans absolutely obliterated at the heels because I'm fucking five-foot-five.

His coal eyes snapped to mine before that courteous, ever-so-slight customer service smile slid onto his face. "What can I get you?"

"I, uh, hope you're ready," I said, fidgeting with my phone as I pulled it out of my pocket, "because it's a bit of a list."

"Shoot."

I sucked in a breath and tapped open the notes app. "All right. I need one vanilla bean crème frap with blended biscotti, one iced chai latte with macadamia syrup, one double-shot espresso on ice, one double-shot hot, one americano, and one hot chocolate with a pump of caramel."

I wanted to take back the last one, immediately feeling like a child ordering a hot cocoa in the midst of the rest of the adult drinks. It did cross my mind to maybe dump a little apple liqueur into it when I got home.

Saint tapped a few more spots on the register.

"You… need me to repeat any of that?"

"Nope," he said, flashing me a confident smirk. "Cash or credit?"

I blinked. Damn he was fast. "C-credit."

He tapped one last button and turned to the machine as I dropped my phone to the NFC pad.

"This is a lot of coffee for an order at 9:30PM," Saint said over his shoulder. "You hosting a late-night study group?"

I rubbed my hands together, slowly pushing the fraying fabric covering the heels of my palms a little further upward. "I'm actually, um… sort of an admin assistant, I guess? My office works nights, so…"

"Oh, yeah? What do you all do?"

"Security work."

"Ah," Saint said, the epiphany sounding clipped over the

thudding of my heart. "So you're the guy Allie mentioned is a regular? I don't think she ever told me your name."

Calm down. It's just your name. Don't think about how badly you want to throw up right now because you've been mentally stalking him for the past two weeks.

"Jules," I said, trying—and likely failing—to sound casual. "I'm Saint."

"I know—" What the fuck, Jules. You *know?* That's creepy as hell. "I know because Allie told me when I came in a few minutes ago. She's, um, the one who usually handled the laundry list of coffee before." Cue my nervous laugh.

But Saint didn't seem fazed by the fumble if he noticed it. Instead, his head bobbed as he flipped on another machine. "So which one's yours?"

Yeah, I regretted that hot chocolate now. Really, really regretted it.

"Erm... the, um... last one." My face suddenly felt super hot. My dad always said that you stopped giving a shit about what other people thought the older you got, but I guess twenty-one wasn't quite old enough for that. "N-normally I get like a frap or a regular black coffee, but—"

"A hot chocolate does sound pretty good right now," Saint said, popping the lid onto one of the finished cups. "I can't blame you for that." He slid the fluffy frap onto the counter, and my pulse quickened. Black nail polish.

Okay, so Saint had to file in somewhere in the alphabet mafia, which meant I wasn't totally out of luck here. And he didn't tease me for the drink, so... maybe I could risk making a move?

He started capping the rest of the drinks and snapped open a brown paper bag, setting it next to them. The way he managed to unfold the thin cardboard carriers was quick and effortless, just like every other precise, graceful movement he made.

Or I should just bury that dream in the graveyard with the others before I make an absolute fool of myself.

Saint set the bag in front of him, all the drinks tucked neatly inside except for one. The damned hot chocolate. I tried my best not to shake the hell out of it as I reached to take it from his hand, immediately telling myself to get a grip when our fingers brushed.

The steely glint in those eyes made my world fall away for a fraction of a second before he said, "Text me if you want to hang out sometime."

Text? Wait, what?

My eyes snapped to my cup, soaking in the black marker pen scrawled on there. A phone number. When I looked up again, still pretty much stun-locked, I found Saint smirking at me as he turned around to start cleaning the equipment.

"S-sure thing. Sounds great." I started to hold up my cup like I was toasting at a dinner party and stopped myself, awkwardly taking a couple steps back before I spun around and hurried out the door.

At this point, I wasn't sure if I should laugh, cry, or pass out. Honestly, all of them were pretty viable options. But I was riding cloud nine, sipping on caramel hot chocolate with whipped cream like a kid who just made out like a bandit during trick-or-treat.

Crosswalk signs blinked and beeped with their countdowns like makeshift siren calls from pavement to concrete, all the way up until I stepped foot in the unmarked gap where the dumpster-filled alleyway for a couple apartment complexes let out. I heard the rustling before I saw the figures, which were already in my peripheral vision when my fight-or-flight kicked in—mostly flight. Me and running with liquids didn't go well together, especially when said liquids weren't for *me*. I tried to reason that my legs locked up to save the coffee and stand my ground. Totally not out of fear.

And totally not because my stomach lurched when a human-like roar and hiss sounded in each of my ears. I gripped the hot chocolate cup like my life depended on it and prepared myself to smack head-first onto the blacktop, not unlike a captain going down with his ship. If the coffee order was going to bite the big one, I might as well go with it.

Something grabbed onto the back of my sweatshirt and hoisted me upright again with a familiar bellowing laugh. "Wound tight tonight, aren't you, Jules?"

A tinkling feminine giggle carried on from my other side. My knees might as well have turned to jelly from the relief that washed over me. "H-hey, Zane," I forced out, my head still spinning with the spike of adrenaline.

Zane's hand moved to my shoulder, shaking it with a near death-grip I'd gotten used to from all the times I'd been dragged along to the boardwalk for drinks with him and Iris. The latter of which, playfully shoved him away.

"Sorry, Jules," she chimed. "We were just having a little fun. Nothing spilled, did it?"

She popped into view, radiating a warm glow with her soothing presence that I'd never really been able to explain. Maybe it was her wild black curls or the single dimple that seemed to have a permanent place on her right cheek from her perpetual grin. Iris was just a cozy soul in oversized chevron-patterned knit sweaters and ankle boots.

Her fingertips plucked at the edges of the brown paper bag, pulling back the edges to peer inside. "Looks like it was packed really well—thank goodness!"

Zane snorted. "Please, Ris, I caught him before anything happened." He slapped me on the back, and I stumbled for a brief second before catching my balance. "You want to hit the town with us later? There's a new club that opened up last week, so the line's way less of a nightmare."

I shot him a weary glance. Partying? Not really my thing. He already knew that though, considering the last time he and Iris took me to one—the two of them looking like polar opposites, as per usual, with Zane's near-seven-foot stature and bad-boy leather jacket getup—I had an anxiety attack in the closet of a restroom. I can still smell the mix of cologne and piss whenever I walk by the place, and I feel the overwhelming urge to sprint a half marathon just to escape the memory.

Zane threw back his head and laughed, clearly getting the message that I had zero intention of repeating that experience, especially after he had to pry my slumped over, alcohol-buzzed body off the sticky tile. He swiped a thumb along his chiseled jaw—damn him—and puffed out his chest. "I guess not all of us can handle the wild life like me."

I had to refrain from letting my eyes roll back into my skull.

Iris slapped his arm away from my back with a scowl. "Don't bully him. At least he has a job, unlike *someone*—"

"Hey! I have a job!"

"Posting gym-bro videos for your one-hundred followers isn't a job! You don't even get any money from it!"

"*Yet.*"

She groaned, and I cleared my throat, holding up my bag. "Maybe we can hang out and do something a little... *calmer* later?" I suggested, hoping I didn't sound too sheepish.

Zane chortled, but Iris patted my shoulder. "Sounds good to me! See you around, Jules." She skipped forward, and Zane gave my other shoulder a soft bump of his elbow, shooting me a friendly smirk before trailing after her.

My heart sank a little as I watched them cross the street up ahead, leaving me there with that little twinge of regret, like I was missing out on something. I made myself take another sip of hot chocolate, savoring the note of caramel, and turned the corner.

A couple blocks later, my arms felt heavy from the delivery, but the duplex was finally in view: a sad, brown-painted thing with one of the original doors bricked up. It managed to stand out and blend in at the same time with how ugly it was versus the lack of Halloween decorations that would've brightened all the original flaws of the modified architecture over time. Little arches over the filled-in windows and the remains of torn down planter boxes did their job of making the place appear less welcome.

I suppose it made sense why the doorbell was rarely used.

I jogged up the steps and set my hot chocolate on the railing to fumble for the keys in my pocket. The storm door squealed open and rammed into my shoulder as I jostled the coffee order to sandwich myself in the entry threshold. When the front door finally swung inward, I didn't even have the chance to quickly retrieve my cup.

"Ugh, *finally!*" The dramatic way I was greeted with my blonde housemate throwing her hands up made me *really* regret not opting to go with Zane and Iris. She stalked forward and wrestled the bag from my grip before carrying it off to the kitchen and staring into its papery depths like the bathroom mirror.

I just stood there like an idiot for a moment until my forehead hurt from creasing it so damn hard. "The fuck?" I whispered, taking a step back and turning around to fight the storm door in an epic battle to retrieve my hot chocolate. *"Thank you, Jules,"* I mumbled. *"You're the best, Jules. You saved my ass, Jules."*

The door scraped the back of my sock on the way inside again, and I bit down on my tongue. It probably wasn't a smart move since the house started to shake with the violent scramble of a dude the size of a linebacker rushing down the stairs. Nothing like the taste of blood to start the night. House: 1; Jules: 0.

Adonis shook aside his shaggy brown hair and stopped in front of me, pointing at my cup. "Is that mine?"

And, out of instinct, I pointed toward the kitchen. "Lux took it."

Now, the difference between Zane and Adonis was that—while they both had that dog-brain status—Zane was a true golden retriever with a bit of a mischievous streak. Adonis, on the other hand, was a rabid chihuahua on steroids that would take my hand off in an instant once he was done pretending to be a half-naked model for a smutty book cover.

"Dammit," he growled. "Lux!" He stomped in after her, his boots thumping against the tile.

"Would you back off, meathead?" she snapped.

"Would *you* take your damn frap and get the fuck out of the kitchen? You don't need to add more condiments to that whipped piece of shit." He made a gagging sound over the pop of the plastic lid and the *whoosh* of fresh, canned whipped cream.

I sighed. At least he wasn't my problem anymore. "Coffee's here," I called out half-heartedly, the wind already taken out of my sails from the vultures. The remaining chorus of acknowledgments echoing through the halls at least let me hone in on the one I was looking for.

I started past the stairs, through the living room, and into the would-be dining room. The owner of the now-office tapped a pen against his lips while he leaned against his desk and stared at a large map of the city pinned up on one of the walls, nearly covering the brick patch where a window has once been. Various tacks, sticky notes, and highlight flags spread outward from downtown.

While Dad didn't spare me a glance, the figure hovering in front of the map with their toned arms crossed over their chest did. The slip of clipped-back blond hair swayed as their head jerked toward the sound of me coming to a stop just beyond the rug.

"Oh, I thought you were Rory," they said, their tone practically a sullen mimicry of Dad's, which I reminded myself likely came from working with him for so long. But it was also a little bit of Charlie's personality: quiet, observant, and commanding. Whether those were traits they'd picked up being in the National Guard or sometime after Dad hired them on, I couldn't remember anymore. All I knew was that my heart sank a little whenever I walked in on them working together.

Charlie's comment finally pulled Dad's gaze away from the map wall. "You didn't see Rory when you got back, did you?"

My fingers pressed a little harder against the thin piece of cardboard separating them from the paper cup. I shook my head. "Just Adonis and Lux. I think I heard him say he'd be down in a minute."

Dad hummed in thought and turned back to the wall. I couldn't help glancing at Charlie then—a mistake, I knew, since they seemed to tune into that awkward energy of me wanting to talk to my dad alone. But they thankfully didn't point it out when they crossed Dad's line of sight, catching his eye before saying, "I'll go grab our drinks."

The sound of their footsteps trailing toward the kitchen gave way to that anxiety churning in my gut. So I opted to do what I do best: rip the bandage off. "I was wondering if I could start training tonight."

Dad's head snapped back to me with surprise that quickly slipped into a scowl. "Jules—" He started to shake his head as he pushed off the desk.

I was *not* going to just stand here and get told no without making an argument. Not after the last time. "I'm asking now because you told me to wait, and I've waited for—what—two, three years now? I'll be twenty-two in December, and you started training Lux and Rory when they were *twenty-one* a couple years ago. I don't really want to be playing coffee-delivery intern forever. I want to *help*."

"And you *are* helping—"

"Bullshit." I slammed my cup on the desktop. "You said this the last time I asked too. What's the excuse this time? Because it sure as hell better not be my age."

He grimaced and forced out a sigh, putting his hands on his hips. "Look, Jules, I think you've been doing a really good job keeping things running around here. That's important.

Without you, there's a lot of things that would've slipped through the cracks because of how crazy things can get with the job."

I motioned for him to continue, waiting for the explanation to back up this flimsy argument. God, it was so thin it might as well be tissue paper.

"You need to understand that what we do is dangerous—"

"I know," I cut in. "Which is why I've been patient. I'm not some kid trying to play monster-slayer make-believe anymore."

He rubbed the stubble along the side of his face. "And I recognize that."

The next word echoed in my mind before it even passed his lips.

"*But*," he said, almost like another breath, "I don't want this for you."

There it was.

I swallowed, trying to clear that lump forming at the back of my throat. "Because of Mom, right?"

His hesitation said it all. I would've spit out a laugh if the sting of that truth he'd continued burying for years didn't hurt so damn much.

"Don't bother," I whispered. "Guess it's fine for you to run around with a bunch of understudies to kill vampires and avenge her death, but God forbid I try to do the same."

I grabbed the hot chocolate cup by the lid, praying it wouldn't pop off and spill everywhere to make my exit horribly awkward. When only the thin cardboard sleeve dropped to the floor, I counted my blessings. I spun around and stopped short to find Rory there with a tablet under his arm. His lidless americano wafted steam past the bags under his eyes, paling his face to an even greater degree, and up toward his mess of reddish-brown hair.

"Sorry," he said, his voice raspy from the probable all-nighter—all-day-er?—he pulled. "Didn't mean to interrupt."

"Nothing to interrupt," I muttered, weaving around him and making my way back to the entryway.

Charlie passed me with a sight, possibly-concerned frown as they carried their latte and Dad's double-shot back to his office. And like rambunctious ducklings, Lux and Adonis filed out behind them. The second I was alone in the kitchen I made a beeline for the liquor cabinet. That green apple spike was exactly what I needed right now, so I dumped a shot into my half-filled cup and dropped the lid into the trash.

The muffled discussion a few rooms over faded in my climb upstairs, every step in the old house creaking under my weight. I passed a couple of doors until I reached my shoebox of a room and flipped the jury-rigged second switch on the wall, illuminating the ceiling in the soft glow of purple from the partially-covered LED strips. A drawer pull, headphone connection chime, and bean bag adjustment later, I was laying back in the corner of my room. The symphonies of video game soundtracks ran over the grooves of my brain as I sipped my caramel apple potion, wanting nothing more for the night to already be over.

2 WAKING NIGHTMARE

Waking up sluggish always meant one thing: I'd made a mistake.

The thudding of what I finally recognized to be the punching bag hanging from the basement ceiling sounded in time with the pounding inside my skull. I opened my eyes and blinked, quickly adjusting to a squint the second the small blocks of daylight coming from the tiny, recessed windows seared into my retinas. At least Charlie typically trained with the lights dimmed or off, and they continued beating the shit out of the bag without sparing me as much as a glance.

I threw my arm over my face and sank into the torn-up leather couch, wishing to disappear. Did Dad talk to them? Did they ask Dad what happened? Did they both have a heart-to-heart because Charlie acted more like the kid he wanted? I tried to shake that projection away from my thoughts, but it'd lingered there for years now. And jealousy was a bit of a bitch.

My fingers twitched when the rhythm stopped, coupled by the blaring of fuzzy music from a dislodged earbud on the other side of the room.

"How did I get down here?" I croaked, cringing when I heard my own voice. Holy hell, I sounded like a mess. The last thing I remembered was falling into the bean bag upstairs, so whatever sort of night I had was probably best forgotten anyway. Thanks, caramel apple concoction.

The earbud noise cut short, and Charlie's footfalls headed straight for me. I couldn't bear to peel my arm back. I didn't want to look them in the eyes like this and have a mental breakdown about how much of a useless son and failure I was. Forever the coffee intern because, in Dad's mind, I was too fragile to do anything else.

"I found you on the porch when I got home."

What the fuck? Okay, I guess I had a night, all right.

I stiffened as they perched on the arm of the couch. "I tried asking you what you were doing, but you, um… seemed to be a little out of it."

"Greaaat…" I said quietly, trying to swallow back the lump in my throat with the mere thought that they'd tattle to Dad about my drunken night. "Um, could you maybe *not* tell Dad about this?" It was worth a shot, even if they'd lie to my face and throw me under the bus for brownie points.

They sighed. "Whatever's going on between you and Mason is your guys' business. I just know that you looked rather torn up earlier, I found you pretty blasted when I got back, and then I carried you down here before anyone else got in for the day. I think the only question I have is: are *you* okay?"

Well, my mom got eviscerated by a vampire when I was

nine and Dad's on a revenge arc that he won't let me join, so no, I'm actually kind of fucked up now that you mention it.

"I'm fine. Just... need to crawl into bed and sleep this hangover off." I grimaced as I threw my arm to the back of the couch and clawed my way up to sit. My head spun while the room swayed ever-so-slightly.

"You're looking kind of wobbly, Jules."

"Give me a sec, all right?" I felt their eyes burning a hole into the back of my skull.

Thankfully, after a long, agonizing moment, they got up. "Okay, well... Let me know if you need anything. I'm going to hit the shower and go to bed."

They lingered for another eternity of a second before my ears perked at the sound of their breathy sigh as they turned to jog up the stairs. Every groan of the floorboards above me made my shoulders drop a little more in relief. I scrubbed at my face and ran my tongue over my teeth, trying to pick up on the flavor of whatever other alcohol I might've gotten ahold of before I pushed myself to my feet.

It didn't matter. What mattered was I'd been caught in a vulnerable moment, and I'd never emotionally recover. My favorite type of humiliation. I tugged on the sleeves of my jacket and crept up the steps to the back doors, one bolted shut and painted over while the other's blinds filtered the lines of daylight along the hallway leading to the front of the house.

A figure moved as I started forward, and my heart lurched. Dad stared down at his phone with a frown on his way from the kitchen, striding across the entry. I quickly stumbled backward and hid in the recess to the basement until I heard him stop on the other side of the wall: back in his office again.

After taking a minute to sag against the doorframe and bemoan my luck that of course Dad would decide to put in some extra hours instead of going straight to bed, I pulled myself together and popped off my shoes to tip toe down the hall and up the stairs in my socks. All the bedroom doors were closed except mine and Charlie's; both were left ajar, though I couldn't help but wonder why I'd left mine that way.

I understood why Charlie did: they'd hit the shower like they said they would, as evidenced by the shuddering pipes and rush of water in the bathroom next door to the one I favored. But I usually made sure that mine was completely shut out of habit—a habit that I learned from Dad. That was my haven, and whatever weird negative energy that lingered elsewhere in the house didn't belong in there, invading my privacy.

My knuckles dipped into the grooves of the door paneling, lightly pushing it open a little further, as if I was an intruder examining a new space. Nothing appeared out of place, as far as I could tell, so my best guess is that I must've been a little out of my mind whenever I'd left. I sighed and placed my shoes and jacket on the floor just inside the doorway before softly pulling the door into the frame.

Bathroom. Bed.

Stealth mission: accepted.

I shuffled over to the free bathroom and scurried inside, closing the door behind me before flicking on the light. And, like any creature that'd been walking around in the near-dark for most of the morning, I winced.

My God, I looked like shit.

My sleeves didn't want to stay above my elbows as I turned on the faucet, but I managed to splash some water on my face before the cuffs got soaked. After going to town scrubbing the dirt off with a washcloth, I dabbed at the circles under my eyes with a towel. It wouldn't fix it, but I at least hoped some of it was just grime until I realized the sole solution would be sleep.

I grabbed my toothbrush, slathered on a little extra toothpaste, and jammed the sucker in my mouth with a silent prayer that it'd wash away any distant memories of last night until I caught a glimpse of something purplish peeking from my shirt collar. My brushing instinctively slowed as one hand reached to peel back the layer covering what I'd assumed was a mystery bruise, only for a little bit of vomit to jump up the back of my throat.

I gagged, dropped the toothbrush in the sink with a clatter that I felt might've woken up the whole house, and my heart went into double-time as I stared at my foamy saliva slipping toward the drain.

It wasn't a bruise.

That wasn't to say it didn't hurt like a bruise, because it *absolutely fucking did,* but I would've killed to have a bruise at that very moment instead of what I feared I'd just seen. Deep breath in. Deep breath out. No need to panic. It was probably just a trick of the light with a hefty dose of fatigue. And alcohol. Lots and lots of alcohol.

I closed my eyes and pushed myself up to level with the mirror, feeling my arms shake and palms sweat even before I forced one of my hands to reach for my shirt collar again. Lifting my head, I counted down from three, my head spinning the second my eyes opened to the yellow light of the bathroom.

An elongated hexagram of pink, irritated skin with intersections running over two *very* dark purple-red puncture marks.

My stomach dropped, even as my other hand shot up to try to scrub the nightmare wound away. It stung, sending little jolts along my skin and making my eyes water. I leaned over the sink and angled it toward the mirror, my eyes tracing over the puffy red ridges, and tried to hold my breath so I didn't fog the damn thing up with my panting.

I'd seen this exact mark before. It was the sort of emblem that surfaced through a magical bond made by a vampire, though I'd never seen the punctures in the pictures look so dark and *brutal*. Dad had shown images of much less painful-looking marks to me when he'd first started researching vampires, and as a twelve-year-old kid, I'd never forgotten it because he'd made sure I didn't. He specifically told me never to trust someone with one since they were loyal to one thing and one thing only: the vampire that marked them.

The mark of a familiar.

The mark I had on my skin right now.

The mark I didn't have a single fucking clue how I'd got.

I gasped for air, unable to hold my breath any longer, and stumbled back against the wall. My mouth still tasted like mint, the side of my neck still throbbed, and my face was still chilled from washing it. This was real. This was *too* real, and I had no fucking clue where to start to come up with an explanation, let alone defend myself from any accusations if someone else in the house found out before Dad did.

A bitter huff of a laugh slipped out as my hand ran

through my hair. Great. So after arguing with Dad about not training me, I'd have to crawl back to him and say that I screwed up because I got drunk and somehow became a familiar last night.

And because I was a pathetic excuse for a son.

I lightly thumped my head against the wall. Ah, yes, give Dad an excuse to go full vampire-hunter mode to track down and murder his son's vampire lord on top of playing general vigilante and trying to find his wife's killer. Awesome.

Then what the hell would everyone do with me? My odds of doing simple things like intern activities would drop to zero and they'd probably lock me in the basement out of fear that whoever my master was might just start playing the little devil on my shoulder and tell me to light the place on fire or something.

I paused and stared at my reflection in the mirror, feeling the blood drain from my face. I'd forgotten that familiars had a psychic link with their masters. My heart hammered a little faster again while I stood stock-still, almost waiting for something to pop into my head at any moment with orders to start killing everyone. Whether or not they could psychically make me do that, I had no idea, but I was scared stiff just thinking about it.

The sudden shut off of the other bathroom's shower made me flinch. Was I really going to spill my guts and give Dad another reason to subtly replace me with Charlie? Or replace me with anyone else in this house, for that matter? I swallowed and slowly clenched and unclenched my fists, staving off that freeze response in favor of fight. My mark throbbed under my shirt collar as if it were a ticking time bomb.

You're smart, I told myself—and not in the sarcastic way I

usually did, like when it came to cute guys like Saint. I'd read a plethora of books regarding vampires and anything related to them. I'd been the one to look up strange artifacts and symbols for Dad before Rory came along and took that job from me. I could figure out how to un-familiar-ize myself and maybe even manage to kill my first vampire in the process.

I could prove that I can get out of my own messes and that I'm worthy of being a vampire hunter too. That warmth that came with an abundance of self-gaslighting built up my hope for all of ten seconds until I realized that I had absolutely nothing to go off of. Last night was a blank, aside from Charlie's mention of finding me on the front porch.

The other bathroom's vent shut off and the door squealed open, so I lurched toward the doorknob, cursing under my breath when it didn't turn. Of course the fucking thing got stuck *now*, at the worst possible time.

Charlie's footsteps halted. "Um, you good in there?"

Fuck me, this was going to be even more awkward having them save my ass. "Er—um, so, the door's pulling off the hinge again, I think."

They jiggled the knob, grumbled something, and then a corner of their towel appeared under the door. "It just needs a bit of a boost. Give me a sec."

I stepped back and noticed my toothbrush still chilling in the middle of the sink basin, so I scrambled to grab it and toss it back into my designated cup. The door made a god-awful noise as paint rubbed against paint in the frame, and Charlie nudged it a little further open.

"Everything all right, Jules?"

I quickly hooked a finger into my shirt collar and pulled it opposite the nasty bite to cover it a little more. "Um, I was actually wondering if I happened to say anything to you when you helped me inside earlier? Like who I was with or where I went? I, er... I noticed my credit card was missing when I dropped everything in my room."

Okay, all right. That's believable enough.

They frowned, shook out their damp hair, and scooped their clumped towel back off the floor. "You mumbled a few things, but you were pretty out of it." They shrugged. "Maybe check your card account and see where you last spent anything? You should at least be able to see if it was stolen if it's still racking up purchases."

They had a point. Even if my card wasn't really stolen, I never really carried cash. So I had to have left a trail, especially if I managed to get my hands on more booze.

"Thanks," I said, slipping past them and rubbing my face with a sheepish smile. "I might have to make a fraud call before bed and lock my card."

The corner of their mouth tugged upward ever-so-slightly. "Sleep well, Jules. Hopefully you feel better tonight." They turned and padded down the hall, ducking into their room and leaving me feeling torn. I couldn't tell if that smirk was mocking or genuine from their well-worn, tired poker face, let alone if their words were condescending.

Pulling up my shirt collar again, I started for my room, jumping at the rush of footfalls running up the steps. I spun on my heel with wide eyes, frozen like a deer in headlights as Dad pinned his sights on me.

"Downstairs."

My mouth worked like a fish out of water for all of two seconds before the next command snapped it shut.

"*Now.*"

I tried to hide my trembling with a nod and jogged down to the entry. When I got to the bottom, I looked back, no longer seeing Dad anywhere behind me. But I could *hear* him though. The chorus of doors being pounded on, opened, and the clash of groggy voices propelled me into the living room, where I nervously adjusted how my shirt fell on my body.

One by one, the rest of the house trailed in. Lux huffed, Rory yawned, Adonis groaned, and Charlie rubbed their arms. Finally, Dad stepped through them and made his way over to the fireplace.

"Well," he said, making eye-contact with each of his students and barely glancing over me, as he grabbed one of the small statues in the line of saints and angels on either side of the Virgin Mary sitting on the mantel, "do any of you care to fess up to what's sitting behind St. Raphael?"

My heart was in my throat for the millionth time tonight. Did I do something when I was drunk? Did my fucking *vampire* make me do something while I was drunk? The entire room remained deathly silent, outside of the anxious shifting of stances and stolen, confused glances at one another. My eyes flicked to Charlie, almost for a little too long, but I forced myself to look away just before they caught me.

Dad tapped the statue. "This is your final opportunity to come clean and make this a whole lot less painful for yourself. If I were you, I'd take responsibility and face the consequences before this turns into a full-blown witch hunt."

Silence.

Well, other than my pulse hammering so hard in my ears that I thought I'd pass out.

"Suit yourself," Dad sighed, ripping the statue off the mantel and spinning it around to reveal a small dot.

My stomach twisted. A hidden camera. One that'd probably gotten a decent view of Dad's office from where it'd been sitting but would be still easily missed between the other statues further down the line and the dark wood paneling behind it.

"It appears we have a mole."

3 SINNERS & SAINTS

tried to rationalize things by telling myself that there was no way I could've planted that camera because Charlie had found me on the porch and later babysat me in the basement. But that was dissolved by my quick recollection that they'd been the first one home.

They'd gotten home first. They'd probably grabbed a little to eat. They'd changed clothes. They'd trained in the basement. And how long had they done all of that without anyone being around?

I mean, I spent most of my time alone in the house, which, right now, was a horrible look. But Charlie always made it a habit to wrap up their hunt early and try to unwind for a bit. Completely unsupervised. That was mainly because I would be eating upstairs and playing a few rounds of some random FPS game of the month or watching a live stream. All right, and *sometimes* I was redecorating my *Animal Village* town, but that's not important.

The point is, it wasn't out of the question for them to have done it. What if they were getting closer to Dad to gather more intel and bring it back to whatever vampire they were really working for? What if this was the perfect opportunity to frame me and get me out of the picture because they saw my bite and believed that I'm working for a rival? Are they just that good at playing dumb?

Adonis was the first one to speak. "Uh, okay? Who put the mole on the statue?"

Everyone's heads turned to him.

"You're kidding," Lux said flatly, crossing her arms over her chest. "There's no way you're *that* fucking stupid."

Charlie grimaced. "The statue doesn't have a mole, Adonis. That's a camera."

"Then why didn't Mason just say so?"

"God…" Rory whispered, rubbing his temple. "What he's saying is that there's a traitor among us."

Adonis's face scrunched up. "Like the game? With the little cartoon astronauts?"

"He's *got* to be faking it," Lux snapped, glancing between me and Charlie. "Right?"

For some reason, she lingered on me a little longer than I expected. But I wasn't going to say shit right now. Yeah, I might've been a little speechless from the morning's turn of events and *yeah*, I'm not Adonis's biggest fan, but I wasn't going to shove one of my possible future teammates—once I got Dad on board, please I'm begging everything in the universe just to let me have this one win—under the bus.

"Faking *what?*" Adonis demanded. "Faking my reaction about this camera thing? I'd think that at least one of you would maybe consider why Jules is being so quiet about it."

"Me?" My voice totally did *not* crack. "I-I'm just as confused as everyone else."

"Confused? Or surprised that you got caught for being a little freak and spying on us because Daddy won't take you to work?"

Okay, I changed my mind. Fuck this guy.

I opened my mouth to hurl back what I'm sure would've been a really good insult, but Dad cut me off.

"Enough."

Everyone snapped to attention again, complete with Adonis's smug smirk in my direction since he'd gotten the last jab in. Dad popped the camera off St. Raphael, letting it clatter against the wood like the proverbial pin drop in our tense silence. Then it met its doom with a *crunch* under Dad's boot.

"Come clean. Now."

But no one moved. No one spoke. And I started to sweat worse than when I discovered my familiar mark in the bathroom less than fifteen minutes ago. Another round of sideways glances passed up and down the interrogation line before Mason puffed out a resigned sigh.

He slammed St. Raphael back onto the mantel. "I trusted you. I trusted *all* of you. I brought you into this house because we had a shared goal: to get rid of the vampires plaguing this city so they can't ruin any more lives."

Guilt settled in my stomach as Dad rubbed his face, mostly around the dark circles under his eyes from the recent long days after longer nights. I couldn't help but continuously ask myself if I'd done this—if I'd either managed to get in and do it before Charlie made home or if I'd somehow slipped away from them in my drunken-slash-possibly puppeted haze.

Had I ruined Dad's entire operation all because I'd decided to drink away my problems and… do whatever the hell I chose to do last night? I tried not to fidget with Dad's 'last chance' look of scrutiny pinned on everyone, but I really *really* wanted to check my phone—to check my credit card—to find any sort of hint as to where I'd gone or what I'd done during those blank hours between settling into my room for the night and waking up in the basement in the morning.

"Frankly, I'm disappointed."

Great. Now Dad had me in a chokehold. The only good thing about those words is that no one could bring themselves to look at him. All eyes were on the floor, directed at the fireplace, or looking somewhere in the middle-distance past him to avoid direct eye-contact.

"Until we figure out which one of you did this, I'm sending all of you down to the basement. You can sleep there for the day while I figure whomever the guilty party is. In the meantime, the culprit will have to face those of you getting punished unjustly because of their actions."

Oh, *awesome.* I was going to totally get ripped to shreds by Adonis and maybe eviscerated by Charlie. I'd be lucky to survive the next hour without getting physically pinned down for someone to discover my mark and being hauled up to Dad for him to fix the problem. I could already hear the bemoaning about getting treated differently for my mistake, paired with complaints about how I endangered their entire mission, despite whether or not I'd actually placed the camera. Not to mention that if I hadn't, I'd make an amazing scapegoat.

I was well and truly fucked.

"Move," Dad ordered, ushering everyone toward the front of the house to begin our walk of shame down the hall.

I hunched in on myself as I padded by the stairs, feeling Dad practically breathing down my purple-marked neck. Quiet grumbling and stolen scowls at one another put me further on edge, knowing full-well that, unless there was miraculously an actual, willing traitor, my time in keeping this bite a secret was severely limited. Which meant I'd be on house arrest for the rest of eternity. Hell, Dad would probably make my room a padded cell and keep me in there until he kicked the bucket.

The basement door squealed open, and I cringed. My palms started to sweat as Lux passed the threshold, leaving only me to follow.

Dad grabbed my arm, and I stumbled backward, causing the procession of hunters to stop and look over their shoulders.

"I'll send Jules down with food for breakfast when it comes time," Dad started, continuing with other instructions I didn't catch because I was too gob-smacked to comprehend anything other than I wasn't going into the dungeon with the rest of them.

The door shut and he flipped the door stoppers in place at the top and bottom, just like he'd done whenever they'd held a vampire-worshiping zealot down there for interrogation.

I stared at him, stunned as I caught Adonis's grumblings of me getting special treatment through the cracks in the door. "Dad... what—"

"You didn't have anything to do with this, Jules. You're not a hunter and putting you down there with them would solve nothing. I brought you downstairs so you'd be aware of it." He put his hands on my shoulders, and I wanted to sink into the floorboards. "I know that you wouldn't ever do anything like that."

The father-son moment was short lived as he pulled away to cover a yawn and motioned for me to follow. Well, if I didn't feel guilty enough before, I sure as hell did now.

I shuffled after him, rubbing my arms. "I think you're forgetting we just had a fight..." The guilt was definitely eating at me by this point.

He sighed. "Fights happen. I think we can put that disagreement on pause until we figure things out."

"Yeah, but..." I bit my lip as we came to a stop in the living room. But what? But I'm pretty pissed that you've kept shoving me aside, and this would be the perfect way to get back at you? But shouldn't you treat me like the rest of your protégés? But I'm a *familiar?* I swallowed.

Dad shook his head before I had a chance to let anything slip. "I trust you, Jules. And I'm not short-sighted enough to believe you'd do this after an argument that can be solved another way."

Yeah, I was absolutely not fine now. I felt gross. Even if I didn't know what really happened at this point, the urge to come clean about the bite had never been stronger. But I held my tongue, reminding myself that this was my only chance to fix things. All I needed to do was find the vampire that bit me, kill it, and bring proof back to Dad to explain everything that happened and how I handled it on my own. I didn't need him to solve my problems for me. I was a grown-ass adult, goddammit. I could do this.

Dad started picking through some items on his desk,

covering another yawn. "I'm going to start with some of their recent reports and make sure everything's in order there. It's possible the timelines might not match up from what they wrote down versus when they actually triggered the doorbell camera or showed up on our phone GPS pings. Could you go get their phones, Jules? I hate to do it, but we probably need to brute force their passcodes and check their calls and texts."

I perked up. That gave me the perfect opportunity to retrieve mine and retrace my steps as well. "Sure," I forced out, heading straight for the second floor without trying to seem too eager.

The second I hit the landing, I jogged to my room, shoving open the door and scooping up my phone. Holy shit that was a lot of notifications.

Two missed calls from Iris.

A bunch of messages in the hunter group chat.

Several emails.

Three credit card purchase notifications.

A call and a voicemail from Zane.

And a text message from Saint.

I don't know which was more mortifying: the fact that Saint and I had been texting when I was black-out drunk or the fact that I'd put a little black heart emoji next to his name. The fact that my hands shook as I unlocked my phone to check on the damage felt pretty damning on its own.

SAINT

How are you feeling?

I blinked, my body numbing with warmth as I tried to fill in the context. My thumb pulled the message thread downward, taking me back to the beginning:

It's Jules :)

I could picture myself struggling to send that, unsure whether or not to use the smiley face, but I couldn't recall actually doing it.

Hey :) You manage alright with all those drinks?

My insides melted. Oh my God, he smiley faced back.

Yep! Just trying to unwind a bit before I need to do some cleaning and camera-watching. Hbu?

Man, the time stamps between these texts probably would've killed me. I counted my blessings that I didn't remember stressing over this.

I'm finishing up my shift in 20 min. When are you cut loose for the night? Did you want to grab a drink?

Well, fuck. Of course I said yes. My dumb little gay brain wasn't going to turn down that offer. At least I now understand how I ended up outside of the house and blasted out of my mind. But now I had the overwhelming fear that I'd made a complete fool of myself in front of Saint.

I skimmed the next few messages that made my stomach twist in anticipation with map links and bar names until, at around 3:35am, I texted:

Thanks for tonight. I really needed it.

I'm glad we could talk some more :) Maybe tomorrow?

I'd like that :)

That was it. After that, there was a new time stamp and Saint's message from 7:00am. I hesitated, trying to think of what to type back since I wasn't *good*, even though that was my default answer for everything I didn't want to talk about. I was honestly feeling like shit between the copious amount of alcohol I undoubtedly consumed over the course of the night—though I strangely didn't have much of a hangover yet—and due to helping lock up literally everyone I lived with because I might've made a bit of an oopsie.

I'm feeling a little worse for wear haha. I think I went a little too hard.

The typing bubbles made my heart stop.

Still awake?

Oh shit. Yeah, I should've been in bed by now, but that plan got derailed pretty quickly.

Haha, yeah. I'm actually winding down to pass out now. You should get some sleep too.

I'll talk to you again when you're up. Sleep well.

You too!

My head was spinning. Was that our first date? Was he asking for another date? I shook the thoughts away. Focus, Jules, focus. I swiped over to the chaotic hunter group chat, finding the usual back-and-forth banter of who was wrapping up and going home, who was heading out, and who needed a bit of backup—all the usual stuff.

I took note of Charlie going solo and heading back early, where they mentioned finding me locked out. Suppressing a cringe, I moved on to look at Lux's note of needing to take a detour to pick up supplies, and then Adonis's text of running a little late because of a street being blocked for a crime scene. Rory only posted a couple of ETAs before asking for assistance, which Adonis sought to about five minutes later.

That kept both Charlie and I at the top of the suspect list, especially since there was a huge gap of time between when I texted Saint a thank-you and when they'd found me on the porch at 7:30am. Four hours. I was still missing four whole hours of time I couldn't account for.

"Jules?" Dad called out.

I tensed. "Sorry," I called back. "Just checking through some stuff while I'm up here."

Shit.

I crammed my phone into my pocket and hurried across the hall. Shoving the door open to Adonis's room, I half-tripped over the small pile of clothes in front of the dresser. The place reeked of sweaty socks, and it took everything in me not to gag. A gym duffle sat by his nightstand, more clothes pouring out of it and trailing to the sliding closet doors that partially popped out of the hanging tracks.

There, on the stand, sat a phone that had seen some shit. The white charging cable looked striped with the amount of electrical tape holding it together, the screen was cracked to hell, and the heavy-duty case—clearly a late addition or else the glass would be in one piece—looked like it'd been crammed in one too many jean pockets with the dark stains on the rubber coating. I collected that bad boy and unplugged the charger from the wall for good measure since that was a fire waiting to happen.

The deep breath I took once I stepped back into the hall made my head spin, and I almost didn't catch my phone vibrating in my pocket on my way to Rory's room at the opposite end of the hall.

ZANE

Dude, are you alive?

I blinked down at the screen, thinking it was Saint until my eyes caught Zane's name printed across the top.

Yeah, sorry. Was just heading to bed. I'll talk to you later, okay?

I shoved my phone into my pocket and nudged the door open to a tranquil, average-looking geeky college boy's room with navy plaid sheets, spare computer parts littering his desktop, and small piles of miscellaneous items in the corners with labels. The PC tower sitting next to his rolling chair slowly cycled through colors with its built-in LEDs. His phone's lock screen was about what I expected: a render of a graphically embellished motherboard and processor with an animated pulsing lock.

Two phones down, two more to go.

My pocket buzzed again, and I juggled between my acquisitions and my own phone.

> Been trying to get a hold of you for hours.
> Where did you disappear to?

I bit my tongue. My *hope* was that he was referring to the possibility that I'd met up with him and Iris last night, but unfortunately, I had to put my phone away again when I heard Dad start moving around downstairs. It'd have to wait.

I jogged in my zig-zag pattern over to Charlie's room, a muted green haven with succulent pillows decorating a makeshift window seat. Their laptop was still open, luring me toward it like a siren's call until I shook my head and hurried to grab their phone. I'd have time to snoop later—a reminder that made me more antsy to quickly dump all these devices on Dad's desk like a sack of hot potatoes.

Pulling Charlie's door shut behind me, I hissed out a curse with my phone's next buzz, alerting me to Zane absolutely blowing the thing up. Instead of checking it, I pressed forward to the next door, letting it glide open to a rose-gold wonderland. Champaign pinks and eggshell whites took over every square foot of the room, matching that tell-tale scent of roses and raspberries that was a welcomed transition from the sweat pit of Adonis's lair. But I couldn't really say I expected anything less from Lux. I strode past her fluffy monstrosity for a bed—at least, I *think* it was a bed, but I could only see pillows and a couple of fluffy throw blankets —and plucked her phone off a pink charging pad that pulsed with little symbols like a pastel goth's store-bought penta-gram. I decided not to think about it too much, despite the fact that it seemed a little satanic, which teetered a little too close to vampire-adjacent.

I mean, maybe she thought it was ironic? Probably. That was probably it.

Fuck-ton of phones in tow, I stumbled back downstairs and let my haul spill onto Dad's miscellaneous paperwork.

"Thanks, Jules," he said, sounding like the wind had been ripped from his sails.

I swallowed, slapping my butt to muffle my phone's new complaint from Zane. "Is there anything else I can help you with?" That was one-hundred-percent the guilt talking.

He paused, the muscles in his jaw flexing until he said, "Do you think you could order us some food? I think it's going to be a long day."

4 MEMORY LANE

'd fallen asleep on the couch at some point. Go me. Fantastic job of staying awake and alert. If it weren't for the knock on the front door, I'd probably still be in my post-bite coma. And, judging by the way Dad jolted in his chair across the dining room-slash-office archway, I wasn't the only one who had ended up snoozing on the job.

I rubbed my eyes and groggily swung my feet to the floor, trying to fight the sway of the room as I headed for the door. Dad grumbled something I didn't catch, my brain wholly focused on checking the time: 6:00pm. Safe to open the door.

So I did.

"Jules!" our guest cheered—a woman my height with her near-black hair pinned back.

The next thing I knew, I was trapped in a hug. "A-Aunt Syd?" I squeaked. Holy shit, what was she doing here?

I heard Dad's scramble to hurry over to us so he could block the view of the office. His quick strides across the wood and onto the rug pounded in time with my thrumming pulse as she started to pull away. "I came over as soon as I got checked into my hotel."

Hotel?

Oh my God. My heart dropped. I'd completely forgotten what day it was, and now I *really* felt like a failure of a son. It was the anniversary of Mom's passing tomorrow. Everything went numb, almost like I was having an out-of-body experience, even as Dad clapped a hand on my shoulder and took over with the talking.

"This isn't exactly a great time, Syd—"

She scowled. "Mason, nothing can be so important that you can't take a couple of hours to join your sister-in-law and your son for a memorial dinner. It's not like this is even a surprise to you since we've done it for the past *twelve years*. You're a workaholic, and even your son has bags under his eyes. I'm dreading to even ask what you've done to him."

I winced. Well, I kind of did it to myself, but she sort of had a point.

Aunt Syd folded her arms over her chest. "Now, you can either join Jules and I for a nice dinner, or you can spend the night working yourself to death with my sister's ghost shaming you."

All right, so it looked like I was locked in whether I wanted to be or not. While I *wanted* to go, the more sensible part of me was screaming that I shouldn't be anywhere near family in public by the time it got dark because that was just asking for my newly acquired vampire lord to swoop in and kill the rest of the people I loved.

But, Dad being Dad, floundered, his mouth working like a

fish out of water before he finally said, "Jules, get your jacket and keep Syd company on the porch while I clean up and check on some things."

Aunt Syd beamed, and I hesitantly nodded, forcing a smile onto my face to mask the sheer panic brewing in the bottom of my soul. I turned on my heel to dash upstairs and trip into my room, where my jacket remained in a puddle on the floor. My mind raced for anything else I might need in case of a vampire attack or something that might help keep my vampire's voice out of my head—a fun new activity I anticipated possibly happening after the sun went down in the next hour or so.

When I came up blank, I admitted defeat and hurried back down, pulling the front door shut behind me when Dad excused himself to "clean up"—hide all the phones and vampire research in his office—and "check on some things"— things like the four twenty-something-year-old hunters locked in his basement like this was a horror flick.

I rocked on my heels, hands stuffed in my pockets like I was that anxious little kid meeting his expat aunt for the first time again. "So… how's Canada?" I asked lamely.

"Cold," she chirped with a chuckle. "But it's beautiful when winter hits. You should really come visit." She glanced at the door and sighed. "I'd invite your father, but he always comes up with excuses."

My heart sank at the sight of her crestfallen expression. Loneliness emanated from her dark eyes, dulling their excited sparkle from earlier. She'd moved up there years ago, right before Mom died. I'd seen pictures of the place: a cabin that looked like it'd been pulled straight from a luxury home buying show with its tall glass windows and modern cabin architecture. It was the picture-perfect place to spend a summer or the holidays since it was right next to a lake.

And now she lived in it for years by herself.

"I… tried to convince Mason to let me take you for a week a couple of times, but he always made the excuse of school, even in July." She rolled her eyes. "I get it, though. He was probably nervous to let you travel without him."

What?

My feet fell flat on the boards. This was news to me. Dad hadn't ever mentioned Aunt Syd wanting to babysit me. Though that did explain why she'd popped in occasionally during the summer when I was younger. The memories of walking down to my favorite ice cream shop a couple of blocks away and chatting with her about the places I'd like to see slipped into showing her all the pieces I'd prided myself on creating in art club. And then all of that trickled into the day Dad and I had gotten into a huge fight after I came out to him—a shock he clearly wasn't prepared for—but I'd mumbled the same words to her while peeling off the paper around my ice cream cone.

She'd asked to take a walk when I was upset. She'd hugged me and said she was happy I would share something that made me so vulnerable with her. She'd said that she loved me when I needed to hear it the most, all when it'd taken Dad weeks to finally bring it up again and apologize for how he'd reacted.

And I just learned that I had the option to have a semi-normal life instead of doing vampire research summer school with my dad. My dad, who said he "didn't want this life for me." Nice.

Aunt Syd blinked with surprise at the sound of my shoes

hitting the porch before her brows knit together. "Did...
Mason not tell you?"

I tried to swallow the knot in my throat, hating how much
it hurt to know that I hadn't even been given a choice. Appar-
ently, Dad thought he could have it both ways: keep me
around for peace of mind and use me as an extra set of eyes,
but also keep me at intern status until I... left, I guess? Or
whatever sort of ending point he'd managed to come up
with, assuming he'd even thought that far ahead of what to
do with me.

"Nope," I said quietly, trying to fight the bitterness to my
tone.

Aunt Syd's expression slipped into concern, her mouth
opening to press further until the front door swung inward
and Dad stepped back outside, nudging open the storm door.
He spun to lock the deadbolt and drop the keys into his
pocket.

"Should be good for an hour," he said. "Did you drive
here or use a rideshare?"

Without missing a beat, she took out her own key—rental
tag and all—and jingled it, beaming with a mask of pride. I
could tell she was itching to continue our conversation when
she threw an arm over my shoulders to guide me down the
steps.

"Jules sits up front with me since *he* didn't try to get out of
family obligations," she said, shooting him a teasing glare.

I tried my best not to shrink under the additional attention, but part of me also silently thanked her for forcing me
out of the awkward position of staring a hole through the
back of my dad's head during the entirety of the drive to
Mom's favorite diner. We turned the block and climbed in

where she'd found a free parking spot on the street. I couldn't bear to check the rearview mirror, let alone spare him a glance once I was seated next to him in one of the teal-covered booths.

It was hard to believe that I used to look forward to these get-togethers growing up, but now I wanted nothing more than for Dad to disappear so I could have a mental break-down in front of my mom's older lookalike. The one major downside to all of this was that Aunt Syd didn't know shit about vampires—a blessing that she wasn't on a warpath like Dad and a curse that she couldn't understand the mess I was in as a familiar.

I fidgeted with the corner of the laminated menu like I wasn't going to get the same meal as I did every year: a grilled cheese sandwich and a side of fries. My ultimate comfort food since Mom always made the best ones. This was the second best, but since she took her recipe to the grave, it'd have to do.

I automatically ordered a lemonade when the waitress asked for our drinks, and I twirled my straw around in the glass while Dad and Aunt Syd chatted about something I couldn't focus on. All I could think about was how I'd been robbed. Robbed of my childhood and my choices.

It wasn't until Aunt Syd cupped my hand from across the table that I broke free of my negative headspace. "Sophie would be so proud to see you now."

No, that's cool, I totally wanted to cry in the middle of the restaurant. I blinked back the tears and told myself to man up because I couldn't afford to be emotional right now. Not with a fucking puncture wound in my neck.

She gave me a wistful smile as she patted my hand before

signaling for the waitress to bring us the final plate we always ordered for the night. The damn raspberry cheesecake. Mom's favorite dessert that she always celebrated with for her big wins. When the slice reached the table, we brought out our forks and divvied it into four pieces. The chunk of gram cracker crust holding up the edge wobbled against the plate. She'd always said it was the best part, so it's the piece none of us dared to touch, almost as if she'd step inside the diner at the last second and apologize for being late.

Dad tucked a few bills under the plate of unfinished cheesecake for a tip, and Aunt Syd scooted out of the booth to pay at the register. The ritual was complete.

I walked outside to stand on the sidewalk and reflect on the last gasp of dusk, basking in the comforting white noise of the city until Aunt Syd grabbed the side of my head and kissed my temple.

"I'm so glad I got to see you both tonight," she said, Dad's footsteps scraping the concrete behind us. "It's tough without her but remember that we have each other."

And *that* I was doubting even more each passing second. I wanted nothing more than to spin around and demand why Dad hadn't told me about Aunt Syd's invitations. It was so fucking tempting to rip him a new one about why I couldn't be a hunter, but I also couldn't go have *fun*. But I kept my mouth shut and my head down on the ride back, letting my rage practically eat me alive.

Next thing I knew, we were on the porch again. The home of where all my problems seemed to start nowadays. Dad moved to unlock the door, and Aunt Syd pulled me into a quick hug. "I'll be around for a few more days if you want to hang out," she whispered into my ear.

My entire body went limp. God, I wanted that so badly right now. If it wasn't for everything else going on, I'd take her up on it in a heartbeat. So instead, I forced out a, "I'll let you know if I get some time to swing by your hotel."

She let go, and I had to resist from keeping my arms locked around her like a vice. I needed that hug more than I realized, but it'd be pretty damn selfish of me to put her in harm's way here in a few minutes once the sun was extinguished. Her grin made my heart sink, despite her playfully ruffling my hair before saying her brief goodbye to Dad. Then she was trotting down the steps, across the walkway, and rounding her car to speed away.

And I felt more empty and lonelier than ever.

That numbness found me again as I followed Dad inside, letting the storm door clatter behind me. I half-expected to walk into a tornado of escaped prisoners, but everything was exactly how we'd left it. Dad groaned and rubbed his hand along his beard stubble, making a scratching sound that pushed me to the edge of my nerves.

"Everyone's probably awake by now, so if you could get them breakfast before we dig back into our investigation—"

"*Our* investigation?" I echoed, my tone even as I teetered on the edge of imploding.

I could be spending time with Aunt Syd right now. I had a cute guy texting me and wanting to hang out tonight. Not to even fucking mention the *bite mark on my neck* that I would've never had to deal with if it wasn't for Dad's adamancy about me *not* needing to be involved in his hunting squad. Which I absolutely *was*. This is where I had to put my foot down. Even if I felt a little guilty about it because I wasn't completely sure if I was the culprit or not, I had to put myself first for once. Full fucking stop.

Dad turned on his heel, his brows knitting together with a surprised, quizzical look plastered onto his face. "What's with the attit—"

"I thought you didn't want this for me, or am I mistaken?" I asked, unable to keep that bitterness out of my voice. "I'll get you guys coffee and breakfast, sure, but if you're keeping me out of official business, then I don't think it's fair to ask me to half do the job you've banned me from. What kind of standard is that?"

"Jules—"

"And Aunt Syd mentioned that she wanted to have me spend a week or two of my summer vacations with her, which I found pretty surprising since I never heard anything about it."

When he grimaced and looked away, I knew it was true. My stomach knotted, but I'd already hit the gas on this motherfucker, so it wasn't going to stop until it hit empty.

"I thought, damn, that's crazy. And then I was like, man, what the hell was I even doing over my summer breaks? Oh *yeah*, that's right—doing vampire research. Like an intern. Like I still am now after over nearly a decade of being your little helper."

"Jules, I—"

"You *what*, Dad? You thought I'd be safer with you? You thought it'd be best for me that I not get a chance to be a fucking kid? You thought I shouldn't get a choice or say what *I* wanted in all of this? Oh, and not to mention when I finally tell you what I want, *then* you can make it known that I've been strung along because that's not what *you* wanted—you just didn't actively discourage it though."

I'd be lying if I said I didn't feel a little bit of pride in seeing my dad slack-jawed over my argument until he gritted his teeth. "I kept you close because I didn't want to lose you."

I couldn't help it. I scoffed. "I think you should be careful about what you say because you're about to with the way you've been jerking me around like a dog on a leash."

It was even more difficult to tell if the remorse in his eyes was because he was actually sorry or just sorry he got caught. "I never intended to make you feel like I was stringing you along, and I was honestly worried about what might happen if I wasn't there to protect you."

"So you decided not to give me a choice?" I demanded, feeling stinging at the back of my eyes. "I used to dream about working alongside you as an equal to get justice for Mom."

"And I'm not just doing this for her, Jules. I'm doing this for *us*—"

I bit back a laugh. "No, you're doing this for *you*."

His face went slack like I'd slapped him.

I swallowed down the rest of the rage slowly choking me in favor of my ultimatum: "This is your mess to clean up. I'll continue running your errands and keeping the house going, but I deserve to have a life outside of all of this if you want to keep me at arm's length. You can't have it both ways."

Right on cue, to heap on the guilt I needed Dad to feel at that very moment, my phone buzzed. I wiggled it out of my pocket and saw Saint's name scrawled across the top of the notification. Quickly flashing him the phone screen, I took a step back to head for the kitchen. "And that would be the date I was going to blow off before I realized I'd been putting my life on hold for you. Now, if you'll excuse me, I have breakfast to make."

I spun around and crammed my phone in my pocket, the silence stretching between us so thick I'd need one of those fancy informercial knives made with Japanese steel to hack through it. When I tugged the freezer door open, Dad's footfalls finally trailed away to his office, moving from wood flooring to rugs and back again until I heard drawers being opened and the locks clicking. Meanwhile, I was unpacking frozen breakfast sandwiches to chuck in the microwave, mixing protein powder into a blender-full of a greenish smoothie concoction, and heating up some instant apple cinnamon oatmeal.

After popping everything into meal prep containers, I made the awkward trek to Dad's office, where I slid a paper-plated sandwich onto his desk. His mumbled thanks only prompted a nod from me before I headed back to bag everything up with some plastic red cups and break out a lidded pitcher to fill with water. Once everything was sitting on the counter, ready to be hauled down, I took a deep breath, letting that pent up stress roll off of me in favor of taking a break.

All I had to do was do a breakfast delivery, and then I could focus on my own issues for a while. And, honestly, it felt *freeing*. Even with the purple monstrosity on my neck I still needed to puzzle out.

I slid out my phone and unlocked the screen to find Saint's newest message resting at the bottom:

How's 3am sound? :)

I bit my lip, trying not to break into a giddy school-girl smile. My thumbs moved faster than my brain, refusing to let me think through the potential consequences of meeting up with Saint in the middle of this mess.

Sounds like a plan.

5 BEWITCHED & CONFUSED

The breakfast catering I offered to the crew was awkward, to say the least. Rory and Adonis were the only two mumbling to each other when I stumbled down the steps, which I managed to catch a bit of since they'd taken up residence near the entry. I guess they'd decided to back each other up since they'd stuck together toward the end of last night, but they didn't appear to be gunning for Lux or Charlie as their prime suspect yet, judging by the way they hadn't won either of their fellow prisoners into their territory.

Charlie's head popped up from the floor in the far corner—by the exercise equipment—and they swiped at their eyes as I laid out the spread of food that I'd carefully tucked into a reusable tote bag to help me haul everything down in a single trip. Adonis grumbled somewhere behind me, Rory remained silent, and I tensed when Lux hopped up from the corner directly across from the entry before jogging over to the squatty storage cabinets I was turning into a makeshift buffet. I assumed that she was making a mad dash for her breakfast, but she grabbed my elbow instead.

I half-spun, guilt immediately clawing at me when her pleading eyes bore into mine. "Jules, I didn't do th—"

A shadow rose from near the base of the stairwell, and my hair stood on end. "Really, Lux?" Adonis snapped. "Damn, you wasted no fucking time trying to plead your case to Mason's minion."

Oof, okay. My fist clenched at my side, and I gritted my teeth. I was very possibly the reason why everyone was down here, so as much as I wanted to fight back, I kept reminding myself that it wasn't worth it. I mean, Adonis didn't even have enough of a vocabulary to understand the word 'mole' in any context other than a dot on his skin.

Charlie began to push themself up, and Lux's grip tightened as her head whipped around. "Fuck off, Adonis," she spat, jabbing her finger at him. "For all I care, *you're* the one that got us locked up down here."

"*Me?* What about *you?*"

"What about me, dickhead? You made buddy-buddy with Rory really damn quick the second the door shut, didn't you? Almost like you're trying to cross your name off each of our suspect lists one-by-one because you have something to hide."

He scoffed. "I don't even know what's going on!"

"Then maybe," Charlie ground out, "you should consider treating Jules with a little respect *because* he's 'Mason's minion.'" They made air quotes to emphasize their disdain, as if he might miss their deepening scowl—a highly likely possibility.

"What? Are we all just going to forget the argument we heard—" He glanced back at Rory.

"Thirty minutes ago."

"The argument we heard *thirty minutes* ago? Because it sounds like little Jules here might have a pretty good reason for wanting to spite Daddy, doesn't he?"

I couldn't stop my teeth from grinding as I took in that ever-so-slight smug smirk on his face. Here I was, exhausted and enduring the sting of my dad's secretive betrayal, and now I was playing nanny to *this* asshole. Sure, I was sweating like hell with the notion that he was strangely on the right track to possibly have everyone here gang up on me, but what could I really say?

A shiver ran through me as I felt something tingle along the back of my skull, working its way into my brain.

Every ounce of guilt I had ebbed to some far edge of my thoughts, pulling in a tide of numbness that left me with unease—an unease that I couldn't shake until a come-back tumbled from my mouth: "Why don't you go *whine* to someone else?" I felt my face crinkle with a snarl.

His eyes went wide, but my body didn't give me a chance to process what had just happened—*I* wasn't in control here. But I couldn't quite comprehend that until I shoulder-checked him and made it to the top of the stairs, the door firmly shut behind me.

I blinked, and I could flex my hands again—shake my head again—unclench my jaw and *breathe.* My stomach twisted, and I tried to swallow a lump forming in my throat.

Oh fuck.

That wasn't me.

That was something *controlling* me.

That was my *fucking vampire.*

I stood stock-still, waiting for something else to happen, trying to go full smooth brain with zero thoughts bouncing around in my head other than: *fuck, fuck, fuck, fuck, fuck.*

An eternity might as well have passed as I listened to my pulse thrumming in my ears, drowning out the hushed hostility just on the other side of the door. In all likelihood, it'd probably only been a couple of minutes before I dared to take another step. Then another.

I kept up that pace going down the hall, taking it one square foot at a time until I was upstairs and in the sanctuary that was my room.

"You're so fucked," I whispered to myself, lightly slapping my cheeks.

The very first thing that I finally allowed to break through the soft static of my brain was about my date with Saint in several hours. If this vampire screwed this up for me, you better believe I was going to kill them with my bare hands.

After the murderous thought crossed my mind, and I didn't feel my body doing wacky things without my control, I forced out a deep breath and rubbed my sweaty palms on my pants. Maybe it was for the best to opt for a nap instead to lower the chances of my new vampire lord deciding to ruin my entire life in one go.

I spun around, locked my door, and tugged my phone from my pocket to set an alarm for 2:00AM. At least getting some shut-eye now would help keep me up a little bit longer into the day tomorrow so I could roam around without fearing that horrible sensation of mind-fuckery. My body made a brief, involuntary shiver at the idea of it happening again, and I sank into the bed.

Plugging in my phone, I hit the remote switch to turn off the lights and trigger the black-out shades in one go. Finally, after hours of hell, I was in the cool, dark embrace of my room. I sighed as I buried my face into my pillow and scooted my arms under it, jolting when the back of my hand scraped something underneath.

I jumped and hit the switch again, the world snapping to that harsh bright light in the midst of me throwing my pillow to the side. In its wake, something rolled down the mattress and stopped when it hit my knees in the indent. It couldn't have been much larger than my thumb, but I dove out of bed like it was a huge spider coming for my ass, and I hit the floor with the loudest sound I could've possibly made. My eyes watered on impact. I winced and rubbed at my backside before I heard Dad's voice carry up the stairs.

"Are you okay?"

"*Fine*," I managed to call out, though it was laced with a squeak of pain. "I'm good."

It took another couple of seconds before Dad's footsteps trailed away from the stairs again, and I pushed myself to my knees to examine what had attacked me: a pink crystal.

Naturally, my first question was: how the hell did that get in here? Followed by: how *long* has that been there? And: *why?*

If my vampire was watching, they were probably lounging on a sofa, enjoying some popcorn, and laughing at my absurd duck-and-cover reaction to a sparkly rock. I pulled my sleeve over my hand and used the fabric as a buffer to pick it up and turn it around in the light.

Okay, so the thing about crystals is that there are the ones that the more holistic pseudo-hippies or wiccans use, which are usually very harmless because it's meant for energies and whatnot, and then there are the ones witches get ahold of. For spells.

And seeing how my luck over the past twenty-four hours had been absolute shit, I wasn't willing to risk gambling that this was a regular, run-of-the-mill, untampered-with crystal. Plus, I didn't know much about crystals outside of figuring out if they're messed with or not because my focus was more on, well, *vampires.*

Sure enough, I twisted in the light, and there was a little sacred circle of some sort chiseled into the very center.

I groaned, letting my forehead collide with the edge of the mattress with a dull *thump.* Awesome. So much for forcing myself into a short coma to keep the vampire away. The crystal dug into my hand through my sleeve as I tried to consider who would've come in here.

My door had been open this morning. I knitted my brows together in concentration. *Charlie* had been home—ugh, but then again, *everyone* had been home by the time I'd woken up, talked to them, and ascended from the basement. My memories spun through each event at double speed. Finding the door open, heading into the bathroom, finding the *bite…*

I hadn't even slept in my bed with this thing in here. And if Charlie dragged me inside… *I* definitely couldn't have done this. I lifted my head and squinted at the offending spelled crystal again. There was no way that we had a *witch* in this house, right? And why would they be targeting *me?*

I ran my tongue along my teeth, trying to imagine the motive someone might have for trying to hex or spell or *whatever* me. Unless this thing somehow made me *forget,* and I *did* happen to make it home and slump over in my bed during that unaccounted-for time between 3:35AM—when I parted ways with Saint—and 7:30AM—when Charlie dragged me off the porch and into the house.

I waited for my vampire to do something to inconvenience my life a little more, but nothing happened. So, I let out a breath and pushed myself up. Sleep clearly wasn't in the cards right now.

My sleeve-covered thumb crested the ridges of the crystal as I worried my lip and turned around to face the door. Someone in this house *right now* had snuck in here. I let my eyes wander, tracing the door frame, the knob, the beanbag, the shelves—every inch of my tainted safe-haven while dread curdled my stomach as I circled back to my final question: *why?*

Why try to put a spell on me? Was it because *I* hadn't been the one to install the hidden camera downstairs? Was it because *this witch* was responsible? Were they working with a vampire? Were they working with *my* vampire?

I hesitated, my fingertips turning icy at the mere thought that I was being used as possible bait. Bait to get to my dad.

Pretty sure I white-knuckle-gripped that pink rock in my hand to the point of shaking. I was so pissed. Here I was, being told that Dad didn't want me involved in any of this, but here were the consequences of his actions. And now I was left to deal with them on my own, whether I wanted to or not.

I shook my head, trying to push down that anger as I crept toward the door and popped it open. Being mad wouldn't solve anything right now, but I could at least redirect those feelings toward finding the culprit who'd tried to screw me over. I stopped on the threshold, glancing up and down the hall from Adonis's room to Rory's at the very end.

That's when I remembered Lux's phone charging pad. I kept my eyes on the stairs as I moved as quickly and quietly as I could to her door, my heart hammering in my chest and pulse pressing into the crystal. I turned the knob, sucking in a deep breath and slipped inside.

Maybe I worked myself up into believing the place would magically turn into a place of satanic worship this time, but it was still the same pink palace I remembered. My back stuck against the door as I eased it shut, my eyes darting around the room for anything else I might've overlooked the first time. But I couldn't see any weird symbols in the abstract pastel art hanging over the headboard—pretty much the only pieces that weren't solid colors.

I swallowed, trying to force down the lump in my throat as I started for the nightstand. The crystal weight heavier in my grip as I hovered next to the phone charging pad. The thing looked harmless. It was something kitschy and cute, rather than menacing and ominous. Maybe a friend of hers bought it as a joke or said it fit her aesthetic.

I looked back down at the crystal. I mean, it's a pink crystal, and the phone charger is a pink witchy circle thing, so… maybe? Biting my lip, I glanced over my shoulder to try to brush away the unsettling idea that something might be in here watching me go through Lux's things. If there was, I certainly didn't see it, and my vampire didn't take over and magically give a shit about what I was doing.

So I tugged on the nightstand drawer. It made a clicking sound as it caught on the latch inside. My brows shot sky-high. Now why the fuck would she lock this? I chewed on my lip and shoved the crystal in my pants pocket before dropping to my knees and lifting up the comforter to peer under the bed.

"Jackpot," I whispered, finding a small box tucked into the corner where the headboard met the nightstand.

With a silent prayer that the key was inside, I dragged that sucker out and took in the top of what had to be a jewelry box. There were worn-down velvet patches that receded into the grooves of the plastic, resembling the facets of the tufted chair she had in front of her desk. I think that's what gave me pause. This thing was old and personal, unlike everything else in the room. I couldn't help but let my fingertips graze the latch on the front, unable to shake that uncomfortable feeling that I was invading Lux's privacy until I told myself that it was very likely that *she* had invaded *mine*.

Thanks to that newfound resolve, I flipped the lid open. A charm bracelet, a pendant, a couple of crumbled hundred dollar bills, and some small, half-folded envelopes took over the hot pink interior. I nudged the items around.

"Dammit," I whispered and shut the box. No key.

Okay, to the desk.

I pushed myself off the floor after replacing the box and tip-toed over to the other side of the room. The thing might as well have been a scene set up for those study-with-me videos with how clean it was. Her tablet-laptop combo was neatly set in the middle of the desk in front of her pink typewriter keyboard and baby pink wireless mouse—all of it set on top of a matching pink desk mat. Aside from the white digital clock setting off to the side with its faux-flipping numbers, that was *it*.

Now to hope that the desk drawers weren't as barebones as the top of this thing. I slid out the top two drawers to find a couple of neatly tied charging cables, pens, sticky notes, and notebooks, which didn't leave me with much hope as I opened the bottom drawer. Well, until I slid it open to a star chart.

I raised a brow as I plucked it out and turned it over to find the astrological symbols with dates for sun, moon, rising, and a bunch of other nonsense I didn't understand. It wasn't proof of witchcraft, that's for sure, especially when my eyes caught the small advertisement on the back for star-sign branded makeup, complete with a smiling girl donning deep blue eyeshadow with connected dots to mimic stars. I muttered a curse and dropped the chart back into the drawer, stirring up a rogue slip of white receipt paper.

Reaching in, I snapped it up and smoothed it out to read the top: *Charm & Rit*. The phone number underneath was scratched through, like it'd seen war in the depths of Lux's purse, and there wasn't a website listed. I skimmed through the line items: OBS CRST— QTY 5, RQ CRST—QTY 5, STR CHRT—QTY 1, and HERB BNDL—QTY 1. When I reached the bottom, there was the final nail in Lux's metaphorical coffin: the date of the night I got bit. The night she said she'd taken a detour in the group chat. The night *someone* had snuck into my room.

CRST. Crystal.

I felt sweat start to break out on my palms as I rocked back to sit on my feet, knees complaining from me putting weight on them for so long. All I could do for a minute or two —maybe even an eternity if I'd let myself—was stare down at that damning piece of receipt paper. Yeah, of course I know that Lux isn't the *nicest* person in the world, but she seemed to take on bitchy as a personality trait more than anything.

She never really actually felt like she was *malicious* to me, at least.

I couldn't help but think about when I'd brought everyone breakfast about an hour ago, when Lux had grabbed my arm and started pleading with me. Was that because she felt guilty? Or was that because she didn't want to get caught? Or maybe she was trying to win me over before I figured out what she'd done.

I shook my head. What *had* she done, exactly? Sure, there was a crystal in my pocket now, but I didn't know what it did or what it was for. Maybe it was something beneficial or completely harmless—a prank, maybe?

God, my eyes almost rolled back in my head. I gritted my teeth and nearly crumpled the receipt. Seriously? A *prank?* No, this was a sign of her betraying the rest of the hunters, possibly getting me bit, and acting as a spy. This was potential evidence.

I reached for my phone in my pocket before I grazed the crystal there instead and ripped my hand out like I'd touched a hot pan. I'd forgotten that I left my phone in my room. The name *Charm & Rit* repeated in the front of my mind as I pushed the desk drawer shut and hurried out of the room, quietly pulling the door shut and tiptoeing down the hall to get my phone.

Once I was cross-legged on my bed with a search tab up on my emotional support device, I found social media link after social media link, all locked behind needing an account. My dad told me that I was forbidden from having one while living under his roof—a rule I was honestly super tempted to break right now—but his reasoning was still pretty sound: it makes it incredibly easy for others to find you. And considering all the shit going on right now, I didn't want to be found.

I threw my head back and groaned before returning to the screen and clicking on a *Yep!* link, where the shop reviews were insanely generic about things like customer service. Aside from one that mentioned purchasing some books, I still didn't have any concrete indicator of what the hell they sold. I scrolled up on the page to the address and hours.

They were open. Right now.

I bit my tongue as the screen dimmed, warring with myself on whether or not I should let myself journey outside with the threat of my vampire possibly taking over at any second loom over my head.

But what other option did I have?

I slid off the bed and carefully fished the crystal from my pocket, finding a tissue to wrap it in so it didn't scratch the hell out of my phone if they were going to cohabitate in there. Shoes, jacket, gloves, and I was heading down the stairs, slowing when I hit the first-floor landing.

"Jules?" Dad called out from his office, muffled footsteps signaling that I needed to get the hell out of this house before he did or said something else to tip me over the edge.

"I'm heading out," I said coldly, wrenching the door open to the chilly night air. At least that would help keep me awake and alert, though I'm not sure it'd matter much if I wasn't in control.

"Just hold on for a second," he said, finally appearing in the entry. "I want to talk abou—"

I shot him a glare. "You may want to, but I'm not really in the mood right now."

Damn. I was sort of proud of myself when the door

swung shut behind me, despite that deep ache in my core that threatened to overwhelm me again. I sucked a sharp breath, letting it anchor me as I jogged down the steps and onto the sidewalk.

I couldn't trust anyone in that house to fix my problems, especially when more than one of them had caused it all in the first place.

6 SHOP OF HORRORS

think I made it a whole two blocks before I started to drag. In a sick, twisted way, I was honestly becoming a little more open to my vampire taking over and navigating me straight to them so I could skip this whole investigation arc, kill them, and pass the fuck out for a week. But, since they didn't magically appear to pilot me like an anime mecha to the final boss, I had to stop at a convenience store for a pick-me-up.

The electronic chime of the door opening made my heart jump a little, even though the guy at the register didn't bother to look up. He seemed far too busy with his phone to give a shit, which at least saved me a little face. I'd rather not be scrutinized right now, please and thank you.

I made a beeline for the refrigerated glass cases and prowled down the aisle as I scanned for my poison of choice: a black and electric green can that promised to keep me awake enough to make it through my 3AM date. And while I was having some reservations about canceling after my recent vampire possession, I still had time to figure something out. Probably. The blast of chilled air helped snap me back to my senses as I plucked out my prize, only for the door to pop shut and leave me with a frosted reflection of quite possibly the worst state I've ever seen myself in.

My jaw hung open as I reached for my hair and tried to smooth it out, but I ended up cringing with how greasy it felt. I wiped my hand on my pants and tugged up my hood, hoping to hide it. But the icing on the cake was how much darker the circles under my eyes looked. I prayed it was just the terrible fluorescent tube lighting in the store, but I questioned if the lighting in any other place I'd end up on my date would help me not look like death warmed over.

Shaking the thought out of my mind for now, I nabbed a protein bar from the end of the shelving units and made my way to the checkout counter. The dude didn't even spare me a glance as he scanned everything, mumbled if I wanted my receipt, and sent me on my way so he could continue with his phone. I guess that was better than seeing his eyes bulge out of his head and saying, "Jesus, what the fuck happened to you, man?"

The second I was outside, I popped the top on the can and knocked back some caffeine to keep me upright for the rest of the trek. My fingers rapped against the tin can at each intersection I was forced to wait at, and I took sip after sip until I couldn't stand the taste anymore about a block away from my destination. I dropped it in the trash and jogged the rest of the way to the door next to a large picture window with *Charm &* *Rit* painted in old-timey block letters on the glass.

When I stepped into the little inlet and pulled on the

handle, it took me a second to register that the sign was flipped to 'CLOSED'. But the door gave a little jingle as it folded inward. And, I mean, the lights were on, so I nudged it open the rest of the way. I winced when the bell rang out a second time as the door shut behind me.

Simple, flat-pack warehouse furniture corners peeked out from tasseled runners and tablecloths cluttered with trays, book stacks, and glass dishes of what looked to be soaps and bath bombs. My sights fixed on the fairy lights strung along the perimeter of the ceiling, leading from towering case to case lined with more tomes and decorative bookends that reminded me of the geodes I liked to collect in one of my cozy video games.

I instinctively reached to pat the crystal in my pocket as I wandered over to the jutted-out cabinet at the bottom of one of the cases, where a display of assorted rocks—*crystals*—sat. Well, fuck. Okay, but that didn't mean anything yet, right? This could just be some run-of-the-mill hippie joint that Lux enjoys frequenting?

Honestly, I was doing a pretty good job at gaslighting myself until I finally saw the gleam of a strikingly similar pink crystal in one of the little dividers. I reached for the description card to get a better look at it, my palm sweating like crazy before I heard a loud *thump*.

I nearly pissed myself. The building shook with the force of that door slamming on the second floor, followed by a rapid jog down the stairs that reminded me of Adonis's stampede back at the house. I whirled around on my heel just in time to find a shadow pouring over the wall behind the checkout counter.

Thinking I was about to meet the biggest, beefiest witch

alive, my whole body stiffened as if the guy might leap over the counter and throttle me for slipping into his shop during after-hours. But instead, a thin woman emerged.

Her eyes narrowed at me with annoyance, glossy pink lips pursed before she stole a glance at the door. The woman's fringe, free from her bun, flew upward with her frustrated breath. "I'm so sorry, I thought I already locked up. We're closed."

I cleared my throat. "N-no, that's my bad. I just kind of automatically pull doors sometimes." I forced out a nervous laugh. "Um, I was actually hoping someone might be able to help me identify a crystal I found—"

She shook her head and waved a hand. "Sorry, but you'll have to come back tomorrow."

I sputtered, mentally grasping to find a better explanation about why this was sort of fucking urgent as I blindly reached behind myself to grab one of the pink crystals from the bins.

Spoiler: I didn't grab the right one.

Whatever the hell I grabbed, it was smoother, and it burned like *hell* the second it touched my skin. But it was sort of too late with how quickly my arm rotated back to try to present it to the proprietress. By the time I opened my fist to show it to her, I was hurling it to the floor.

"*Shit.*"

It smacked against the wood as I shook out my hand like I'd scooped a burning coal out of a fire pit.

She stared down at it.

I stared down at it.

The blue-green-yellow streaked black mass remained motionless.

The soft static of my brain overtook whatever explanation

I had now because this whole damn crystal shop was probably run by witches, shopped by witches, and cursed by witches, which meant I needed to fucking leave.

I cleared my throat. "I'll just see myself out."

My shoes squeaked as I made a sharp turn and took all of three steps before I was knocked off my feet. I slammed against the floor, much like that stone-crystal-thing, my shoulder driving straight into the leg of one of the tables. Rocks shifted in their boxes, threatening the entire integrity of the display.

Then came the angry stomps of the woman—*witch*, yep, she was a fucking witch, for sure—that'd barreled down those steps moments ago.

I winced and scrambled to my knees as fast as I could.

"You damn vampire pets just don't know where you don't belong, do you?"

My heart stopped. Oh my God. Oh my God, she *knows*. I held up a hand as she slid a dagger from under the back of her shirt. "W-wait, I'm not—"

"Shut the fuck up and *die*."

The bell jingled, and her head whipped around. A blur of a person rushed in, tackling her to the floor. With the quickest one-two-punch knockout I'd ever seen, Iris turned to me, panting, and asked, "Are you okay?"

I sat there, slack-jawed, staring down at the woman's prone form, out cold. The dagger must've been somewhere under the display furniture because it wasn't anywhere to be seen now. But the worst part of the entire sequence of events is that someone had immediately clocked me as a familiar and immediately turned on me. And I couldn't even react. I'd fucking froze.

"Jules?" Iris asked again, peeling herself off of my attacker and shaking my shoulder. "Come on, let's get you out of here."

"Y-yeah," I finally managed, my legs shaking as I pushed myself off the floor. I couldn't bear to look Iris in the eyes, so I used the table I'd been rammed into to stand. Well, right before I accidentally grabbed the edge of one of the crystal boxes and sent a shit-ton of rocks clattering all over the floor.

Once we were outside, Iris guided me down the street, arm looped through mine as we walked for a half-block in silence. Silence that consumed every fiber of my being as I replayed that moment over and over again, trying to antici-pate what I would've done to combat psycho-witch's knife from plunging into my heart.

"You're really lucky I walk this way every night," she finally said, breaking me out of the prison of my thoughts. "Why were you even in there? Zane and I have been really worried about you since last night, you know?"

Change the subject. Change the subject— "Shouldn't we, um... you know, call the police?" I asked, pointing a thumb behind us.

She skidded to a stop. "Jules, I am not about to tell the cops that I ran into a place of business and punched out a lady who looked like she was threatening you. You don't really expect that to go in either of our favors, do you?"

I awkwardly looked away, rubbing the back of my neck. I don't think embarrassed is the right word for how I felt at that very moment, but it was pretty fucking close. It shouldn't even have been a question in the first place because I should've been able to handle the situation without Super Iris swooping in to save my ass. But I guess that stupid mentality of trying to call for help was still my default.

Iris clicked her tongue. "That's what I thought. Now why have you been ignoring us? What's going on? Is this related to whatever happened back there?" She squeezed my arm, worry crossing her face out of the corner of my eye.

"I'm, um... Sorry about missing your calls." Yeah, that was kind of the worst deflection ever, but what else could I really say? Oh, sorry, I was busy becoming a servant to an evil vampire lord and now my life has spun out of control? "I don't think I've been in the right state of mind for..." How long had it been now? Less than a *day?* Holy shit, it felt like at least a week. "Um... Since I picked up coffee and ran into you two."

Iris stole a glance toward the crystal shop and looped her arm through mine again. "Come on, let's get out of here and then you can lay it all out for me, okay?"

Her soft smile temporarily made me forget about all the shit I'd been dealing with for the next ten-ish minutes. The chilly night air pushed its way into my lungs to keep me from folding like a lawn chair on the sidewalk from pure exhaustion in combination with coming down from that rush of adrenaline.

I think we were about halfway there when I realized where she was taking me: her favorite twenty-four-hour diner that she'd infamously dubbed her 'post-party pad.'

The yellow lighting poured from the windows of the place left a halo on the sidewalk like a red carpet greeting when we arrived. Neon signs all around the door in various shapes and sizes screamed 'ALWAYS OPEN' and '24/7' and 'WELCOME' with reds, blues, greens, and purples.

Iris let go of me and jogged over to the door with the biggest, giddiest grin as she held it open, its pre-recorded chime beckoning me. I stuffed my hands in my pockets as I shuffled to the center of the entry and glanced around at the people in booths and at the bar enjoying breakfast for dinner with some burnt coffee.

She slid past me, tugging on my sleeve, and guided me over to a booth along the far wall.

"So," she started, sliding into her seat, "what's been eating you?"

Well, *that* was certainly a choice of words. I forced my hand to stay pressed against the booth seat to stop it from absently toying with my shirt collar. "Well, uh... Dad and I got into a bit of a fight, so... I mean, we weren't really fighting last night, but it kind of turned into that a little earlier."

"I'm not going to lie, you seemed pretty plastered by the end of the night, so I was a bit concerned because that's not really like you." She worried her lip. "I was kind of freaking out when you vanished on us. I thought you might've passed out somewhere dangerous or got hurt and couldn't get to your phone."

I tucked my hands under my thighs. The edge of my hood grazed my ears as I shrank into it. Damn, I've been an inconsiderate dumbass because of this whole mess. "Sorry for making you worry, Ris. I honestly didn't mean to stress you and Zane out—"

She shook her head. "You're okay now, and that's what matters. *I'm* sorry you're going through it. I know your Dad hasn't exactly been the easiest to deal with from what you've mentioned here-and-there. But you know that you can talk to me about that sort of stuff, right? I'm not just a good-times-only party girl."

Her worry ebbed into a hesitant smile at the arrival of the waitress, who saved me from squirming under her gaze while trying to decide what I could actually tell her. The girl asked if we needed water or coffee as she passed us laminated placemat-style menus. As much as I wanted another jolt of energy, I didn't want to push it if I had another run-in with a crazy witch that might make my heart pop out of my chest, so I stuck to water.

"I'll take a coffee," Iris said, beaming at the waitress to see her off.

The stress of just *knowing* that Iris was about to peer into my soul again made me focus on the glossy list of pancakes, waffles, and all five million ways you could have your eggs cooked. My thumb pressed into one of the menu's sealed, rounded corners until it must've turned white when she folded her arms on the table and leaned forward to try to regain my attention.

"I hate to ask, but did you get any sleep since we last talked?"

I winced. "Uh, not really..." Look, *I* wouldn't have believed myself if I'd lied, so she could win this one. "My aunt showed up earlier and I had a hard time falling asleep before that."

"How about after some food, we head back to my place and you get some shut-eye, hm? Then you don't have to deal with your dad, and you can chill for a bit."

I think I almost cried with how relieved I felt to get that offer, even if that little voice in the back of my head reminded me that my vampire might fucking kill her if I took Iris up on it. I swallowed back that pain. "Thanks, Ris. I'll see how I feel after I get some food down first."

"Sure thing," she said, a smile crawling back onto her face as she wiggled out of the booth. "Give me a sec to hit the restroom. If the waitress comes back before I do, just tell her I'll take some bacon and eggs, okay?"

"Yeah, no problem." I couldn't help but smirk at the bounce in her step as she headed somewhere behind me.

Damn, I wish I could be as confident and quick-thinking as her.

Instead, I was staring down a menu, unable to read anything on it because my brain was too busy replaying how I reached for that rock, dropped it, and then got hurled across the room—all in under thirty seconds before I'd been staring down a knife. I tried to shake it out of my head, but it wouldn't fucking disappear.

My palm turned up as I glanced to check it. No mark, which I guess was a bit of a blessing in these trying times. But that didn't exactly put my mind at ease since now I knew there was a weird-ass way to be able to tell if I was a familiar.

The buzz of my phone in my pocket pulled me out of replay mode just long enough to fall straight into idiot gay mode.

Saint's name, complete with that little black heart emoji, took up a notification on my screen.

> Hey, there's an issue with the building's water, so the shop's closed tonight for repairs. Which means I'm also completely free now. You able to meet up earlier, or...?

Yes. Oh my God, yes. I really needed a win right now, and

this could absolutely be it. Well, it *was* going to be a win until I stopped my little thumbs from typing back an incoherent reply because I realized that I'd be ditching Iris. *Again.*

I groaned. There were two choices here: stay with Iris—like a good friend—and risk snapping her neck when she inevitably drags me back to her apartment, *or* go on an earlier date with Saint—I mean, come on, it's *Saint*—and avoid any and all dangerous activities for a bit while I re-evaluate my current situation.

I was fairly confident that I would be safe from my vampire making me hurt someone while in public. Anywhere out in the open or places with cameras would be a risk for them. While it's not completely out of the realm of possibilities, it would be a hassle to clean up a erratic, violent mess with witnesses. And vampires don't randomly make people into familiars either. It's intentional. Strategic. Though that train of thought gave me pause regarding why a vampire would choose *me*. Either way, it meant I wasn't wholly expendable, which was both rather comforting and extremely disturbing.

I tilted my head back and forth as I stared down at my phone. Being in public was safer. *Staying* in public was safer. And I wouldn't be going anywhere private with Saint—not during our second time hanging out together. With a quick glance behind me to the restrooms, I sighed.

Where do you want to meet?

"Sorry, Ris," I mumbled, sliding out of the booth. "This is for your own good tonight. I promise to make it up to you."

The phone buzzed again.

In front of the shop?

See you in 15 :)

See you then :)

I grinned stupidly to myself as I pushed open the diner door to the crisp night air, hoping to finally clear my head for the first time tonight.

7 LOVE OR WAR

I didn't even get a chance to respond to Iris's text before my phone screen lit up with a circle-cropped photo of her grinning from ear-to-ear while she made a peace sign. No way was I going to be an asshole and decline it after straight-up ditching her.

So I exhaled, swiped to answer and put the receiver to my ear.

"Jules? Are you serious right now? Why did the server tell me you left while I was in the bathroom? I've been sitting here for the past several minutes thinking that you went to hit a stall and fell in."

"Um." Oh boy was I glad I'd already come up with a good explanation for this one. "Sorry, my dad called, and he wants to talk. He made it sound pretty urgent, so I'm going to head home and try to hear him out. I'm *really* sorry, Iris. I feel really shitty, but I had to go."

Her sigh might as well have been her punching a hole through my chest. "Are you sure you're good to talk to him right now? I'm not so sure it's the greatest idea since you've been kind of out of it, and you admitted that you're running on no sleep."

"It's fine, Ris, really. We'll talk, and then I promise I'll go to bed before the sun comes up, okay?"

The groan on the other end told me exactly how she felt about the entire situation, but I wasn't about to put her anywhere near another supernatural being tonight, including myself.

"Fine," she said. "But I'm going to require *one thing*."

Well, fuck. I rocked on my heels at the crosswalk, holding my breath as I stared two blocks ahead to the edge of that familiar storefront next to where Saint was waiting for me.

"Please text me when you make it home, all right?"

I could've collapsed on the pavement with relief. "I can do that. I'll be there in the next five minutes."

"Thanks, Jules. Please let me know if you need a place to crash if things don't go well with your dad, okay?"

"Will do. And I'm really sorry, Iris."

"Yeah, yeah. I'll make sure you make it up to me later, so don't think you're getting off so easily." The light in her voice bled through, bringing a smirk back to my lips again.

"Have a good night, Ris."

"Be safe, Jules."

The call ended, and the crosswalk sign blinked to white. I stuffed my phone in my pocket and jogged across, tugging my hood up over my head with the hope that it would make me look a little more presentable for my date. God, my heart still fluttered when I thought about it like that.

I silently prayed that my vampire wouldn't fuck this up for me in whatever non-violent, humiliating ways that were still on the table for them because that was the absolute *last* thing I needed right now. When I finally reached the corner, I saw Saint playing with his phone in front of the café, the lights dimmed except for the bright beams pouring out from the back of the place. A flush crept up my neck as I crossed to the other side and realized that Saint was donning a leather jacket.

When he looked up, I did a stupid little wave and couldn't suppress my nervous, giddy smile. I'll admit that the nerves were starting to get to me, especially since I didn't have any liquid courage in my system and my memory was shot. But I think what fucked me up the most was Saint's reaction once we stood face-to-face.

"Jules, are you okay?"

Well, I tried. I guess my appearance was beyond saving.

Worry clouded Saint's perfect, beautiful face as I reached to nudge my hood a little further over my hair.

"Y-yeah. Just haven't really slept well and had some personal issues to deal with." I waved a hand like it was no big deal, even though it was a fucking *huge* deal that was currently ruining my life. "But I think I'd rather just forget all of that shit exists right now if that's okay?"

I tried not to squirm under Saint's gaze, my gut twisting at the hint of pity there.

"Are you sure? I can handle talking through personal stuff, Jules."

What the fuck? This guy was too fucking perfect to be

real. I hesitated, considering giving into the offer and trauma-dumping until I reeled in my composure.

I shook my head. "It's fine. Really. They're my problems, and I don't think that's fair to drop all of that on you for our second time hanging out together." Not sure why, but I couldn't say the word 'date'—it just wouldn't fit into the vocabulary I could use around him just yet. Like speaking it in his presence would summon every bad thing in existence to come and kick the hell out of me for having something nice for a change. Or worse, have him laugh in my face and ask if that's what I thought this was.

"Then... how about we get something to eat?" Saint asked, sliding his phone into his jacket. "And if you change your mind after that, you can talk my ear off, okay?"

Okay, now I was about to cry. No one was *this* nice. Seeing how I'd just ditched one of my few opportunities to eat something of real substance tonight, I nodded, unable to get any more words out.

"Come on, there's a place not too far from here that I wanted to try." He took a step, keeping at my side as I turned around to join him. "You like pub food?"

I stifled a moan, mainly because I feared it would sound far too sexual in the presence of a guy I was still trying to keep my cool around. Not that I was succeeding, but I at least wanted to *try.* "That sounds amazing right now."

Saint chuckled. "Perfect."

On the way there, I made a mental pros and cons list about whether or not to get a beer. And considering my current vampire problem and almost getting stabbed to death, the cons won out. It was a good thing I decided fast because reaching the pub had only been a five-minute walk.

Saint, like a true gentleman, held the door open for me to shuffle inside. I immediately hunched in on myself and texted Iris a lie about making it home to avoid being the one asked about complicated things like party size or booths versus tables that my pea-sized brain didn't have room to handle right now. It worked, because the wait staff asked Saint instead, who happily answered everything and got us seated across from each other in a green-cushioned booth at the back of the place.

I slid in, my attention drifting to the dark wood décor and a chalkboard menu with handwritten selections of beers on tap. The temptation was at an all-time high. It was time to distract myself from getting blasted and ending up with fifty more problems to deal with.

"Um, so, how'd you end up working at *The Crown Café?*"

Saint gave me a look, a bemused smirk tugging at the corner of his mouth. "All right, so if I answer your question, that means I get to ask my own. I don't want you deflecting the whole night to make this all about me."

Well, fuck. Why did I have to find a smart guy too?

I chewed the inside of my cheek before I surrendered. "Okay, that's fair." Most of it would probably be cover-story lies anyway, but there wasn't a whole hell of a lot I could do about that.

Saint blew out a breath, drumming his black-painted nails against the paper menu. "Well, I sort of needed money to get a place, which required a job, so that's the main reason. Didn't exactly want to stay in this town, but..." He half-shrugged, his eyes skimming the selection of drinks. "How are things as a late-night admin assistant for that security company? Do you plan on staying there?"

I barely had time to register the fact that he'd asked me a question with the gut-punch that he was clearly trying to get the hell out of here. I pulled the cloth napkin from my silverware roll into my lap to fidget with as a member of the wait staff stopped at our booth, giving me a second to clear my head before I spiraled about the idea that I could very well be Saint's temporary distraction.

After Saint ordered a water, and I decided not to let this conversation steer me away from my pre-made decision to stay away from alcohol, I followed suit. She left, saying she'd be right back, leaving me to finally answer his question.

I absently rolled the napkin against my jeans. "I, um… don't know." I didn't know anything about my plans for the future after I'd last spoken to Saint, let alone if I'd have one with the way things were currently going.

Saint cocked his head, his brows knitting together in a way that made my insides twist. Either he was pretty fucking good at faking sympathy, or I'd magically hit the jackpot of all reasonable guys to ever date in my entire life.

I tried not to squirm under his gaze. "Well, um, I don't really *mind* the job, but I don't think I have many other options. Didn't really go to college or teach myself anything career-worthy, so…"

He smirked. "You could always come work with me at the café."

Despite it likely being mostly a joke, my heart decided to try to beat out of my chest again like a wild animal. As clumsy as I was, I knew me plus hot drinks seemed like an absolutely terrible combination, but my dumb little brain latched onto the idea of working alongside cool, collected, attractive Saint on a nightly basis. And that sounded a million times better than continuing to work for a bunch of hunters who kept me at arm's length.

What if Saint and I got serious? Would we move in together, work together, and spend every waking moment together until he would undoubtedly get sick of me?

The waitress returned, breaking me out of those thoughts with two glasses of water placed onto the table top. She slid out her little handheld order device, and Saint tapped something on the menu. I didn't catch what he'd said because I had to force my brain to hurry up and make a decision. I definitely panic-ordered their signature sandwich with some onion rings, immediately regretting the rings when she'd walked away.

No way in hell Saint would want to kiss me now.

I shoved those thoughts aside, reaching for my water. "You implied that you want to leave? Why?"

He chuckled through a cringe. "I was sort of hoping you'd forget that comment. It's not something I like to talk about, but I was in a bit of a toxic relationship before I moved to this side of town. I'm not exactly thrilled to live in the same area as said person either. But I don't really have the means to go anywhere else at the moment, so..." He shrugged. "I'm still here."

My heart squeezed. Well, fuck. "I'm sorry."

"Don't be. It's my problem, not yours. Plus, if I didn't compromise by moving and working at the café, I probably wouldn't have met you."

Heat crept up the back of my neck. The way Saint looked at me then made me feel like I was the only person in existence. I almost forgot I was sitting in a pub with a few other stray diners, let alone that I had a fucking vampire bite on my neck.

"Now that you've heard a bit of that sob story, do *you* have any evil exes that I should know about?" That teasing smirk was back.

Awesome. Now I have the terrible privilege of admitting that I'm a loser. I grimaced and stared down at the table like I'd find a way to answer that wasn't a complete and total lie. "Um, you're actually the first person I've, um..." Don't say 'date,' Jules. Don't fucking curse yourself. "...started seeing, I guess."

I could've sworn I saw Saint breathe a sigh of relief out of the corner of my eye. However, since I was super fucking nervous about his reaction, I went in for the next question instead of giving him time to process.

"Um, so if you didn't have any sort of obstacles, where would you *want* to be living right now?"

"Oh boy..." He hummed, drumming his fingertips on the table as he stared off at some point over my head. "I honestly don't know—not specifically, anyway. I would definitely live in the heart of another city. A bigger one. Some place that has more of a variety of places open late at night."

I laughed. "Forever a night-owl, huh?"

"Definitely."

I jolted when the first plate scraped the table, my eyes catching on the sandwich melt I was more than happy to see at that moment. My mouth watered, ready for some real *warm* food. Then I glanced over at Saint's steaming bowl of soup and felt a little bit envious.

With a chipper, "Enjoy." The waitress was gone again, and I made the mistake of taking the biggest bite of my life.

"So, how did I end up being the lucky winner to date you first?"

I nearly choked. My eyes watered as I chewed a little faster and knocked back some water. In all honesty, I should've slowed down and mimed a shrug to avoid the question entirely, but instead I stupidly, awkwardly, wiped my mouth with the napkin while I stared down at my plate.

"I..." I cleared my throat, trying to push down the still-bitter part of me that had lashed out a few hours ago. "My, um, my dad wasn't exactly thrilled when I came out to him. He still doesn't really like to talk about it. And I... I think I just tried to avoid it because I didn't want to rock the boat even more."

All teasing had evaporated from Saint's beautiful angel face as he set his spoon down and reached across the table, palm up. A silent request to take my hand.

"I'm sorry, Jules."

I gently dropped my palm into his, shivering as his chilled fingers slid along my wrist. I prayed my fingers didn't feel nearly as cold as I rested them against his skin. The last thing I wanted to do was give him a surprise icy finger against his veins when he was trying to comfort me. His thumb ran up and down the edge of mine, making me melt in my seat as hours of built-up tension started slipping from my body.

"I didn't mean to hit a touchy subject," Saint said quietly. "I understand how difficult that can be. I never really told my family about being bi because I was afraid they would disown me, so I just... never did. People can be intolerant, and it really sucks. I'm also sorry if I crossed a boundary there—"

I shook my head. "It's fine, really. Um... I think if it were anyone else, I don't think I would've answered. My friends have teased me about it on occasion, but that's just because they want me to be happy, so it's a bit different. But it's something I've tried to keep close to my chest because it honestly kind of hurts, I guess."

Saint squeezed my hand. "You shouldn't have to feel like you're doing something wrong by being yourself, Jules. I don't want you to feel like that, especially around me. Because I think you're... special?" I raised a brow, and he chuckled, shaking his head. "Sorry, I'm really bad with words sometimes. I'm trying to say that you have a presence about you that makes me feel better than I have in a long time."

My throat constricted. No, that's cool, I totally wanted to possibly cry in front of Saint, the hottest guy in the universe. I coughed into my napkin to make it stop. "That actually makes me feel a lot better after the day I've had."

"Tell me about it," Saint said, tapping my wrist. "I can handle it, I promise."

This would normally be the part where I cracked my knuckles and lied my ass off, but staring into Saint's big, gorgeous, puppy-dog eyes, I folded. "Well... my dad owns the company I work for, so..."

Saint hissed like he'd been burned. "Oh no..."

"Yeah... But it gets worse because I've been trying to stand out to get promoted, and he's declined my promotion *again* because I'm 'not ready' after way too many years of learning and working under him." I paused, taking stock of Saint's perfect, turned-down mouth. "I'm never getting that promotion, am I?"

Saint slowly shook his head. "Probably not."

My gaze drifted down to our hands, Saint's icy fingers finally warmed by leeching off my body heat. I think that's when the real questions began—between me and myself, anyway.

Did I even *want* to hunt vampires? Or was that to simply make Dad proud?

Would Mom even want this for me? Or would she beg me to move on and invest my time into making a life for myself and let her joyful memories live through me?

Should I seriously be wasting my time on revenge when I could be falling in love?

"Hey," came Saint's velvety whisper to break my torrent of emotional thoughts, "if you need a place to say, you're welcome to stay at my place for a bit to take a breather."

My vision swam as I choked out a laugh. "Thanks. I already had a friend offer the same, but I... I can handle it. I appreciate the offer though."

"It'll be on the table if you ever decide you need it, okay?"

I nodded, trying to paste on a smile so I didn't burst into tears. I'd needed that more than I realized. And while I could've had a heart-to-heart with Ris about everything, it felt more affirming to have it come from someone I was still getting to know.

Saint gave my hand one last squeeze before he pulled away. "Let's finish eating before it gets too cold."

I chuckled and dug in, grateful for the warm meal and easy silence between us. It just felt *nice* to be in his presence, and after his earlier comments, I really did hope he meant that he felt the same about me. Well, despite me currently looking like a raccoon that'd just stumbled out of a dumpster.

Saint snatched the check before I had a chance to, which

left my stomach in knots after his admission of wanting to leave the city but not having the means.

"Let me pay you back," I said, wiggling in my seat to fish out my wallet.

Saint shook his head. "I got it. Don't worry about it."

"Are you sure? I mean, you said that you want to move, and—"

He waved a hand. "Really, Jules, let me get this one. And don't worry about that, okay? A few bucks for a nice night is worth more than scraping it into savings and living a joyless existence because things don't change overnight." The pen scratched against the receipt paper as he added a tip, and I sighed.

I'd have to pay him back with something nice later. Or maybe a dessert or drink tonight. I scooted out of the booth when he sat the pen down and folded the receipt back into its little black folio.

When I pushed myself to my feet, the world wobbled, and I grabbed onto the edge of the table to steady myself.

"Careful," Saint said, quickly slipping out of the booth and grabbing my arm. "Are you okay?"

"Yeah," I breathed, the word a puff from my lips as I forced myself to let go and shake off whatever had made my head spin.

But that was a mistake.

My body seized, heat stabbing into my neck from the bite. *Something* crooned my name in the back of my mind, running its icy claws along the edge of my brain.

I've been searching for you, Jules.

There you are, Jules.

Stay there, Jules.

Keep still, Jules.

And while I was being assaulted by a chorus of demands only I could hear, I guess I was falling. Because the last thing I heard was Saint calling my name before I blacked out.

8 CURSE SICK

When I opened my eyes, the last thing I expected to see was the sad, droopy potted plant above *The Crown Café*, complete with smiley face, sitting on the ledge of a bay window. I racked my brain for an answer as to how I'd gotten here, but the last thing I could recall was talking to Saint—

My heart stopped as I shoved myself upright on the couch. The terror quickly smothered the embarrassment I felt from blacking out in front of Saint when he rushed over.

Oh my God. I was in his fucking apartment.

This was a nightmare.

If it were any *other* situation in which I dramatically passed out like a damsel in distress and woke up here, I'd be furiously blushing and ruining all sense of self-preservation. But right now, my mouth was dry, and I was sweating all over. My vampire was trying to find me, and I was in the absolute worst place possible.

Jules, you're a dumbass who's going to get your maybe-boyfriend killed in under forty-eight hours. Good job.

"You should lay back down," he said, gently cupping my shoulder. The pressure there indicated that I'd have to fight back against his instructions. Being the submissive wet noodle that I was when it came to anything related to Saint, I let him push me down against the couch cushions.

"Um," I squeaked. Very tough of me, I know. "How... did I get here?"

Saint grimaced and rubbed the back of his neck. "I told the pub staff that you had a bit too much to drink earlier and it finally hit you. I debated having them call an ambulance, but you were breathing and your pulse was fine, aside from being a little elevated." He cleared his throat. "I did CPR training for the café about a week ago. Guess it came in handy tonight. But anyway, you were fine and came to for a bit, so I helped you walk back here. I'm guessing it's likely got something to do with the bags under your eyes."

My throat constricted with panic before the memory of Saint pulling me off the floor bobbed to the top of my bucket of blackout memories. Everything still blurred together, but that phantom touch of Saint grabbing my waist to steady me made my head swim. So, yeah, it was a good thing I was laying down.

"T-thanks. And, um, sorry for scaring you. But I'm fine, really." I pasted on the best, carefree smile I could muster in the midst of my fear that I would lose control at any second now and witness my vampire dispose of Saint because he was inadvertently keeping me from them.

Saint frowned, folding his arms over his chest. "Even if

that's the case, I took anything you'd need to leave because you really need to rest."

The second he turned his back on me, I shot up again. "You took my wallet and keys?" I instinctively patted my pockets, even as Saint stopped at the little peninsula of the kitchen and patted my wallet.

"Wallet, keys, and—" He picked up another item and my heart dropped straight to my stomach. "Your little emotional support rose quartz."

I might've given myself the Heimlich maneuver with how hard I threw my torso into the back of the couch. "Don't touch that!" I held my arm out, straight as an arrow, like I might be able to dive and grab it from five feet away.

Saint blinked before a teasing smirk tugged at the corner of his mouth. "Jules, you don't have to be embarrassed about it. I think it's cute that you think you need a little talisman to keep me around."

Wait, what?

My fingers curled in my outstretched grasp. "Er, you, um... Know what it does?"

He raised a brow. "Are you saying that you *don't?*"

I forced out a nervous chuckle and started to pick at my ribbed-knit sleeve cuffs. "Well, a friend gave it to me, but she didn't really say how it'd help. Something about good luck?" I gave a bit of a shrug, trying to act as cute and clueless as possible.

Somehow, that fucking worked because Saint laughed and shook his head. "It's a superstitious way to try to make someone fall in love with you."

For love? What the fuck? Why would Lux be trying to

make me fall in love with her? She knows I'm gay. That doesn't make any sense.

I stared at the counter top, barely registering Saint placing the crystal down again.

Focus, dammit. Here I am, being held hostage by Saint, who unwittingly decided to put himself in harm's way, and I'm worried about Lux's weird crystal bullshit.

Saint's phone buzzed, and he swiped the screen. "Perfect timing. Just got the all-clear that I can use the water again. I'll make us some tea to help you relax."

I shit you not, that man went straight for the damn sleepy time tea. Fuck no.

Pushing off the back of the couch, I stumbled to my feet on wobbly legs and muttered a few curses under my breath before I slid across the wood flooring next to the counter. I scooped up my keys, and Saint spun around with the kettle in his grip.

"Jules!"

"I'm *really* sorry, but I have to go—it's important."

"And you passing out *isn't* important? Your health should come firs—"

"It will! I promise!" I quickly exclaimed. "But I have to... um..."

"You have to *what*, Jules?"

I grimaced, the excuses slipping through my fingers like sand. "God, it sounds really stupid..." Come on, Jules. What would make sense right now? My brain ran through all the trauma I'd dealt with and hooked onto something I could work with: "I lost my company card last night when I tried to use it instead of my actual card. I think I put it on a table or something, or it fell—I don't know, but my dad will literally kill me if I don't get it."

The way Saint's face fell with pity might as well have been a kick in the teeth. "Jules…"

I swallowed and rubbed the back of my neck. "I, um, didn't really do myself any favors with this, so it's my fault. So… yeah. I was planning on hunting it down after…"

"Our date," Saint finished with a sigh. That fact that he'd said it warmed my heart, even though his disappointment rippled off of him in waves. He set the kettle down as I slid my wallet off the counter and into my pocket, deciding on how to handle the quartz. Well, that and how to handle saying goodbye to Saint for the night without leaving on bad terms.

"I don't want to think I'm blowing you off or anything." Great choice of words. That was totally going to be in my top cringy interactions that kept me awake in bed later.

Saint slid the crystal over as if it was a peace offering, my stomach forming knots as I cupped my sleeve around it. No point in risking another incident like back in the crystal shop. Then he rounded the counter, which set off alarm bells in my head, the volume of them cranking up when he opened the small entry closet and pulled out a black pea coat.

"Um…"

"You just passed out, Jules. If you're hellbent on getting this credit card back, then I'm coming with you to make sure you're safe."

Well, this had backfired horribly.

"Y-you don't have to—really! I can call my friend to meet me on the way, and she can look after me if you're worried."

A lie, because there was no way I'd drag Iris into this either, but I didn't really have many cards to play here.

One arm was already in a sleeve. "You can do that, but if she's going to meet you on the way, I'm going to at least walk with you until you're with her."

So maybe there was a downside to having a potential partner that cared. Because now I had to figure out a way to ditch him without him worrying or hating me, which was an impossible task.

My head lulled back, eyes closed. Okay, look, o-great-vampire-lord, I just need you to leave Saint alone in all of this and maybe we can work this out, man-to-man.

"Jules?"

I snapped my neck back into place and fished out my phone. "Yep! Sorry! Let me, um... get those addresses..." I tapped through to get to my credit card notifications, hands sweating so bad that my fingerprint didn't register against the screen. Eventually, I saw the pending transactions populate and clicked through some searches to the IDs I couldn't find names for.

A bar. A florist. A convenience store—the one down the street from the two.

What the fuck had I been doing?

I plugged the bar into my maps app and grimaced. Fantastic. A twenty-minute walk of agony to not pass out or snap Saint's neck and have his blood on my hands for life because he might be actively pissing off my vampire. Cool.

I cleared my throat. "It's a bit far."

Saint grabbed the apartment door's handle. "Lead the way." Of course he wasn't deterred by a bit of walking.

The app disconnected and reconnected once we climbed down the stairs and stepped outside. I shivered and tugged my hood back up. This was probably going to be the most awkward walk ever after trying to ditch him countless times, so I kept my eyes on the GPS and prayed Saint didn't decide I wasn't worth the trouble by the end of the night.

New plan: try to lose Saint.

I hated how my insides twisted into knots thinking about how horrible of a person I was being. Was all of this even worth it? What the fuck am I even doing? Is this how I want to spend the rest of my life? Just fucking lying to my could-be-partner about hunting vampires on a nightly basis?

That thought tumbled into another sad reality: I'd probably never see Saint if I ended up hunting with Dad and everyone else. Dad would also probably get bent out of shape if I moved in with Saint anyway. That was a thought I had to shake from my head almost immediately because of how my heart started to speed up. Of course my mind had gone straight to curling up in bed with him every dawn or—well—just *not* going to bed right away.

My face started to heat.

Saint elbowed me, and I fumbled to catch my phone.

"S-sorry, what?"

"You good?"

"Yep! Fine!" I flashed him a smile, but his brows furrowed with concern.

"I guess I'm just worried that you think you have to handle all of this stress on your own."

I hated how the pressure built at the backs of my eyes then. Of course I had to deal with all of this myself—who the fuck else would? I mean, other than the bite issue, the rest of it was too personal—too *intimate* for anyone that wasn't someone I trusted with my entire existence. I love Iris and Zane to death, but they're the kind of people that try to 'fun' everything away. I certainly couldn't talk to anyone in the house about this shit because they'd use it against me. And, even though Saint seemed to be sinking his claws into me and managing to get me to spill my guts to him, I couldn't push myself beyond that just yet.

Well, maybe not until I had the entire vampire thing sorted and I was bite-free.

I shook my head. "Look, I'll get this stupid credit card, go home, and have a talk with my dad. Hopefully we can just figure out a way to set aside our differences."

"I hope you can too," he said.

My grip tightened on my phone. Every light and store-front turned into a new point of small talk during the agonizing trip. I waited second after second for my vampire to beam me a new signal that they were approaching my destination to collect my ass, but we managed to make it to the bar without incident.

Various big-name beer names on neon signs cluttered the windows, practically demanding for me to step inside. That's probably why I'd stopped in at some point.

"Do you mind waiting outside for a sec?" I asked, playing with the edges of my phone case. "I promise I'll be quick."

Saint scowled, but pulled his hand out of his pocket. He held two fingers up at chest-level. "You have two minutes. Anything longer, and I'm going inside to make sure you didn't crack your head on the bar, okay?"

I gave him a thumbs-up and jogged inside.

That sense of déjà vu hit me like a semi-truck—the scent

of beer, vapes, and fried food transported me to another dimension. I scanned the collage of photos and signs covering every wall, like a few license plates and sports flags would somehow give me all the answers I was seeking.

Two minutes didn't feel nearly long enough to patch all the holes in my memory.

I started toward the bartender, trying to ignore the rowdy patrons loudly singing on the far side of the room. "Excuse me, I think I meant to get a receipt from last night, but I must've lost it or something. Would you be able to print a new one?"

"Sure," the guy said. "Know what time? Cash or card?"

I wiggled my wallet free and flashed him the last four digits. Before I knew it, the receipt was in my hand, complete with a single drink order: a gin and tonic.

That was something I've never ordered before.

I quickly thanked him, something familiar prodding at the back of my mind as I tucked the receipt into my wallet and hurried out.

"Not here," I said, pulling out my phone to type in the address for the florist. "Next stop is a block or so away."

Saint followed me like a duckling as I racked my brain as to why I'd ever consider ordering a gin and tonic. There was clearly still a piece missing, but I tried to reason that I had time to figure it out. Even if the chain of stops still made zero fucking sense.

It was a bit of a shock to find a florist open so late, but the woman running the place didn't bat an eye as I pushed my way inside, abandoning my knight in shining armor once again. She popped out an earbud in the middle of boxing something and greeted me with a, "Oh, hi again! Do you need a dozen instead?"

I stopped short, immediately confused. "A dozen of...?"

"The carnations? You asked for one the other night and said it was for someone special. Are you back for more?"

That sensation was back, the mention of carnations placing the answer on the tip of my tongue. "N-no, sorry. I was actually here to check which one I got again because it slipped my mind."

"Oh, of course!" she said, beaming. "You wanted the pink one. That one's been pretty popular with all the homecoming activities going on."

"I see. I'll, um... I'll keep that in mind. Thanks."

She waved, and I saw myself out. The gears of my mind turned as Saint scooted next to me. "You find it?"

I jolted back to reality. "Oh, no—Sorry. It must be at the... the convenience store."

And I already knew I'd magically 'find' it there. I let the GPS lead me two more blocks away, past a wrought-iron fence that wrapped around the parameter of a grassy plot I felt I'd been to before. I slowed, stopping at the light as the red hand commanded me to wait.

Saint started onto the crosswalk before I realized the signal had changed, my heart squeezing when he glanced back to check on me. The air hung thick and heavy, making me feel like I was walking through a dream. Even the chime of the convenience store's door sounded dull and unreal.

I walked up to the clerk behind the register, who barely looked up from their phone.

"Hey," I said, hating how hoarse I sounded. "Were you here last night?"

They slid their eyes over to me. "Oh, yeah. I think I remember you. The guy that bought a bottle of wine, right?"

"Y-yeah. Do you happen to remember what kind it was? My friend was asking about it, and I forgot to note the label after a celebration party..."

"I think it was a rosé or something? It had a bear on it." They pointed to the back corner of the store. "Should be along that wall."

"Thanks."

Sure enough, after prowling the case of wine, I found one matching the description: a pink moscato. I sighed, rubbing my face as I tried to hold back the tears. I didn't want to cry tonight, dammit. Why the fuck was everything trying to make me sob?

But I understood why I'd made this weird trek now, even though it had fucking nothing to do with my vampire, as far as I could tell.

I pulled out my wallet and slid my company card free to complete this charade of an evening. When the door chimed as I stepped back out into the chilly night air, I held it as triumphantly as possible for Saint, who smirked, seemingly relieved.

"So, um, you said you can handle talking about deep shit, right?" I asked, nervously tapping the card against my fingertips.

"Yeah," Saint said, those soft, kind eyes watching me.

"Could we maybe make a bit of a detour? I think... I think I'd like to talk about another thing that's kind of been eating at me."

He nodded. "Of course. What's going on?"

The lump in my throat really didn't want to go away, but I

somehow managed to get the words out after I stared down at the concrete and shuffled a little closer to him. "It's the anniversary of my mom's death."

My mom, who, according to my dad, had loved gin and tonics and pink carnations. But clearly I couldn't stand the former, so I thought pink moscato would have to do in her honor.

9 RAGE ROOM

needed the burnt coffee to keep me awake through all of this, so I was glad that Saint was cool with going to a shitty diner another block over. Mom's cemetery fence was still in clear view, but I didn't have the courage to go back there and introduce her to my two-day relationship with Saint.

Not yet.

Maybe after a few years when my heart didn't do weird things when we held hands, and I could properly tell her I'm gay. I like to imagine that she'd be as supporting as Aunt Syd. Or that she'd snap at Dad for being weird about it.

I guess that's what really hit me then, after walking out of that convenience store with the recovered knowledge that I'd carried out an entire fucking moscato bottle and likely ended up white girl wasted in a cemetery, that the one parent I needed the most right now was buried under six feet of earth.

I swallowed down the lump in my throat. "So, um... My dad, he, uh... he threw himself into work after my mom died.

I was nine." I stared down at the hint of my reflection in my coffee, unable to look at Saint and whatever horrible, pitying expression might be there. "It took him a few months before he could gather up the strength to tell me that she was murdered. So he took some training, quit his job, and started a security service with the conviction to not let someone else be killed on his watch."

"That sounds like a really noble thing to do in her honor," Saint said, doing his best to avoid the awkward apologies for a twelve-year wound that decided to gush open.

"Yeah." I huffed out a bitter laugh. "It started out that way" —it hadn't, but I couldn't exactly tell him he started a *security company* for revenge— "but I felt more and more obligated to help him after school. Like I needed to chip in to cheer him up or make him remember that I was still there."

That old ache returned. I squeezed my mug, my thumb absently tracing over a chip at the base of the handle. "I was like his first employee. I helped him run things around the office. Made him lunch when I packed mine so he didn't forget to eat. I was probably the dream kid everyone wishes they had because I cleaned the bathroom without needing to be told."

Saint chuckled. "Probably. I think the least I could've done was thaw the chicken after school now that I realize how busy they both were. My name suits you better than me now that I know that."

Heat crept along my ears. "I wouldn't go that far." I rotated my mug, hands shaking with nerves. "But, um, yeah. I did everything I could for him like it'd somehow make up for losing Mom. I felt like I needed to shoulder that burden because taking care of me turned into something that often slipped his mind. Taking care of myself turned into a new normal, and taking care of Dad turned into second nature."

"It sounds like it cost you your childhood, Jules."

My eyes burned.

"And, honestly, maybe more than that. You didn't go to college. You didn't try to teach yourself new skills. You invested your whole being into your dad, and... I don't want to be a dick, Jules, but it sounds like he's using you as a crutch. Has he ever asked you about what you want?"

Well, that cut me deeper than I expected. "Nope," I rasped, trying not to add salt to my coffee, though that was getting harder by the second. "I'd like to turn back time. I want Mom back, but I'm not a kid. I know that isn't going to happen." I finally lifted my head to blink away the tears blurring my vision. "Sorry. I really didn't want to dump any of this on you."

Saint shook his head. "We're adults, Jules. And you're going through a rough time. It's okay to lean on others."

"Doesn't really feel great if I'm being honest."

"Because you're not used to it. And probably because it's strange for you because you're used to doing everything on your own." He half-shrugged. "But I want to help you if you need it. You're probably one of the nicest, but definitely the *cutest*, people I know."

And the heat moved to my cheeks, probably turning them insanely red. "I-I-I don't think—"

Saint's melodic laugh shut me the hell up. "*You* might not think so," he said, pulling the unspoken words from my lips, "but I do."

That soft, warm smile made my heart do cartwheels as I melted into my booth seat.

"Well," he said, tapping his nails against the mug with a glance outside. "I guess maybe now would be the best time to ask: what do you want to do?"

I wasn't sure why now would be a good time for that, so I started to shrug, my mind wiped blank from Saint calling me cute. He shook his head. "No, Jules, I mean, you haven't been able to choose what you want to do. So, if you could do anything right now, what would you want to be doing? What do *you* want to do?"

Oh. *Oh.*

"Um..." I bit my lip. "In what kind of sense? Job? School?"

"Preferably something we can do tonight, but if you want to talk about goals and aspirations, I wouldn't mind." He brought the mug to his lips, and a stupid little part of my brain went to: do you think he'd put his lips on yours if you said that's what you wanted?

The more sensible part of my brain was still clinging to that sorrow and pain, which was slowly feeding that well of rage I'd unleashed on Dad earlier. I guess that meant it was being replenished with the validation that I craved, even if I didn't feel right heading back home for good old round two of dragging his ass.

"You know, I'd think a rage room would be rather nice about now," I said, honestly feeling good just *mentioning* the idea. With everything going on, it sounded exactly like something I needed. Well, minus the fact that I might accidentally hurt Saint with or without the help of my vampire because I don't think I could be trusted with something like a sledge-hammer. "But I'm pretty clumsy, so maybe that's not a great idea. I'd probably injure myself."

Saint grinned. "All right, I can respect that since I'd rather you didn't hurt yourself. However... if you're looking to blow off some steam, I think I might have an idea..."

He pulled out his wallet, and tossed some cash on the table with a twinkle in his eye.

"You up for another detour?"

———

When the rideshare car stopped in front of a *Workout Galaxy*, I frowned. I'm not a working-out kind of guy. I had pulled my hamstring once when I was trying to get a bit of muscle and it put me out of commission for a few weeks. By the time I was pain-free, I'd already gone back to my normal routine of being a coffee boy, thankful I wasn't hobbling to and from the café.

Saint stepped up onto the curb next to me as the car started down the street, sealing my fate for whatever weird religion of gains and protein I was about to be dragged into.

"What?" he asked, a laugh bubbling out.

"When I said I wanted to go to a rage room, I didn't mean a room full of rage."

He snorted. Damn. Even his snort sounded cool. How the fuck did he do that?

"Okay, I have a guest pass, and I promise you that we're not going to go shoot up steroids in the locker room. No pumping iron. No running on treadmills. Nothing like that."

"Then, what exactly is there left to do here?" I asked, sliding him a suspicious look.

He rolled his eyes and led the way. A single security person manned the front desk, too busy watching and liking videos of scantily-clad girls on his phone when Saint scanned us in. We roamed through the halls, past windows of gym equipment—only a couple of people using anything in there—and brought me to a separate room.

It was probably a quarter or less of the big workout tank room, the floor covered in soft mats, and punching bags hung periodically from the ceiling. Saint held out his arms, as if showcasing the space. "Welcome to the alternative rage room." He flashed me a smile. "Nothing sharp or heavy, and you get to wear gloves so you don't bust up your hands. Jules-proof."

I was speechless. This was easily in the top ten nicest things someone has ever done for me. How the hell was I supposed to hit something after my body turned to gelatin because Saint was too damn perfect?

He'd already shimmied out of his coat and collected gloves for me by the time I could manage, "Thank you for this."

"I know it won't solve all your problems, but I hope it'll help you feel a little better." Saint held the gloves in offering, waiting as I shed my jacket. I'd almost pulled off my hoodie until I remembered the bite and thought it was for the best to leave it on to help obscure my neck. The way his fingertips gently pressed into my arms to help me strap on the gloves sent chills through me—the good kind that made my head spin from him being so close.

The main problem was that my brain had begun chanting 'kiss, kiss, kiss' when Saint's face hovered anywhere close to mine. What did this guy actually see in me? How the fuck did I end up with *Saint?*

I jolted back to reality when his hand pressed between my shoulder blades, my heart hammering wildly as he guided me to one of the punching bags. Then his chest met my back, his arms guiding mine, as I tried to focus every ounce of my attention on beating up the thing in front of me instead of the fantasy that Saint would start trailing kisses along my jaw.

"You got it?" Saint asked, the tutorial over after both an eternity and split-second.

I cleared my throat, praying it removed any squeak that would've sounded. "Yep." It did, thank God. So, with more confidence than I felt the moment Saint stepped back, I began my assault.

Every jab's impact was a punch to the metaphorical face of a problem: Mom's death, Dad's choke hold on my life, my fear of Charlie being the child he'd always wanted, my frustration at not understanding why Lux had sneaked into my room and planted that crystal, Adonis calling me a minion and treating me like I was beneath him, Rory's disdain whenever I barged in on one of their meetings.

The anger ramped up, greedily collecting every morsel of rage I poured like gasoline on a fire.

Another punch for not being able to go to Aunt Syd's while I was growing up to take a break from a life of studying vampires. One more for having to lie to Saint and my friends about what I actually do or I'd get hauled off to a mental institution.

A heavy *slam* of my padded fist against the bag for the throbbing bite on my neck—my mind unraveling that I'd gotten it somewhere between the bottle of pink moscato and the journey home. For that vampire deciding I was easy prey. For *being* easy prey. For wanting a fucking *normal life*.

I stumbled back, panting.

That's what I wanted: a normal life.

A life where vampires were fantasy creatures in movies, TV, books, games—all make-believe. A life where I could go on carefree dates—fuck yes, *dates*—with Saint and not worry about putting him in danger. A life where I didn't have to lie about what I did and never get the recognition or thanks I deserved for busting my ass to help everyone my dad saw as worthy to fulfill their goals of revenge.

Saint crept back into my periphery, arms crossed as he took one slow step at a time toward me, as if I might go back in for another round. "How you feeling?"

"Better," I breathed.

That wasn't a lie, unlike so many other things I'd told him tonight. I fumbled with the velcro by my wrists before he strode over, gently taking my gloved hand and freeing it from its stiff prison. Every action toward me was so gentle that I couldn't help but stare at his face—that perfect, beautiful face that I couldn't believe watched me with any form of interest.

The rational part of me chided myself for letting the thought creep in that I'd be walking away from my dad by choosing my maybe-boyfriend, who I'd known for all of two days. Eventually the honeymoon phase of the start of the relationship would wear off, right? Would the two of us still be happy then? Would I regret the decision of leaving behind everything I'd grown up learning to—I don't know—become a barista and worry about mundane things like rent?

The other glove slipped off, and Saint held them both up. "I'll put these back and get us another driver. We can head back to my place and watch a movie or something? Anything to let you get in some extra time before you have to deal with your dad and work bullshit?"

My mouth twitched as my eyes flicked to his lips. Really,

Jules? You want to kiss him *now?* In the middle of a *Workout Galaxy?* This is where you want your first kiss? Then again, the struggle I had years before reaching this milestone was worrying if the guy I went out with would think I should be the one to go in for the kiss. Saint was clearly the leader of the two of us, right? Surely he'd be the one to initiate any sort of base-running baseball-metaphor stuff.

"Yeah," I said, barely able to comprehend the question with my mind immediately clouded with thoughts of puppy love. "That sounds nice."

My brain quickly pumped the brakes once Saint grinned and started for the cubbies of gloves. The vampire bite, you idiot. Did you forget that you're dealing with a crisis and were desperately trying to escape his apartment to begin with? I had to pull the plug on this somehow, but I'd really screwed myself here unless I could come up with an excuse.

I needed to think, and clearly, thinking was next to impossible in his presence because I was turning to putty whenever he touched or looked at me. I glanced around the room, my eyes catching on a sign above the two doors along the wall behind me.

I cleared my throat. "Saint, I'm, um—I'm going to go clean up right quick if that's cool." I jabbed a thumb toward the locker rooms as he turned around.

He hesitated. "Okay, but you have three minutes. Any longer than that, and I'm heading in there to make sure you didn't pass out again. Don't bother with the shower, you can use mine when we head back."

I silently cursed him for the timer. And the mention of using his shower. My face heated as he eyed me with a warning glare while he pulled out his phone. I spun on my heel and jogged to safety to compose myself again.

When I pushed open the door to the men's locker room, the lights flicked on to a U of lockers against the walls and a hall jutting off the left of bathroom stalls, urinals, sinks, and probably showers a bit further down. From the way another hall intercepted it, I guessed it connected to the door by the hallway by the workout tank we'd passed to get here.

Fortunately, it was empty, based on the lack of noise, stuff, and the fact that the motion-sensor light had been off in the first place. I made my way over to the sinks, my face looking like I ate a whole lemon when I caught a glimpse of my reflection.

Do *not* think about showering in Saint's apartment. Worry about that later. *Think*, Jules. Fucking *think*.

I reached for my phone and my heart dropped. It was in my jacket. Right next to Saint's in the boxing room. I groaned. There went that idea to invent someone calling or texting me to tell me to get my ass home ASAP.

I stared down at the drain and chewed the inside of my cheek. I didn't want to deal with this anymore. I'd already decided that. But I think it finally kicked in that it also meant something else: I no longer needed to prove myself to Dad.

There wasn't a point in taking on my vampire myself. I wasn't cut out for this. Hell, I almost got stabbed by a witch earlier. I was out of my depth here, and if Dad wanted to continue playing vampire hunter, then the solution was simple: I had to go home and tell him.

Sure, he'd lock me up for a while until he took care of it, but after that, I could leave. I wouldn't have to feel guilty.

He'd get the satisfaction of saving his son, and I could finally close the door on that chapter of my life for good. I could have that normal life. I didn't have to risk dying to do it either.

I closed my eyes, forcing out a deep breath.

Everything would be all right.

However, before I could formulate the escape portion of my plan, a door swung open, and I jumped.

"Jules?"

I spun toward the other entrance's hall, a stretch of sinks between me and a duffle bag-toting Zane with the biggest grin. This was the worst thing that could happen right now. I really needed the universe to stop throwing the people I cared about at me so I could possibly put them in harm's way tonight.

"It is you!" He moved to close the gap between us. "Ris said she ran into you earlier, but you ran off. Is everything okay? You seemed a little out of it yesterday."

"Did I?" I asked nervously. "Sorry, man. I've been dealing with some shit." I forced out an awkward laugh as I tried to brush aside my hair like it'd somehow miraculously look less greasy. "W-what are you doing here?"

Zane lifted the duffle, beaming. "I live here for about half the week. Where else can I get good influencer content?"

Ah, yes. His *job*.

I rubbed my forehead. "Um, could you maybe help clear something up?" There was something about his mention of me being out of it that didn't sit right. From retracing my credit card transactions earlier, I'd left Saint around that 3:35am text and wandered around because I was willing to bet I didn't want to bother him by clinging to him the rest of the night, but I also didn't want to go home. So I wasn't drunk yet, but I was definitely a bit buzzed at a couple of points until that damned moscato likely took me the fuck out.

"Sure," he said, his cheer spearing a hole in my balloon of questions. "What's up?"

"When did the three of us hang out last night? You, me, and Iris." I motioned between us. "My head's been a little fuzzy, and I think I lost something. I'm trying to retrace my steps." Might as well stick to the lost credit card lie since it'd gotten me this far.

He shrugged. "I think like three or four? Can't remember after the wild party we went to."

Wait, what?

"Wild party?"

Zane laughed. "Yeah, it was a new place Ris talked about. You don't remember?"

That... wasn't possible. I was with Saint at three. By four, I had to be blubbering to Mom, right? Or at least on my way over there. I blinked, unable to piece it together. I wasn't going to call Zane a fucking liar because he was probably just mixing up his times. "Are you sure it wasn't earlier?" It had to have been. I had to have been a little buzzed from the hot chocolate cocktail—that would explain it.

He hummed, his fingers bouncing the zipper of his bag, and shook his head. "Nope. Pretty sure. You were swaying a lot, so Ris and I had to keep you upright. Kind of hard to forget since we were trying to get you back to her place to rest it off before you vanished on us."

So I just got smashed in a graveyard, somehow ended up partying with Zane and Iris, and got bit before I made it home? I somehow *escaped* a vampire in trashed mode?

I must've been staring at him for too long because his smile slipped. "I fucked it up somewhere, didn't I?"

My heart stopped. I didn't know exactly what that meant, but I didn't like where it could go.

Zane sighed. "Look, Jules, I'm just trying to look out for you. And right now, I need you not to panic."

I swallowed. Okay, I was absolutely starting to panic. I spun on my heel to run, gasping as a hand clamped around my bicep and yanked me toward the sink. My hip screamed as it smacked against it, and I choked back a pained cry.

"Sorry, sorry," Zane said, wincing apologetically. "No more running. I got to take you back, or else both of us are going to get into some serious trouble, okay?"

This is the part where I wished bathroom mirrors were still made of silver. I would've been able to clock Zane being a vampire the second he'd stepped inside. But modern technology is a bit of a bitch, and silver is fucking expensive.

I tried to peel his hand off my arm, gritting my teeth. "Did you do this to me? I thought we were fucking friends, Zane."

I would've felt bad for the wounded expression that followed, but—well—*vampire*. He doesn't exactly get a pass, especially if he fucking bit me. I didn't know what hurt worse: the betrayal or the pain radiating from my hip.

"I didn't bite you, and you *are* my friend."

"Then *who* did?"

Spit it out, Zane. Feel a little bad for me and give me something to work with if I manage to get the hell away from you and back to Dad. My guts churned with the thought that I was running to Dad to solve all my problems.

"My maker."

"Your *master?*" Well that was *something*, I guess.

His nose scrunched up. "That's really outdated and offensive language."

"Sorry," I said, bitter sarcasm seeping into my tone as I tried to pull free, my sneakers squeaking against the bathroom tile as I slowly lost the battle. "Not very vampire-progressive of me, but they kind of violated my right to consent and all—"

The door swung open behind me, and my stomach lurched.

Zane loosened his grip just a bit, likely to what I'd estimate to be the strength his *should* have if he wasn't fucking undead. I scrambled to right myself, sweating profusely as Saint walked in on me just—you know—having a casual chat with my bestie, Zane, who totally wasn't in the process of kidnapping me or anything.

Saint paused, his eyes locking on Zane's firm grasp of my arm.

I wasn't quite familiar with exactly what jealousy looked like because usually I was usually the one dishing it out. But, based on the way Saint's eyes darkened and how quickly his serene, cool demeanor shifted to something more serious, I feared that I was in deep shit.

"S-sorry!" I blurted. "I just ran into my friend, Zane. He was worried about me because I've been acting a bit off, so he was checking in on me."

Please don't be mad. If Saint was mad and thought I was cheating on him, I would stake Zane myself. I was going to throw up. Everything was terrible.

Saint stopped next to me, a million pinpricks shooting up my spine as he placed his hand on my back. "Hey, Zane." His name sounded cold and sharp on Saint's tongue. "Would you please let go of my boyfriend's arm?" The way it sounded was *far* from a request.

I felt like I was in an old western, stuck in a triangle of three dudes pointing guns at each other until one of them moves. Then it registered: boyfriend. He called me his *boyfriend*. The screaming in the back of my head was quickly silenced by the realization that my *boyfriend* had just threatened a fucking vampire. Like he could fight him.

I sputtered. "Z-Zane saw I was getting a bit wobbly and was trying to help. T-that's all. I'm fine." I prayed Zane would get the fucking hint and let go as I shot him a look, hoping it would say something like: *hey numbnuts, don't screw this up for me, and we can deal with this one-on-one.*

His grip loosened again, his hesitation making my breath catch.

In my defense, the next couple of seconds were a bit of a blur, but I'm pretty sure this is what I saw go down.

Saint lifted his leg and stomped Zane's arm against the edge of the sink counter top. Zane actually *yelped*—I'm assuming from surprise—and I got shoved back a few feet before Saint grabbed Zane's duffle from the counter and rammed it into the side of his head.

Needless to say, I just kind of stood there, dumbfounded, until Saint grabbed my hand and ran us back into the boxing room. He ordered me to get my jacket as he collected his, and then he dragged me through the hall, past the locker room as Zane stumbled out.

Saint didn't stop to acknowledge him. Instead, we blew past the security desk—the guy manning it too hot and bothered by his video feed to look up—and pushed through the doors to the sidewalk, where our ride idled on the curb.

I probably would've had another moment of swooning when Saint opened the car door for me, but I was too busy scooting over to let him pile in. Coats in our laps, Saint firmly told the driver to go. When the car shifted into gear, Zane stepped out, trying to flag us down.

"Ignore him," Saint spoke up when the driver checked his mirrors. "He's some crazy guy that thinks I owe him money."

I slid down in my seat, quietly questioning my existence for the remainder of the ride.

10 UPSIDE DOWN

Zane was a vampire.

Zane was *my* vampire's... creation?

I don't know the best inclusive word for it, but Zane was essentially the new Adonis in a parallel universe in which my dad was a vampire who decided to turn everyone but me.

Which fucking sucked.

This is probably what people meant by 'always the bridesmaid, never the bride,' but I didn't even want to be the 'bride' in this case—I just wanted to be left the fuck alone. I didn't want to start going on blood runs instead of coffee runs or carry Zane's stinky dufflebag to the gym.

The worst part was that if Zane was a vampire, Iris was probably a vampire. They were vampire siblings in a fucked up vampire family. And I'd been lured in because I thought they were my friends.

My heart ached. No friends for Jules. I squeezed my jacket to my chest like it might stop that emotional pain. The punching bag couldn't save me now, partially because I sure as hell never wanted to step foot in *Workout Galaxy* again and partially because I was about to let myself cry in front of Saint.

I didn't think I could stuff down my sobbing anymore. It'd just built up to a new level every hour, and at some point, I had to uncork it.

The car rolled to a stop in front of the café, and Saint pulled out his phone to tip the driver before sliding out. I climbed out after him, wobbling on the sidewalk. He shut the car door before I got a chance. Then his hand found mine, and the water works threatened to turn on right then and there.

"Was that really your friend back there?"

I shook my head. Not anymore. My throat was too tight to speak, so I stayed quiet as we walked to the entrance. I didn't try to make an excuse to leave. I know I should've, but I couldn't fathom running to my dad to sick him on the two people I'd once enjoyed spending time with outside of work. Hell, it was entirely possible that Zane and Iris were heading to my house right now—the two of them getting ready to camp out and intercept me on my way home. But they wouldn't know to look for me here.

"Did he hurt you?"

That was a question that put me at a crossroads: do I lie and act stronger than I actually am? Or do I tell the truth and risk seeming like I'm too much work to be worth it?

Saint paused, watching me as I stared down at my sneakers with each step. I opened my mouth to finally lie, but it was too late.

"Where? Your arm?"

We started up the steps and I winced. Saint quickly stepped down.

"My hip," I breathed. "It hit the counter really hard."

Saint let go of my hand and pulled my arm around his neck, his hand snaking around my waist. "I should've checked on you sooner. I gave you a couple extra minutes because I was afraid I was rushing you."

Relief flooded my body when we reached the landing, everything level before one last painful set of stairs.

"A shower doesn't sound like it's a great idea for you anymore," Saint thought aloud. "But I don't have a bathtub."

I grimaced as he guided me toward the first step. "Standing: okay. Walking: okay. Stairs: bad."

"You're sure?"

"Yep," I squeaked, pain shooting from that joint.

I could breathe again once we made it to the top, Saint's apartment door mere feet away. He pulled out his keys with the sweetest jingle I'd ever heard and let us inside. I would've taken off my shoes, but trying to kick one off hurt like hell. I wanted nothing more than to forget everything that was happening. To turn off my brain. To hold onto the one person that seemed to actually give a shit about how I felt and what I wanted.

Saint flipped on the entry light and slid my jacket from my hands. "Lift up your shirt. Show me where it hurts."

I flushed, but he just moved to put our outerwear in the closet like he didn't just ask me to expose skin. Even worse—I pulled my shirt up to see the injury's fun discoloration wasn't anywhere to be seen unless I pushed down the side of my pants. Of course, just as I did that, Saint hooked his finger near where mine were to check, and every cell in my body screamed in horrific euphoria.

"Let me get you some ice. Try to get comfortable on the couch, okay?"

I nodded, my hands trembling as he started for the kitchen. Breathe, Jules. Breathe.

The journey to the living room was like a fever dream. Everything around me might as well have been on fire. And then there was Saint, who managed to smother all of it for a moment before something else caught ablaze.

Once I eased myself onto the couch, I let my body sink into the cushions, ignoring my bruised hip's protest until Saint handed me a bag of ice wrapped in a cloth. "Thanks."

He perched next to me. "I wish you hadn't got hurt..."

"I'm really sorry," I said. "I—"

"Why are you sorry? Jules, I should've been there sooner." His hands curled into fists on his lap, his eyes squeezing shut. "I was stupid and didn't think that anyone would bother you because there were only two or three people there."

He's blaming *himself*?

I moved to console him and hissed. Alarm taking over as his eyes widened. "Hold on, Saint. It's not your fault. I don't want you to feel like you have to take care of me because that's not fair to you."

"Yes, but—"

"I don't want to be a burden on you with whatever weird shit my life throws at me, okay? I..." I sighed, wincing as I rubbed my face. "I feel like so much of it is because of my dad and this job. I... After tonight, I think I want to talk to him about" —I swallowed— "about quitting. And maybe getting a new job. Maybe at the café—which I know was maybe just a joke, but—"

Saint cupped my face. "Is that what *you* want? Or is that what you believe will make *me* happy, Jules? Those are two very different things."

My heart sped up. Were they though? I *liked* Saint. I wouldn't find another guy like him *ever*. The fact that he was touching me was fucking bonkers. A guy like him being nice, humble, cool, *and* sweet was impossible. He might as well be a unicorn if they were real. I wanted to be with him—to have someone that looked at me like I was the best thing on the planet. Someone that I could care for and be cared for in return.

I was about to say something borderline cringe with all of these thoughts bouncing around. My breath hitched, his cool fingers pressed along my jaw. The way his eyes searched mine told me that what I was about to say was true, no matter how quickly we were moving.

"I want you."

The air left my lungs when he kissed me, the room spinning as I sank into the pillows, falling into the corner of the couch. Every kiss grew more urgent and wanting than the last. My brain short-circuited when he leaned over me. I was sweating like hell in my hoodie with how quickly my body temperature spiked—the little gremlins in my head smacking the pleasure button like there was no tomorrow.

I shivered as Saint's hand slid under my shirt and—much to my embarrassment—moaned when the kisses moved from my mouth to my jaw. Now, you're probably thinking: Jules, did you forget about the bite on your neck? You know, the one that Saint is currently making a kissing trail toward?

The answer would be a resounding: *absolutely*.

I was too busy writhing in hormonal ecstasy, thinking that I was probably going to hit a home run with the most gorgeous man in the universe that I forgot that I'd be fucking bitten by a vampire.

When Saint reared back, the confusion kicked in. I blinked, searching his face to understand what was going on. It was like staring at a blank slate. "Saint?" I asked quietly.

His pupils flicked over to me, and then the horror kicked in. I reached for my neck, slapped my hand over it like it was a bleeding wound. "H-hold on. I-I'm okay, I-I j-just..." The rest got caught in my throat. Well, now my night was *officially* ruined.

How the fuck was I going to explain my way out of this one?

Saint's mouth worked. "When?"

Okay, I can answer that. Maybe I could write it off as something weird that he'd accept. "Sometime last night. I-I'm pretty sure I went to see Mom's grave and then I drank a bit too much, and it was there when I came to after I was home."

He leaned in closer. "Jules, did the guy in the gym do that?"

My blood ran cold. "What?"

This wasn't happening. He didn't just ask what I thought he asked. My entire world tipped upside down in a heartbeat. I pushed him off, surprised he didn't fight back as I tried to free myself from our tangled legs and smacked against the floor. *Hard.*

It almost knocked the tears loose before I scrambled to my feet, stumbling backward to avoid Saint's advance. I was such a fucking idiot. He worked the night shift. He was always cold. He beat the *shit* out of Zane. But of course I didn't question *any* of it because I'm a dumbass.

I didn't want to question if he was too good to be true because I was afraid of what I'd find. And fuck me, I found it, all right. So much for reading books about vampires for the past decade when I can't deduce the ones right in front of my face.

"Stay the fuck away from me," I snapped. Fear and hurt coursed through me, pushing my body to its limit.

Saint held up his hands. "Jules, calm down. I'm not going to hurt you."

"I've known Zane for years and fucking threw me against a sink. Did *you* do this to me? Are you fucking gaslighting me to keep me here because—because—I don't know! Something, something, I have to kill your dad?"

Saint blinked and stared at me like I hit my head. The fact that he was still putting on a show of caring about me was starting to piss me off.

"I don't work at a security company, Saint! That's a lie or else a normal person would laugh and get me hauled off to the loony bin. My mom was killed by a vampire and my dad *hunts them.*"

"Okay," he said slowly. "Things are making a lot more sense."

"No they're fucking not!"

"Jules—"

I took a step backward and winced, grabbing onto the wall for support.

"*Jules,* please just listen to me. I'm not trying to keep you here against your will."

"Good, because I really want to leave."

"*Who* bit you? Do you not know?"

"No! It could be you. It could be any vampire in this damn city who hates my dad's guts and wants to fucking stick it to him." I somehow made it to the entry without eating shit and reached for the closet handle.

"Let's talk about this."

"About *what*? About you being a vampire? A-about me be *bitten* just because I decided to take one fucking night for myself because I'm not worth training to fight or useless enough to let go so I can pursue my own dreams?" I ripped my jacket out, shaking uncontrollably as the hanger bounced against the tile. "I was going to go home tonight and finally tell my dad that I fucked up and got all familiar-ized so he could take care of it. And then I was going to give all of this shit up to be with *you*."

I couldn't see. My vision was so blurred that I didn't have a choice but to blink. I felt so incredibly weak when the first drops rolled down my face, and I could see Saint's face again. Well, I'd done it. I cried in front of him after all. But not for the reason I had expected.

"Jules, I never lied to you," he whispered.

"I can't fucking get away from any of this, can I?"

I shakily unbolted the door and hurried into the hall. My hip screamed as I jogged down the steps, but I bit my tongue. When I was outside, I tugged on my jacket and swiped at my face, speeding up my walk to put as much distance between me and the café as possible.

Maybe it was a good thing that I was going to confess to Dad tonight. It'd give me enough time to find a new coffee place and figure out what to do with the rest of my life since I almost slept with a vampire after a whole two-day romance.

Cue the second round of tears.

I continued wiping my face as the blocks passed, praying Zane or Iris wouldn't happen to find me as I zig-zagged through weird side streets. When I made it to the crosswalk two blocks from the house, I burst into tears. I ducked into the steps of a boarded-up doorway and just let it out.

My friends were vampires.

My boyfriend—*ex-boyfriend*—was a vampire.

And I'm a familiar.

All I had now was Dad and Aunt Syd—the former, I really didn't want to talk to, and the latter, I couldn't see or else I'd put her in danger.

I probably sobbed for a good thirty minutes, listening to the occasional car go by while I tried kept an eye out for my former friends to try to take me to their leader. I curled inside my jacket, playing the part of a homeless person trying to stay warm. Anything to turn invisible for a little while. It would probably be the last time I'd go outside for a long time. I sucked in a lungful of crisp night air, trying to tell myself that the pain I felt would eventually pass.

Whether I believed that or not didn't matter. I simply had to pretend it was true long enough for me to find what I wanted, even if it hurt that it wasn't Saint.

Once I was done with the initial wallowing, I stood, dusted myself off, and prepared to start my prison sentence. I pressed the button to the next crosswalk as I formulated my impromptu speech that would get everyone hauled out of the basement and me thrown in.

Something like: *sorry Dad, I'm a huge fuck-up.* Or: *oops.*

Everything was jumbled, so I figured it was in my best interest to go straight to: *I got really upset about you blowing me off again, got depressed, visited Mom, and got bit at some point because I was trashed.*

Yeah. That was probably the winner.

I rubbed my arms, the chill finally seeping in as I reached the porch. Fishing my keys out of my pocket, I pulled open the storm door and paused in the glow of the porch light. But the front door was already cracked. I pressed my palm to it and pushed. It creaked open, the keys jingling helplessly in my hand.

"Dad?" I called, my voice sounding too small—too scared in the darkened entry.

"Well, well."

I froze, peering up the stairs, my ears perking at the familiar voice. I finally noticed his frame then: the bulk and muscle of Adonis sitting on the steps.

"How are you..."

"Out of the basement?" He chuckled. "While you were away doing fuck-all after your little fight with Mason, would you believe we got attacked?"

My heart dropped. Oh no.

"And while we were here, fighting for our fucking lives, I thought about how convenient it was that you weren't around. How *weird* it was when you snapped at me earlier. What was it that you said specifically? *Whine?* Honestly, that's pretty fucking clever." He waved a stake in the dim light. "But I don't think you could come up with that on your own. Or that you believed any one of us would actually turn on Mason. But you're his little boy who can do no wrong."

I wanted to argue that was far from the truth, but I opted to keep my mouth shut as he stood. His boot thumped on the first step in his descent.

"The nervous looks."

Thump.

"The subtle jabs."

Thump.

"The fights."

Thump.

"And taking the night off."

Thump.

He stopped, his eyes practically glowing as we stood about five feet apart in the entry. "You're the spy, aren't you?"

I started to shake my head. "What would my motive be?"

He smirked, emitting a raspy laugh as he glanced to another random point in the dark—I guessed the statue that had held the camera in the living room—before returning his attention to me. "You're a familiar."

"I-I'm not," I said, trying to choke down my fear. Sweat broke out along my collar. "I don't understand the logic here, Adonis."

Oh, I did. And it looked *really* fucking bad, but some of the stuff he was saying didn't make sense. Yet.

"Where's Dad?" I asked again, my pulse pounding in my ears. If I'd lost him in all of this too, it'd be the inevitable start to my comic book style hero origin story.

"Dealing with the mess you made, familiar. But don't worry." Adonis stepped forward, irises glowing a bright gold like the reflection of an animal's eyes in a camera lens. "I'll make sure you can't feed those bloodsuckers any more information."

My stomach dropped as his fingers cracked and elongated into claws.

Werewolf.

Adonis was a fucking goddamn werewolf.

Seriously?

I burst through the storm door and sprinted across the porch, Adonis's footfalls pounding on the planks after me. A car screeched to a halt in front of the house and the driver leaned over, popping open the passenger door.

"Jules! Get in!" Lux screamed.

Out of all the people I expected to find coming to my rescue, *Lux* had been at the bottom of my list. But I didn't argue. Instead, I threw myself inside, slammed the door shut, and held on for dear life as she hit the gas.

11 TRUST EXERCISE

"Where did you come from?" I demanded. I didn't really care where she was driving us, so long as Adonis the werewolf didn't bust through the car's moon roof.

"I've been circling the block because Adonis said he wanted to kill you!" Lux exclaimed. "I tried calling you once I escaped and found my phone on Mason's desk."

"What?" I twisted in my seat and slid my phone from my pocket with a hiss. Yep. My hip was still pretty pissed with me. When I clicked the screen on, sure enough I had a few missed calls from Lux. "Okay? But *why?*" I narrowed my eyes at her.

"Um, I don't know. Maybe because you're my boss's son, and I don't want you dead?" Lux scoffed. "Is that so hard to believe?"

I pulled the crystal from my pocket, wincing again, and shook it at her. "Why the fuck was this under my pillow, Lux?"

A sheepish smile. "I was trying to look out for you. You seemed a bit out of sorts lately, so I thought I'd help you out."

"By making me fall in *love* with you?"

"What? No!" she squeaked. "It was to help you and Mason get along!"

"Isn't this for like, love *love?*"

"No, Jules. It can be for other types of love." She huffed.

Oh. I stared at it, sighed, and dropped it in one of the cup holders. Maybe I was wrong about Lux. Seeing how great of a track record I had going for me so far, I was heading into 'fuck it' territory and throwing caution into the wind. "Where did Dad end up? I need to talk to him."

"He followed the vampire he thought was leading the attack once he broke down the door to let us out." She turned as the light flipped to yellow and drove a little further, slowing by a parking garage entrance. "Then we got the rude awakening that Adonis was a werewolf who was screaming about you being a familiar. Most of us decided it was probably best to bolt." After a quick dip down a ramp and rolling into a spot, she shifted the car into park and leaned back. "So... yeah. Fun night."

"Tell me about it," I mumbled.

"You look terrible, by the way."

I snorted. "Yep. Already heard that one."

The car fell silent for a moment.

"Do you think we'll have to put him down?"

I scowled. "Huh?"

"Adonis. Do you think we'll have to put him down?" Lux repeated. "Like when a dog bites too many people."

I groaned and thumped my head against the seat.

"Look, I'm just trying to lighten the mood of a very

serious situation while my phone finishes charging a bit more."

"I'm calling Dad." I flipped my phone over again and scrolled to his number.

She shrugged. "Fine. If he doesn't pick up, he's probably in the middle of a hunt. I think Charlie said they were going to tell him about Adonis, but I don't know if they have yet or not."

I tried to block out her yammering as I pressed the receiver to my ear. One ring. Voicemail. It hurt to hang up, mainly because he was my only lifeline and I wouldn't know what to do if he died. Considering I got into this mess in the first place because I went to see Mom and couldn't handle being sober to do it, visiting both of them would probably give me alcohol poisoning, at best. I absolutely couldn't drag Aunt Syd into this for her to start the whole cycle over again. Someone in this family had to be a normal, sane, human being. I glanced at Lux, who was tapping through some pink screens on her phone.

Yeah, I was having some serious doubts about whether or not Lux was someone I could trust, but my options were pretty slim right now. I tried again, praying that Dad would answer if a second call would make it seem urgent. Two rings. Voicemail.

I let the phone drop into my lap. "Lux."

"Hm?" She looked up.

"Do you have that tracking thing on your phone?"

She shook her head. "Mason said it's a security risk if one of us gets compromised. All tracking stuff is back at the house."

I pressed my lips together in a thin line. "Great. That's just fantastic."

She pushed herself up in her seat and unplugged her phone. "This might be a bit of an awkward question, but because *Adonis*, of all people decided on it, I sort of *have* to ask—"

"Can you just spit it out already?" I probably would've regretted snapping at someone because of my lack of sleep and the never-ending chain of bad luck, but Lux was part of the problem.

"Yikes, okay. Are you a familiar?"

"No." Lux didn't need to know that. I didn't need to confirm that with anyone but Dad—not when someone in the crew had decided they were going to skewer me without any physical evidence.

She pursed her lips. "You're, like, *super* sure?"

"Lux—"

"Because, like, I don't know— Adonis is kind of dumb, but when he comes up with something, it's usually right."

"I'm *not*, though!"

"So I can check your neck?"

I threw up my hands. "*No*. I don't consent to any neck-checking. I don't really want anyone to fucking touch me for the foreseeable future."

"Fine…"

It was like I could think again when her questions stopped, letting myself try to start formulating a plan for how to yoink Dad's laptop without Adonis ripping my guts out. But, like everything else tonight, that moment quickly ended as Lux threw herself across the car and pinned my neck against the seat with her arm.

I flailed, trying to push her off of me as she grabbed a chunk of my hoodie's collar.

"Oh, Jules..." The pity in her voice spiked my adrenaline. Either she was pretending to me sad because she had to kill me, or she was *actually* sad that she had to kill me. Neither was what I needed right now.

"Get *off*—" I pushed her away and quickly yanked on the handle to stumble into the parking garage. Considering that she knew where we were, and I was an idiot passenger along for the ride, when her car door slammed in time with mine, I decided to face this problem head-on and stand my ground for once.

"What?" I demanded. "Do you want to show off one of your fancy tricks like Adonis did? Go ahead, throw me across the garage with your witchy magic. That was a *ton* of fun earlier when I got rag-doll-tossed by another witch when I was trying to figure out what that crystal was for."

She stopped short, wilting under the comment. "So you found out..." The way she uncharacteristically grabbed her arms and folded in on herself extinguished the small flicker of fight I had in me.

"Yeah," I mumbled, sighing. "Look, Lux," —I motioned to my bite region— "*this* happened last night. I don't even know what vampire did it, and then I find a weird crystal under my pillow... Ugh, I'm *really* tired and *really* fucking scared. I don't want to have been the accidental spy, but if I was, then whoever my vampire is, he barely has anything. This might just be to get back at my dad for ruining their plans or something."

Her arms dropped to her sides as she drew a bit closer. "You know we all heard your fight with Mason, right?"

I looked away. I'd rather pretend none of them had, but I didn't want to tell her to shut up and forget it. She grabbed my bicep and gave it a gentle, reassuring squeeze, despite my flinch. Part of me waited for her to have super vampire strength like Zane and fuck my day up a bit more.

But her ghost of a smile had me locked in her clutches of kindness. "I may have been a little tough or impatient with you, and I'm sorry. I thought you honestly wanted to keep doing what you were doing and not step up, but I was clearly wrong about all of that. It's not fair of him to treat you differently," —she waved a hand— "aside from you being his son. I get that's a special bond, but you're not made of glass, Jules. I can see your potential, and I feel like it's going to waste because he's being stubborn."

I think that was the confidence boost I'd needed tonight. Every breath came a little easier as her thumb traced small circles against my arm before her hand fell away. "Thanks."

She shrugged, a smirk taking over. "Sometimes you have to lie a bit on your hunting resume to get the job. Being a witch turns into a black mark because the motive is a bit different, but we're all trying to accomplish the same goals, right? I don't think this familiar slip-up should be counted against you either."

To be honest, I didn't exactly understand the *why* of Dad being adamantly against witches joining, aside from the risk of them casting evil magic on other hunters. But she had a point: if we *wanted* to help fight, we should be allowed to, right?

"Come on," she said, starting toward the parking entrance. "Let's go get some energy drinks and figure out what to do next."

We walked about a block to a convenience store, where Lux bought me a bottle of soda. She opted for a neon pink and yellow can of something that would probably kill me if I took a sip with the poor shape I was in. Leaning against the building next door, we sipped like a couple of people on a smoke break.

"You know," I started. "I had this crazy thought that I could go take down my vampire myself to prove to him that I could do it."

Lux made a sound into her can that was a cross between an entire classroom of kids finding out you're going to the principal's office and a gaggle of girls learning you have a crush. "What a rebel." She elbowed me playfully. "Don't tell me you're chickening out of the idea—is that why you're telling me?"

I hesitated.

She clicked her tongue, pulling the can away from her lips. "Jules, the only way for Mason to understand that you're an adult is to stand up for yourself. I think you should go for it. I'll back you up."

That... wasn't what I expected to hear. But for once, I felt like I was finally accepted by one of the people I'd been living with. My heart swelled with the idea that I might actually have someone to help me through this. Honestly, she was right, too. As much as I'd started to abandon the idea of taking on my vampire myself, I took this on to also prove to myself I *could* do it, right?

"Thanks, Lux."

She beamed. "Of course. I think some parents forget that when their children are adults that they're responsible for their own actions. They're their own people now, and that can be a tough pill to swallow until they see your accomplishments without them."

I nodded, capping my soda and turning to yawn.

"Tired?" she asked.

"Yeah. It's been a long night. Been dealing with trying to figure out who my vampire is and..." I mentally slapped myself when the image of Saint's wounded face popped into my head. "And all the fun stuff that comes with it."

"I think I know a place where you should be safe to nap for a bit." Lux knocked back the rest of her can and tossed it in the trash, motioning for me to follow.

I wasn't going to turn that offer down at this point. She could stuff me in a trashcan to sleep, and I'd do it. My feet dragged the further we walked, passing by the parking garage entrance and across another street to a familiar-looking storefront: *Charm & Rit.*

Jogging to catch up to Lux, I grabbed her arm and pulled her back. "*Please* tell me we're not going there." I pointed to the shop up ahead.

Confused, she glanced between me and her shopping haven. "What? I know the owner. She's a friend. *And* she has an apartment upstairs you can crash in."

"You remember the whole bit about being thrown by a witch I mentioned back in the garage?" I hissed. "She fucking *knows*, Lux. And she tried to kill me."

"Goddess," she lamented, tipping her head to the sky. "Okay." She held up her hands. "Just follow me and let me take care of it. I'll talk to her."

"And if she tries to kill me *again*?"

"Then run to the car, and I'll park us somewhere for you to nap in the backseat."

Honestly, I was cool with that. I let go, and she patted me on the arm with a reassuring smile. It felt even creepier to approach with the shop's lights off, but there was still a glow emitting from the windows above it. When we reached the door, she tugged on the handle. This time, it jiggled in the frame instead of swinging wide open. But instead of pulling out her phone or navigating to another entrance, she tugged on her necklace and pulled a key out from under her shirt.

I must've been staring because she glanced back at me and gave a shrug. "What? Never hurts to be prepared."

Can't exactly argue with that.

Lux unlocked it and ushered me inside, locking up behind us. Well, *that* would screw up the plan to run, wouldn't it?

"Stay here," she said quietly. "I'll be back in a minute."

"Um..." I pointed to the door. "How am I supposed to escape if she decides to finish me off?"

Lux softly clapped her hands together, pleading. "Please just trust me here."

I squirmed, unable to demand she unlock the door. "Fine."

"I'll be quick."

Before I could say anything else, she disappeared behind the counter and up the stairs. I rocked back and forth on my heels, trying to keep myself from passing out. Every yawn ticked by another few seconds I was fighting sleep, knowing that my body was an hourglass running out of sand.

Finally, two sets of footfalls trailed down the stairs, and Lux reappeared. Her thin witch friend stood next to her, hands on her hips with a look of irritation.

"Fine," the woman said in a huff. "Come upstairs."

Relieved didn't even begin to describe how I felt in that moment.

I strode over to the counter as Lux gave her friend a quick hug before motioning to me. "This is Jules. Jules, this is Drew."

"I, um, I would say nice to meet you, but…"

Drew rolled her eyes. "If I had known that you're a friend of Lux, I wouldn't have done that earlier. That's my bad." Her words were so dry that I couldn't tell if it was meant to be an apology or not.

So I tried to shrug it off. It must've worked since she led the way upstairs. My hip wasn't exactly thrilled about the climb. When I reached the top, my eyes watered as I scanned the main living space. It was small in a cozy way, decorated with fairy lights, plush rugs, and a sectional sofa that fit neatly into the rectangular alcove off to the side.

"All right," Drew said, motioning to the couch. "Have at it. Just try not to drool on the cushions."

Say *less*.

I dragged myself over to it and flopped down, passing out the second my head hit one of the plush pillows.

———

I don't know how long I'd been out for, but it wasn't nearly long enough before the sound of talking started to drag me from sleep. However, I can tell you the exact moment I'd snapped awake: whenever I heard that horrible *zip* of a plastic tie before I felt a band of pressure around my wrist.

"See?" Lux said. "Told you the spell would last long enough."

My eyes flew open, grogginess slowing down my thoughts as I lifted my head to look up at Lux. She startled, but quickly regained her composure and put her hands on her knees as she bent to look me in the eyes.

"Hey, sleepyhead. Drew's finding you a travel pillow, and then we'll leave you alone."

I tried to move my arms, realizing they were bound to a chair. "W-what's going on?" I tried to lift myself up, but my legs were fastened to the chair too. Panic shot through me, replacing utter exhaustion with fresh adrenaline.

"Shh, Jules—you're fine, I promise." Lux squeezed my arm. "This is just to make sure your vampire doesn't try anything, okay? So, you're going to stay here and rest while I go find and kill your vampire, and then this will all be over."

"What? B-but you said—you *encouraged* me to go after him myself—"

"Oh, I know," she said, wincing. "But I thought on it, and that's kind of a risk I'm not willing to take right now because, well, the vampire could control you and kill you, which would really throw a wrench into things."

Huh? There was something I was missing here.

"I-I don't understand..."

Lux took a deep breath and grabbed a rolling stool from under the desk shoved into the corner that looked like a crafting mom's paradise. She plopped herself down in front of me and worried her lip. "So I might've lied about the crystal."

What the fuck.

I blinked rapidly. "Lux, I'm gay."

"Okay, look, I understand that, but it was meant more to have you bond to me in more of a *familial* sense, rather than a lovers sort of deal." She bounced her legs. "Oh boy, basically, when I met Mason to interview about hunting—"

"I was there Lux, what about it?"

"Yep! You were there," she smiled, as if I perfectly understood what she was getting at. "And I saw Mason was basically using you as a secretary, telling you to get us water or to file something." She leaned forward. "But there was a brief second when my hand brushed yours when you handed me that glass, and I felt *it*."

My stomach twisted into knots as I silently begged for her not to say she was madly in love with me. I really couldn't handle a stalker on top of everything else.

"Jules, you have dormant magic running through your veins."

My brows shot up. That was probably the biggest twist of tonight if it was true. To be honest, I didn't even know if I *wanted* it to be true. I licked my lips. "W-what does that mean, exactly?"

"Not everyone has the potential to be a witch like Drew and I. But *you* do."

Me? A witch? I squirmed, eyeing her with uncertainty. "Are you sure?" After all, this was *me* she was talking about. To say I actually had some sort of magical powers or abilities felt like a huge reach.

She nodded enthusiastically, every facet of her face brightening with excitement. "Do you understand how rare it is to find someone like us? Our coven is so small now that we've been searching for more witches, and that's why I took Mason's offer. I joined because of *you*, Jules." Her smile tapered off. "I honestly thought you didn't have any intentions to join into anything like Mason's crusade, so I got a bit discouraged. Then I decided just to go for it, but it looks like I messed up my timing. If I'd just talked to you sooner, none of this would've happened."

I shook my head. "Lux, I—"

The gentle way she cupped my face in her hands brought a pang of sadness with it. Sadness because I didn't know who or *what* I was anymore, let alone what I really wanted.

"We're going to fix this, Jules." Her thumb stroked my cheek. "Then you'll pledge your body and soul to our goddess and become a member of our coven."

I'm sorry, what now?

Alarm bells started going off in my head. "Um, what if I don't want to do that? Can I have a bit to think on it?"

"Sorry, but no." She patted my cheek and rolled back, standing in one single, fluid motion. "Our goddess needs more worthy servants, and you're kind of at the top of the list."

"Wait, hold on," I said, my face scrunching up. "So you're telling me that I'm being *volen-told* to basically become the equivalent of a familiar to your goddess?"

Her hand flew to her chest. "Don't you *dare* compare the two! *Anyone* can be a familiar—this is entirely different!"

Drew stopped in the office doorway, travel pillow in hand. "Found it."

"Perfect," Lux said, her tone turning sour as she peered back down at me. "When I get back, we're doing the ritual. No more wasting your true potential."

I squirmed, my wrists screaming as the zip ties pressed through the fabric of my hoodie. Lux was already grabbing the pillow from Drew's hands so I could sleep through the rest of this nightmare and wake up to a new one.

Lux skidded to a stop, her head snapping around with Drew's as a crash echoed from downstairs.

"What was that?" Lux asked.

Drew vanished into the next room. "You locked the shop up, right?"

"Um, yes—"

Crunch.

Every hair stood on end when the apartment door buckled. Drew shouted something over the muffled pound of footsteps, and then the door must've swung free with the loud *thump* of wood on plaster.

"Drew?" Lux called.

But Drew didn't respond. Instead, after several painfully long seconds, another figure stood in the office doorway.

Saint.

12 DAMSEL IN DISTRESS

What the hell was Saint doing here? I wasn't sure if I should be angry that he'd probably been stalking me or grateful that at least someone was going to try to stop me from being forced into joining a coven. One issue, though: Lux was a vampire hunter.

My heart lurched when Saint didn't waste any time lunging at her, throwing caution into the wind with fangs fully on display. Witnessing him streak across my vision with elongated canines and eyes shifting to pure black made my stomach drop straight to hell.

I'd *kissed* that.

Well, now I'd probably never sleep again. Because that guy could've taken the biggest chunk out of my throat while I was moaning on his couch like a love-struck fool. My heart went into double-time as Lux dodged him and kicked the rolling stool between them.

I can see the argument that looking away from this fight

would be really stupid, but if they were going to occupy themselves with each other, I sure as hell wasn't going to wait around for the winner. Gritting my teeth, I tried to wiggle free, rocking the chair with the hope that I could escape before they were done.

A *crack* ripped my attention back to the fight, where I found the source of the noise: two halves of Lux's stake laid on the floor.

"You son of a bitch," she seethed.

Okay, back to escaping.

I yanked my arms upward as hard as I could, squeezing my eyes shut against the pain. My wrists felt like they might snap in half before I heard a *thump*. I gasped, gulping down air I didn't realize I'd needed until I stopped fighting the zip ties.

Sprawled out in front of me was Lux.

My time was up.

Fear clawed at my throat as I tore my eyes away from her prone form and found Saint, whose back was to me as he grabbed something from the craft desk. When he turned around with a pair of scissors in his hand, my mouth went dry. Maybe breaking up with a vampire was a poor life decision, even if he'd seemed relatively harmless after I'd ran from him earlier.

"Saint," I squeaked, despite the fangs and blackened eyes being nowhere to be seen.

That kicked-puppy look returned as he started toward me. "It's okay, Jules." I flinched as he knelt down and opened the scissors. "I know you probably don't want to see me right now, but I was worried." He pushed my arm to one side and the first zip tie snapped free.

I yanked my hand away, grabbing my other sleeve.

Unbothered by my jittering, he moved to the next arm. "Some vampires do some... pretty fucked up things to familiars. I couldn't stand the thought of your vampire finding you and you not having any way to defend yourself."

I swallowed. "So you *stalked* me?"

He cringed, the scissors stopping mid-cut. "That's a word for it. I can't really deny that."

The second tie snapped free. I tried to move my legs and Saint grabbed my knee.

"Hold still." He flicked the scissors open. "I saw you in a car with the blonde witch and followed you from the parking garage." The pressure on one leg eased as he cut down the duct tape. "I got really nervous when she took you in here because witches aren't typically fond of familiars. They prefer killing them. So I tried to wait it out for thirty minutes." Another release of pressure. The scissors snapped shut.

I only got a whole thirty minutes of sleep? Are you fucking kidding me?

At this point, I was afraid to move my legs, but Saint didn't budge from his crouch, like he was waiting for me to finish freeing myself.

I cleared my throat and moved my finger to point at Lux. "Is she..."

"They're both knocked out. I'm not a fan of killing unless it's absolutely necessary."

"Okay," I mumbled, cringing at the sticky pull of duct tape peeling from my jeans.

He rose and stepped back when I started to push myself up on shaky legs.

"Did they hurt you?"

God, I wish he didn't look at me like he cared so damn much. My heart played tug-of-war, fighting over whether or not to throw myself into his arms and pretend like he didn't just demonstrate he was an apex predator.

My eyes went to the broken stake on the floor. While it wasn't completely useless, I was a bit disappointed I couldn't quickly swipe it to use as a self-defense item since it was so short. That was just asking to get my arm snapped off.

"No," I said quietly. "I don't think so. They, um—I think they were trying to convert me to their witchy-religion though."

Saint glanced back down at her, and I shuffled to the side, giving myself enough room between us to actually move toward the door. I told myself to pretend like he wasn't silently creeping behind me as I trailed through the living room. I walked around Drew's unconscious body, grabbed my coat and phone, headed down the stairs, and stepped through the broken door of the shop.

Saint left a buffer between us as we stood side-by-side on the sidewalk. "Are you going to be okay? I thought you were going home?"

"I was—I mean, I *did*." I dropped my head into my hands and groaned. How much could I even say to him at this point? I couldn't trust him, could I? My hands fell. "Saint, how do I know that you're not working for my vampire? It's not like you're incapable of lying. And I can't exactly stop you from following me around, even though I really, *really* don't want to talk to anyone but my dad right now if I'm being completely honest."

Saint bit his lip, glancing away.

Dammit, heart, stop doing that thing whenever he looks cute. He's the *enemy*.

"I don't think there's anything I can say to fix that trust. You're scared, and you have every right to be."

I gave him half a trust point for that. At least he *sounded* genuine with that answer. I dug my phone from my pocket. New messages from Iris and Zane—swiped those off the screen—but nothing else. My thumbs went for Dad's number again, and I put the phone to my ear. One ring. Voicemail.

I sighed and ended the call. Anxiety wormed its way into my core as I pulled up my text thread with him, debating whether or not to send something. Text messages could be sent by anyone though—Dad might not be the one replying if I sent something sensitive. Hell, even if I told him to call me, I could end up with the rude surprise of a vampire taking advantage of that request if they'd gotten ahold of his phone, ready with a well-composed script of lies to further fuck up my night.

What I needed right now was his phone's location. Which was back at the house on that damn laptop. Guarded by a psychotic werewolf that wanted me dead.

Saint's head tilted when I looked to him, the screen dimming in my hands. "Do you really want to make sure I'm safe?" I asked.

"I'd like to, yes."

I shoved my phone into my pocket. "Come on. I'm probably about to put myself in peril, but I don't exactly have much of a choice."

———

"A *werewolf* might be in there?" Saint repeated, the two of us standing on the sidewalk outside my house-slash-workplace.

"Yeah..."

"And how did a werewolf end up in your house, Jules?"

I gave a halfhearted shrug. "I guess someone fucked up the background check?"

His brows knit together as he surveyed the building again, probably debating if he'd made a mistake by stalking me. "What, exactly, are you going in there for?"

"I need to grab a laptop." And some hunting gear, but I decided to omit that. If he wanted to risk his ass for me and had possible ulterior motives like quite literally everyone else I'd stumbled into tonight, then I wasn't about to show him my hand to give him the advantage here. I was kind of done playing damsel in distress and still somehow ending up with a new villain in the process.

Saint's shoulders fell. "Okay. Let's get this over with, then." When he strode up the walkway, I almost collapsed with relief—thank God I wasn't going in there alone—until I remembered *why* he was heading in first. Good old Adonis could be sitting on the steps again, waiting to rip my head off.

By the time I scrambled onto the porch to hover behind Saint, he'd already nudged the door open. No eyes peered back from the shadow of the stairwell. He crept inside, and I reached through the doorway to feel for the light. A quick toggle of the switch and nothing happened. Either the vampires had cut the power, or they'd shattered the entry light. Judging by Saint's dead-silent footsteps, I was guessing the power company was going to be pissed about repairs.

"I don't see anyone," Saint whispered, so low I almost didn't hear him.

Oh, right. I guess he didn't need the light. Vampire things.

"Upstairs?" I whispered back, motioning to the yawn of darkness ahead. I jabbed my thumb to the left. "His room's that way—two lefts." I quickly spat out the last bit to avoid him trailing into *my* room. That had a strict 'no vampires allowed' policy. Whether or not that may have already been violated by the last fanged freaks that threw a party in here was something I didn't want to think about just yet.

Saint's form disappeared up the stairs, not even a *creak* left in his wake, which sent chills through me. I rubbed my arms as I pulled the storm door closed behind me, stifling its squeal. I hated how scared I felt in this house now. Like the one last safe haven in the world had been ripped away from me. There was a sickening aura of malicious intent coating everything that I wasn't sure would ever come out, not unlike a particularly stubborn stain on a rug.

I crouched, trying to stay on high alert as I rummaged through the sideboard by the entry. Flashlight, flashlight, flashlight—

Finally, I pulled it from one of the soft storage cubes and flicked it on. The state of the living room and Dad's office formed a lump in my throat. I ran the light over the couch I'd taken a nap on earlier, finding the cushions ripped to shreds. The statues on the mantel had been smashed or toppled. The map was torn down. And Dad's desk had been cleaned off— everything previously occupying it now littering the floor.

"No one's up there."

I seized, biting down on my tongue. When the fuck did Saint get back? Holy hell. "Good," I forced out, trying to hide a sniff before I started toward the office. Once again, I had no idea if Saint was giving me some distance or kept on my heels as I traversed the wreckage until I rounded the desk, searching for the laptop.

Saint had stopped on the wide threshold, as if he was waiting to be invited in. The irony wasn't lost on me—vampires didn't need an invitation. Months of reading helped me come to the conclusion that it was more of a literary metaphor-trope-thing that equated to inviting evil or sin into your home. But a vampire was a *person*, despite being undead. People do whatever the fuck they want, no matter the intention.

That's also absolutely how all of these vampires had gotten in. The only reason they likely *hadn't* before this was because they'd be descending on a house either with no one or a bunch of hunters, depending on their timing. Neither seemed all that great of an idea because if they showed up to an empty place and wrecked it, they were asking for hunters to find them, or the alternative: they fight to the death because everyone's prepared.

I pulled open drawer after drawer.

Did the mole start this? Did that camera start this chain reaction? If whatever vampire had compelled someone to place it here started watching the house and realized no one was coming and going, aside from Dad and I, then they must've realized something was up.

I couldn't help but reconsider me being the mole—but everything leading up to me being a familiar and coming home didn't add up. I was too drunk to even let myself in, and I was probably exhausted from the walk. I couldn't have done it.

Which left Rory and Charlie.

"Fuck," I muttered, pushing the last drawer shut. Shoving

Dad's chair aside, I dropped to my knees and rolled up the rug.

"Everything okay?"

"Just peachy," I grumbled, tucking my finger into the small semi-circle cut in the floorboard. It popped up, and there was *almost* everything I needed: the backup drive for the laptop and a vampire-defense go-kit. "They took the laptop."

"So what do we do now?"

I stuffed the external drive and cable into my hoodie pocket. "*We* don't do anything. *I* am going to go find a computer and fucking fight back." I grunted as I yanked the case from its tight squeeze of a nook.

By the time I put everything back the way it was, grabbed the case, and got to my feet, Saint stood in front of me, arms crossed over his chest.

"What?" I demanded. "You've even admitted that there's nothing you can do to make me trust you. In case you forgot, you're a vampire. I'm a hunter." I held up the case and jiggled it.

"You're a hunter's *son*, Jules."

"And? Sorry if that's the closest thing I got right now. I'm going to find my dad and hope we can fix this. Because even though he's kind of been a bit of a shit-bag, at least his heart is in the right place. You and I have only known each other for two days—I *don't* know where yours is."

Saint ran his tongue over his teeth before he clicked it. "Okay."

Thank God that wasn't much of a fight.

"Okay," I echoed, the gay gremlins controlling my brain crying out in agony because they were all too obsessed with his presence, even after that nightmare flash of vampire they witnessed. "We have an understanding." I moved to leave.

"Question."

I stopped and turned. "What?"

What the fuck? Why was I even entertaining this? Just *go*, Jules.

"Where are you going to find a computer? The library?"

I hesitated. Fuck. I really needed this guy not to poke holes in my plans. "L-look, I'll figure something out. Dad could really be in danger right now if these blood-sucking dipshits have the laptop. I'm *hoping* Charl—" The thing about the mole cut me short. Maybe it was *bad* for Charlie or Rory to have it right now. I swallowed. "I'm hoping that *Dad* still has it, but there's a strong possibility that's not the case."

"So you're flying by the seat of your pants?"

I pressed my lips into a thin line.

Saint's arms fell. "I have a laptop. The sun will be up in an hour. You can start looking and then, if you find your dad's location and feel he's in imminent danger, you can leave and try to get to him in the daylight."

Dammit, that was a solid plan. I just wished it didn't drag me back to Saint's apartment to suffer sitting on the could've-had-sex couch. But it wasn't like I could camp out here or break into a library before opening hours.

I absently pushed back my greasy hair and cringed. "Okay. Fine. Lead the way."

13 OLD WOUNDS

When Saint offered to help me up the flight of stairs to his place, I really wished I hadn't let my stubborn pride get to me. But I did. And my bruised body fucking screamed the entire walk up.

I covered another yawn when Saint got out his keys and let us in. Of all the places I imagined to be my sanctuary tonight, a vampire's apartment had been at the very bottom of my list. I shuffled inside, letting Saint lock up while I awkwardly decided where to put my vampire hunting kit. It felt super disrespectful to bring it all the way inside, especially when Saint was offering me a place to occupy for about an hour, so I pushed it up next to the wall by the entry closet.

Considering Saint had been the only person I'd ran into so far that hadn't tried to directly attack or restrain me—well, aside from consensual restraining for our heated make-out session—I felt pretty confident that I shouldn't have to use the kit on him anyway. Hopefully. I'd been wrong a lot tonight, so I prayed this wouldn't come back to bite me in the ass.

He vanished into a room—his bedroom, if I were to take a guess—and reappeared with a laptop, which he took over to the coffee table. My hands slid into my hoodie pocket, gripping the hard drive.

"It's all yours," Saint said, motioning to the computer as he moved to close the blackout curtains. "Do you need anything to eat? Drink? I don't have much, but I can at least offer some tea or water now."

"I'm fine," I said, partly because I didn't want pity drinks and partly because I was pretty sure Lux did something to my soda earlier. And I didn't care for a repeat of waking up tied to a chair.

"Just... let me know if you change your mind." He wandered into the kitchen and popped open the fridge. A disturbed part of me wanted to follow him in there and see if he was sneaking out blood bags or some shit to help justify why I shouldn't trust him.

Focus. Find Dad.

I moved around the couch and slid out the drive, I didn't really stop to consider if I was making a huge-ass mistake by plugging it in. Saint could be a super computer hacker or something, but I honestly didn't care. I was too tired to care.

A few taps of the trackpad, and I had the special keys for the tracking software. Now it just had to download and install. And run about seventeen updates. I slumped on the couch, playing with my hoodie strings as I waited.

"Any luck?"

I jumped, straightening in my seat. "Y-yeah. Just downloading updates." And regretting that we didn't use different tracking software that I could just use on my phone. Fuck the risks.

Saint hummed in answer, so I sank back into the couch, wanting it to swallow me whole with how nice it felt. God, I was so exhausted. My eyes started to cross as I watched the little blue loading bar take its sweet old time to crawl across the screen.

"Jules?"

I jolted, my head snapping to where Saint had appeared at the arm of the couch. "W-what?"

He didn't look at me, instead he was staring down at the opaque cup in his hands, like the liquid within gave him answers to the universe. "Do you have *any* idea who your vampire might be?"

"No." There wasn't really a point in lying about that. It wasn't like I had any clue who Zane's vampire maker was. Every variation of a 'why' question popped up in the back of my brain until I asked: "Do you?"

I know it was a fucking long shot, but then he hesitated.

"I'm *afraid* that it could be a certain vampire. I don't know if it's him though."

My throat bobbed. Saint set his drink on the far end of the coffee table and my eyes snapped to it, totally disregarding the figure dropping to sit on the floor by the arm of the couch. I leaned over. It was water.

Dammit. So much for finding a reason to be disgusted and appalled.

Saint reclaimed it from his new seat, his black nails tracing the side while he stared ahead and chewed on his lip. I didn't care for the contemplative silence, especially because it made me squirm. What new horrors awaited me with whatever Saint had to say?

He sighed. "When I told you about my ex..."

Oh, what the fuck. "Don't tell me he was your mast— maker..."

"Unfortunately."

That... certainly framed things in a new perspective for me. Saint said he hadn't lied about anything when we talked, and even though those doubts still lingered in the back of my mind, the mention of him wanting to leave town to get away from his ex really struck home. Did Saint not have any money when he left? No wealthy vampire status like most of the other ones Dad encountered and 'leveraged' funds from to keep the lights on in the house? Saint also couldn't travel in the daytime, so that probably caused a few extra issues. No car either. He was honestly kind of *stuck* the more I considered it.

My eyes drifted to the curtains, thinking of the potted plant on the other side with its little happy-face on a stick. An attempt to keep something alive to take care of in an empty apartment with barely anything to his name. Living above the place he worked. Sure, he had people to talk to there, but he couldn't really *talk* to them—not in a sense that mattered. Something I knew all too well.

He was alone, too.

And I was feeling bad for a vampire. Granted, a vampire I'd started to get to know as a person and I'd been falling head-over-heel for before I knew how stupid I was being, but a *vampire*.

The morbid curiosity finally got to me. "Um... *how* did it happen? You being turned by him?" I internally rationalized that I needed anything and everything about this guy if he was, in fact, my vampire nemesis. If my answers could be right in front of me, no matter how much it'd make me feel sorry for Saint, I needed them. Dad always said to know your enemy. Might as well use Saint to figure that out before I never saw him again.

Saint scoffed. "I'm going to out my age, but I guess that doesn't matter."

Oh, boy. Time to find out how many hundreds of years Saint has been roaming around, having his hot guy summer.

"It was the 90s."

Hold up. "The 1790s? 1890s?"

The slow way he panned over to me with his perfect nose scrunched told me that he meant exactly what he said. "Jules, I didn't tell my parents I was bi because I didn't want to get kicked out of the house, not because I was afraid they'd send me to jail or shoot me."

I cleared my throat. "Sorry. Continue."

Saint shook his head. "I was twenty-two when I met him. I didn't go to college because my parents were rather... overbearing. So, I stuck around, took odd jobs—mostly anything that sent me home with tips."

Damn, I bet he got a *lot* of tips too.

"Yes, I am painfully aware of my looks."

I straightened, fidgeting with my hoodie sleeves. "I-I didn't say—" Did he read my mind? What the fuck?

"I don't have to be a mind-reader to guess what you're thinking," he mumbled.

I would've argued that, but I decided to keep my mouth shut in favor of more information.

Saint took a sip and set the cup somewhere next to him

out of my view. "And when you look a certain way, you're bound to get attention. I waited on Aaron's table during my late shift, and he asked when I was off. That's how it started."

Aaron? I mentally flipped through all of the names I'd memorized of the city's most wanted vampires on Dad's list. I'd never heard of an 'Aaron'—unless the guy was a footnote somewhere. I really hoped Saint wasn't trying to pull a fast one on me.

"It was hangouts with his group at first. Then dates that weren't labeled as dates because guys don't do that with guys. I overlooked his tendency to boss everyone else around because he was always a little gentler when he talked to me. Initially.

"I think it was after he got away with doing little things like wrapping his arm around my waist or having our noses nearly touch that he realized I wasn't going to stop him from crossing that boundary. And I let him because there was an air about him that drew me in—like tasting freedom for the first time. I didn't have to pretend to be someone else like I did around everyone. I shouldn't have told *him* that though.

"He fucking turned me the night I said how glad I was to finally have someone I didn't have to be fake around."

His bitter tone ebbed into silence, letting that feeling stew. I started to guess the feelings that would come next though, remembering the fear after finding my bite.

"I woke up in a new city, hours away. I gave myself a burn because I tried to look out the window in broad daylight. I cried because I was fucking scared and confused about being able to see in the dark, how I couldn't keep myself warm, about feeling that insistent pulse that I didn't quite realize was the need for blood. I hadn't asked for any of it, but Aaron reassured me that it was for the best—that he would take care of me.

"I was honestly just a fucking trophy for him to drag along wherever he went. I'd rest and wake up in a different place on a weekly basis. I won't go into the details, but I eventually stopped getting special treatment. If underlings fucked up, they'd get beat. And when Aaron was still angry because of their fuck-ups, I got beat—maybe not in the same way, but..." He shrugged, running a hand through his hair. "The way he treated familiars was the worst part."

My heart caught in my throat.

"That's why I went after you, Jules. I remembered his empty promises to turn most of them when they did their time—specifically one that never stepped out of line. I... I don't want to say that he was my favorite, but he felt like an actual friend. I asked him why he wanted to be a vampire so badly, and his reason was because he wanted the freedom to be whoever he wanted. I tried to encourage him to leave after that, but he insisted on staying because his hard work would eventually pay off, right?"

Saint stole a glance in my direction, and I knew what came next.

"Aaron snapped his neck in front of everyone because he found out he'd been talking to me alone. And now that was against the rules. I was for Aaron. Not for anyone else. I felt guilty about that ever since." He looked away, his mouth working. "The first time you walked into the café, I thought you felt familiar. It was because you reminded me of him. Like the universe was giving me a second chance to enjoy the company of someone who deserved the love I wasn't previously allowed to give."

My fingers dug into my knees. Ouch. The gay gremlins were chanting again, screaming to give him another chance with this newfound information. Saint was a victim, and I'd been desperately trying to paint him as a villain because of something he didn't have a say in.

I hesitated, then told myself to fucking commit as I scooted a bit closer to him and slid off the cushions onto the floor. My hip hated me, but sitting next to him felt *right*. And Aaron's familiar—an alt-universe me—had *died* so I could have Saint's number scrawled on a coffee cup.

Saint fiddled with a thin, black bracelet instead of acknowledging me, possibly so he didn't scare me off. "When we finally moved here and Aaron declared this was where he wanted to climb the ladder, I tried to settle in for as long as I could. Ever since that familiar's death, I'd started taking my anger and despair out on punching sandbags while pretending it was Aaron. Then one day I snapped. I punched him without a second thought. I didn't stop until he surrendered and told me I could leave. He also said he'd never bother me again, but I doubt he'll stick to that."

I tore my gaze away from him and stared at the carpet. The silence gave me time to mull all of that information over until my brain snagged on something crucial. The blood drained from my face.

"Um," I squeaked. "You said his name is Aaron, right?"

Saint nodded. "Yeah, but he started going by something else when we moved in here. What was it..." He closed his eyes. "It was stupid, so me and the other original crew refused to use it. Did it start with a V or an S...?"

I almost choked, silently begging him not to confirm it as I asked: "Severin?"

He snapped his fingers and my heart dropped. "That was it. Severin."

"Oh fuck," I whispered, my head spinning. "Your *ex* is this city's top vampire." It wasn't a question, but Saint took it like one.

His brows knitted together as he considered it. "Maybe? I wasn't exactly told much unless it was something to do with internal affairs. I wasn't much more than property."

I shook my head. "He *is*. My dad's been after him for years now." My hand went to my bite. "And I found my bite the night you and I went out for our first date."

His eyes widened with alarm. "You think Aaron—"

"You just said you doubted he wouldn't ever bother you again, right? Do you think he's stalking you? Do you think he saw us together, got pissed, and decided to fucking bite me?"

Saint's hands roamed over his face. "If this is *my* fault, I can't even begin to tell you how sorry I am."

Watching Saint's cool exterior crumble before my eyes made me go from distraught to pissed. I wasn't going to let myself turn into that familiar that fucker killed, and I sure as hell didn't want to see Saint be miserable for the rest of his undeath.

"I'm going to fucking kill him," I whispered.

"Jules," Saint shook his head, his hands finally leaving his face. "I need to be the one to deal with him."

"If my dad gets involved, then he might kill you."

Saint blinked in surprise. "I... thought you'd be relieved to get rid of me."

"No, I mean, at first, yes, but now that you told me that you were kidnapped and turned against your will, which is horrifically similar to my whole familiar situation, I've sort of changed my stance on the whole you being a vampire deal. Granted, I'm not exactly thrilled about you being a vampire, but we're likely stuck on the same Severin bullshit cruise."

"Something tells me your dad's going to be more upset that you're colluding with and protecting a vampire instead of dating a guy."

"Fuuuck."

Saint chortled.

The back of my head hit the couch cushion. "I really wish my life was normal right now. I don't want to be downloading software updates to fucking find my dad. Or be afraid of going to my house because of crazy werewolves. Or go through a roller coaster of emotions because everyone's stabbing me in the back to drag me back to their vampire maker or goddess or *whatever*." I huffed. "I want to go to bed and wake up to something mundane."

"You must be exhausted," Saint said quietly.

I covered a yawn, right on cue. "I really fucking am." The laptop chimed, and I pulled my head from the couch, wordlessly typing in passwords until the map popped up with a bunch of little pings. I felt Saint looking over my shoulder, but I didn't mind—not anymore. It wasn't like he could do anything until it was dark again.

I clicked on one of the icons that started to move and relief washed over me. Dad. When I zoomed out, he was smack in the middle of downtown, walking down the street. I tugged my phone out of my pocket and dialed his number, my heart racing in my chest. If he hung up on me now, I wasn't sure what the next plan of action would be.

One ring. Two.

"Jules?"

I could've cried if Saint wasn't sitting next to me. "Dad? What's going on? Where are you?"

Saint pushed himself off the floor, taking his drink with him to the kitchen to seemingly give me a bit of privacy— something I made a mental note of and gave him a couple more trust points for.

"Jules, don't go to the house. I need you to listen to me—"

"I already did. Did someone tell you about Adonis?"

"Unfortunately. Are you hurt?"

I hesitated. It was now or never to bring up the bite if I wanted to bow out of this entire mess. I turned my head to find Saint busying himself with kitchen cleaning. Did I want Saint to risk his life to fight his maker? To take on the big-bad of his story with the possibility of dying for real? To never be able to talk to the one person I'd felt a weird, instantaneous, deep connection with ever again?

"Um, yes and no," I finally said. "That's why I've been trying to call you."

14 SANCTUARY

ad's sigh was the final punch to the gut as I tried to ignore Saint staring directly at me from his reclaimed spot on the floor. The former was exasperated by a new problem and the latter wasn't thrilled with me handing the reins of his revenge plot over to a hunter.

"You think it's Severin?" Dad asked again. "You're sure?"

"Pretty sure," I said. "He's been pissed about you for a while, right? I think it makes sense he would take the opportunity to take it out on me." Saint shook his head out of the corner of my eye, clearly not enjoying my half-baked truths to protect him. "I just can't place myself being the one who planted the camera because I was a bit too out of it to get back in the house on my own. I think that's the one issue I have with everything that's happened."

Dad's low hum made me tug on one of my hoodie strings as I stared at the laptop screen. He'd found a café with a corner to sit in—just enough noise to mask his conversation from anyone else zipping in and out for morning coffee, but not too much that I couldn't hear him.

"I think you're right," he said. "It looked like it'd been there for a bit. And I do think Severin's vampire lackeys were the ones who attacked, so it does add up. I just don't know the motive. Both Charlie and Rory have been in contact with me, and we've met up a couple of times..."

The way he trailed off indicated that silent 'but' was on its way.

"But," —right on cue— "there were a couple of disruptions. Some vampires following us."

"So it's likely one of them."

"Likely."

"What do you want me to do?"

"Bunker down wherever you are. Do what you can to secure your location now while Severin and his minions are resting. I'll come get you when it's taken care of."

I thought about arguing and demanding to help, but all the fight in me was gone. I was exhausted and running out of safe spots to carry out Dad's only order for me anyway. As much as I wanted to meet him as someone he could trust to finish cleaning up this mess, I also didn't want to fuck things up even worse if Severin decided to kill me so Dad would have to put another name on his people-to-avenge list.

"Okay," I breathed. "Please be careful. I'm sorry again, and I love you."

"I will. I love you too, kid."

The call ended, and I sucked in a shuddering breath before I had to take on Saint.

"Explain," Saint said sharply.

And my time was up. "Dad was going after Severin

anyway," I began, knowing that if I didn't start with the obvious, I might make a quickly-crumbling, confusing argument for cucking Saint out of eviscerating his ex. "I know that seems like a flimsy excuse, but I'm bitten and because of that, you *just* decided to take this matter into your own hands. The sun is up, which means you have about twelve hours until you can actually do anything, and I'm *spent*. Neither of us are in any condition to kick this guy's ass right now."

I checked my notifications to see a couple more texts from Zane and Iris. "My God do I want to kick his ass though, trust me. What kind of sick fuck makes someone think they have friends and then shatters your whole reality overnight?" I swiped them off the screen and looked back to Saint, his elbow propped up on the couch cushion with a hand in his hair as he stared at the laptop.

That deep, horrible sadness radiated from him as I realized what I'd said and just how applicable it was to us both in that moment. I set the phone face-down on the coffee table and leaned back. "I don't want to get in your way, but this was a *me* problem until now. Plus, I..." I chewed my lip, trying to figure out how not to mess up the delivery on the next bit. "I don't want you to end up dying because of this. You got the shit end of the stick for so long that you didn't actually get to live, and that fucking sucks."

Saint huffed a mirthless laugh. "I could say the same about you and your hunter quest. It's still a choice I get to make, isn't it?"

"But you're making it *because* of me, right?" I asked, pain lancing through my soul as I turned to him. "Because I made you feel a certain way—because I made you think of someone that kept you sane—made you happy for once. But you're not getting that you also just did that for *me*."

I caught him lifting his head from his hand just as I bowed to avoid eye-contact. My throat started to restrict with the sentiment that Saint had probably been the only person I'd been able to *really* talk to in such a long time. Iris and Zane's friendship had always felt casual—superficial in the way that I could enjoy my time around them, but I had to keep them at arm's length with work. And while Saint started out like that at first, I ended up feeling comfortable enough to spill my guts to him before knowing he was a vampire. Here I was, doing it again, but with everything out on the table. No secrets left between us.

"I-I don't have much left, Saint. I don't want to lose you too—vampire or not."

"Jules," he said quietly, that gentle tone a melody to my ears. "You know I can't give you normal, right? That normal that you said you wanted before you ran off—it can't happen with me around."

I sniffed, swiping at my puffy eyes. "I know. But I don't think anyone's going to let me fucking have that if I'm honest with myself. I'd at least want a friend I can talk to if that's still a possibility?" I probably looked super desperate—mainly because I felt it—but I didn't care. I'd figure out my definition of normal at some point, so long as I could somehow keep Saint, the one unlikely person to help me sort through some of my issues in the past forty-eight hours.

Saint's breathy chuckle filled me with hope. "You realize you labeled my following you around as stalking earlier, right? I don't think friendship would be on the table if I hadn't been trying to chase you down in the first place."

I don't think there's a good enough word to describe the joy I felt from a response I normally would've deemed disturbing. "Thank you, Saint."

"And thank you for giving me another chance to explain myself." He glanced at the curtains with a sigh. "You should probably get some sleep."

Fucking finally. I didn't even bother with another word as I climbed onto the couch and curled up, closing my eyes as the world around me faded to white noise. Warmth enveloped me after a few moments, along with the brush of soft fabric grazing my hand. Shortly after, I was gone.

———

I woke to the sound of my phone buzzing wildly against the coffee table before it suddenly cut short. My head felt like it'd been stuffed with cotton as I reached for it, flipped it over, and groaned when the display didn't sear into my retinas. Perfect. It was dead. And in the middle of its important final mission to deliver me a message from someone.

I pushed myself up and squinted my bleary eyes at the microwave. 5:23PM. At least I'd gotten some decent sleep, which was more than I could've asked for. Pushing back the incredibly soft blanket that I wanted to cuddle into again, I rubbed my arms and wandered to find a spare charger. Or Saint to find said charger.

Seeing how he was nowhere to be found and his door was shut, I surveyed the shadowy parts of the room before throwing in the towel and timidly knocking on his door. It opened immediately. With the energy of a small child who was telling their parents they'd just thrown up, I sheepishly held out my phone. "Do you have a charger I can borrow?"

"Oh. Yeah." He took it. "I was going to come wake you up in a bit, but you beat me to it. Did you want to take a shower?"

I was painfully aware of the new boundary we'd wandered into, but I wanted to kiss him just for hearing those words. He didn't have the right to be this thoughtful after I'd given him emotional whiplash.

"Holy shit, I would love a shower."

He snickered and pointed to the bathroom door. "Towels are under the sink. I'll see if I can find some spare clothes for you."

"You don't have to—"

"It'll help you feel a bit better. Trust me." His smirk faltered for a split second before he tapped my phone to his neck. "Is it still there?"

I reached for the bite, feeling that now too-familiar pulse of pain. "Think so," I muttered, locking onto my phone. "I'll be quick. I think Dad might've been trying to call me when it died."

"I'll plug it in now then. Hopefully it'll have enough juice to work when you get out."

I nodded, my confidence in the original plan starting to waver as I U-turned to the bathroom. Despite how cramped everything was, at least the shower was hot. My skin was pink from scrubbing away the grime of my nightmares from the last couple of days by the time I got out. When I wiped away the condensation on the mirror, I secretly hoped the bite mark would magically be gone and I could let myself relax.

It wasn't.

Towel wrapped around my waist, I checked outside the door to find a neat, folded pile of Saint's clothes waiting for me. Trading my torn up jeans and hoodie for crisp black skinny ones and a white-with-black-sleeves baseball tee made me look like a completely different person. Granted, everything was a bit too long, so material bunched up around my ankles and the shirt hung a bit lower. But I sort of *liked* how I looked. Sure, I wasn't anywhere close to reaching the appearance of Saint-level cool, but it gave me a small confidence boost.

I stepped out, ready to take on whatever new horrors awaited me after my call with Dad. Saint had left his door open, where he sat on the edge of his bed and stared at the phone perfectly balanced on the wall charger.

"Did he call again?" I asked, already starting for it.

"No," Saint said quietly. "I don't even know why I'm watching it, but I guess I'm letting my nerves get the best of me since Aaron clearly isn't dead yet."

I bit my lip once my knees hit the carpet. Just as I thought, Dad's number was the last missed call. I tapped the button to call back.

Dad's first words were: "What happened?"

"What? Oh, sorry—my phone died when you were calling, so I had to quickly find a place to charge it. Are you okay?"

Dad's relieved sigh made my anxiety spike. Did he do something to piss off Severin?

"I went to his lair, but when I got there, there was no sign of him or his minions. I'm guessing he decided to relocate after last night to regroup."

Well, fuck.

I grimaced, avoiding making eye contact with Saint. "So what now? It's going to be dark in about an hour. There's no way you're going to find him before then."

"Not unless I call Charlie and Rory to meet up again at two separate times, call off the meeting, and tail them. There's a chance one of them might lead me straight to him or his new hiding spot. That'll likely bleed into dusk, but it's all I have to work with."

The suck-up in me wanted to mention that I could track them, but I was almost positive there was no way either of them would be that bold to take their phone with them to meet this asshole vampire unless they disabled the tracker.

I locked eyes with Saint, covered the receiver, and mouthed: *check the laptop locations*. He rose and vanished from sight. I cleared my throat. Bad son mode: activated. "That doesn't sound like an amazing idea if I'm being honest. Heading right into a nest of vampires at night with no back up is going to get you killed, Dad."

"The alternative would be to wait until the morning to locate him," he said, avoiding Severin's name like he was in a public place again. Or he was just being extra paranoid. "I'm not going to do anything until I have some daylight."

"Promise?"

"Promise. As long as you promise to stay put for tonight."

I crossed my fingers. "Promise." The call ended.

Sorry Dad, I gave you twelve hours to handle this. I'm sort of over having a bite mark, and my vampire ex-boyfriend is likely going to be out for blood. I put my phone back on the charger, holding my hands over it as it teetered.

"What did you want to know about the locations?"

Holy fucking shit. I really needed to start anticipating

Saint sneaking up on me. I bit my tongue, trying to make my heart understand that I wasn't being hunted like a wild animal. Twisting to look up at him, I leaned against the wall. "Were any of the markers missing? There should've been five."

Saint shook his head.

"Were any stationary? Moving?"

"One was moving, the rest weren't."

"Well, I guess let's see if it's an important one," I muttered, pushing myself off the carpet. Saint wordlessly followed me back into the living room, where I hunched over the laptop and located the moving culprit. "Man... it's just Adonis. What a dumbass, still carrying around his phone." I clicked on another. "Looks like Lux is still at the crystal shop."

"Good." Saint folded his arms over his chest.

I smirked and clicked on another. "Dad is at a bar, Charlie's at a motel, and Rory's at a diner. So that's all a whole lot of nothing to work with."

"You mean feeding information to your dad?"

"Yeah, no..." I started, closing the laptop. "Twelve hours ago, neither of us could go after Severin, so the plan was to let Dad deal with it. Now he's trying to see if he can follow someone to find Severin to try again tomorrow."

Saint's face contorted in confusion.

"I'm assuming we can't do that," I said slowly. "Because if Severin followed us both before familiar-izing me, then he's had to have figured out we're here, right?"

"I'm killing him," Saint said, as if he were manifesting the concept into existence. "Tonight."

"Don't you have to work?" I don't know why I thought

this might be the one thing that could stop him while I stormed off to slay this metaphorical dragon for the two of us.

"Not tonight. Even if I did, I'd absolutely lie to Allie to get this over with. Aaron doesn't like making more of a scene than he has too, but he'd disrupt work anyway if he really wanted to bring me back."

I guess I didn't really have any way to talk him out of it now, especially since neither of us could stay barricaded up here. I unplugged the hard drive and crammed it under a couch cushion. "Then *we're* killing him tonight," I corrected, shoving myself to my feet. The hesitation from the way he opened his mouth to argue made me shake my head. "I meant what I said last night, Saint. I'm not going to let you get yourself killed. We do this together."

His jaw worked, his eyes clouding with a sense of unease. I could almost picture him replacing me with that now-dead familiar, fearing history might repeat itself. I grabbed Saint's arm, feeling the chill through his sleeve, and squeezed it. "I'm not him, Saint. I'm the son of a hunter, remember?"

"That doesn't really help."

I shrugged. "Well, I got a vampire hunting kit and about a decade's worth of knowledge about how to kill vampires. I think I deserve a bit of credit for that."

Saint tried to suppress a smile and failed, loosing a laugh. "Fine. Just *please* do what I tell you if things start to go to hell."

I let go, cramming my hands in my pockets. "Works for me. I don't exactly want to die either. That would be the cherry on top of this shit sundae... Do you have any idea where Severin-slash-Aaron might go as a backup lair?"

Saint chewed on the inside of his cheek. "No. Didn't

exactly have the privilege of knowing any of that. I was typically moved on a moment's notice if something happened."

I hummed, rocking back and forth on the balls of my feet. "Well... we could re-trace my steps after we separated the night I got bit and see if there might be any indication of where I was *supposed* to go. Maybe he planned on taking me somewhere else to lure out Dad? Either that or I could call up Iris and Zane and use myself as bait to take us to him."

Saint's eyes nearly bulged out of his head. "A strong *no* to the second option."

"Retracing steps, it is."

15 REMEMBERING

Seeing the place where Saint and I had our first date gave me a horrible sense of longing to remember what we talked about there. It also really sucked that I couldn't hold his hand, even though thinking about holding a *vampire's* hand felt weird. Plus, my mind latched onto this horrible idea that if Saint and I had continued our couch make-out session that he might've accidentally killed me during sex with his vampire strength. Nothing like my first time being my last time. So that gave me a rather healthy dose of fear to keep him in the friend zone, despite the hormonal gremlins' protests. My brain was still trying to find that sweet spot that let me use the words 'vampire' and 'friend' linked together, which was enough of a struggle.

I exhaled a puff of smoke in the cool night air, letting it anchor me while I examined the hole-in-the-wall pub. It wasn't nearly as big as the one we visited last night, but it was cute. Little designs were carved into the wooden façade, mimicking some of the wholesome graffiti that ended up on bar tops and booths.

Saint nudged me, and I spun around to find what he was looking at. "My guess is that he was on the roof of one of those buildings across the street. You can get a decent angle without being seen, and the dark covers you really well. Plus, no one really looks up if they feel like they're being followed. They just look around."

My brows knit together and I took a half-step away from him. "Noted, but mega creepy you came up with that so quickly."

He straightened his coat. "Where did you head after this?"

"The bar. Where I was" —I made air quotes— "looking for my lost company credit card."

"So that was a lie?"

"Yep," I said, popping the 'p.' "I was following my personal credit card notifications. I went there, then to the florist, then to the convenience store."

"Okay..." Saint said, following me as I started us on the ten-minute journey back toward the scene of the crime. "And you made these stops because...?"

"Because of Mom." Another puff of cold smoke curled around me. "I must've checked the date and didn't want to head home just yet. So I tried a gin and tonic, according to the bartender. Dad said it was her favorite drink."

"She had good taste."

I laughed. "I like to imagine she would've been a little more accepting of the whole gay thing like my aunt—her sister." I wrung my hands, wishing I could say something cheesy about her maybe liking Saint as my boyfriend, but I was slowly picking apart those knots. It was like he said: Saint couldn't give me normal. And normal would entail me not having a stake strapped to my back under my jacket like it was right now.

"She'd probably be proud of you for keeping everything together without her."

My throat constricted. "Thanks, Saint."

We walked the rest of the way in silence, letting me hold tight to that sentiment. After the last few days, I think I tossed that notion aside because of the mess I'd gotten myself into. But the more I reflected on it, the more I thought about what she'd say if we were sitting across from each other at her favorite diner and splitting a slice of cheesecake. A few bad days shouldn't erase years of effort. Effort to learn, to grow, to support—even if I'd done it all without much of a reward or recognition.

She'd probably tell me it was time to move on—to let go of Dad's goals and find my own. I couldn't stop myself from thinking of what Saint and I talked about last night, or keep myself from a quick peek out of the corner of my eye to find him staring straight ahead. I understood, deep down, that I was trying to grapple with the rug being yanked out from under me when it came to Saint, but it was hard to tell myself that I needed time. Time and maybe distance, once this whole nightmare was over. Assuming that the universe would even allow me to walk away from the supernatural of vampires, werewolves, and witches.

Saint slowed when the bar popped into view, tearing me from my depressing head-space. I glanced around, pin-pointing the other two stops.

I worried my lip. "Do you think he followed me into the bar?" I pointed over to the florist. "If he sat by the windows on the far side, he'd have a clear view of me heading in there." Shuffling around Saint, I moved to the corner, looking to and from the convenience store. "He'd be able to see down there too, right?"

Thankfully I could *feel* Saint leaning over my shoulder this time, like I'd finally adapted to having a human-sized cat silently following me like a shadow.

"That would make sense," Saint mumbled, his voice drifting away as he rocked back on his heels. "He could follow you in if you were distracted at the bar. Pick a spot. Stick around to give you enough distance when you left, and then decide when to pick up following you again."

I shivered.

"Cold?"

"Fucking creeped out." I rubbed my arms.

"Where do you go next? Home?"

I shook my head. "Remember how I talked to you about Mom at that diner when I miraculously found my card?" I jabbed my thumb toward the wrought-iron fence just beyond the nearby shops.

"Oh."

"Yeah. Oh." I hit the crosswalk button. "Time to go to the one place I'm only guessing I must've gone because I didn't have the balls to do it with you earlier." It took me a second to realize Saint had shifted next to me, and my face heated. "Oh my God, that came out wrong."

"No comment," Saint said, awkwardly glancing in the opposite direction.

I sped-walk across the street, likely blushing furiously because I just crammed my whole foot in my mouth. Why couldn't I have phrased that any differently? Why did I have to accidentally turn visiting my mother's grave site into a sex joke? What the fuck is wrong with me?

My bruises complained as I jogged up the steps to the main path beyond the cemetery gate, Saint's shadow painting the ground next to mine. This wasn't how I wanted Saint and I to come see her, based on my normal-life fantasies, but I had to return to the scene of the crime and at least apologize for screwing up a bit. I carefully moved around the decorative headstones until I reached hers, taking in the blocky, carved letters that made up 'SOPHIE'.

Saint stopped next to me, barely in my periphery as I motioned to the single carnation. "Florist." And the moscato bottle, empty and knocked over at the edge of the headstone. "Convenience store."

"Oh, Jules..."

"At least I now know, without a shadow of a doubt, what I'd been doing before I got bit," I muttered, rubbing the back of my neck.

"So Aaron must've followed you back here."

"With Zane and Iris—two of his lackeys and my supposed friends," I grumbled. "Zane said that I wandered off somehow, though, which is the part I can't quite wrap my head around in all this." I outstretched my arms toward the bottle again. "I mean, there's no way I downed that sucker and managed to outrun two-to-three vampires."

Saint tiled his head and folded his arms. "You had time to drink the whole thing, so Aaron must've made a call during that. They had to have brought a car, right?"

"I don't think Zane and Iris can *drive*. If they could, you'd think that Zane would've maybe gotten in a car and followed us from that *Workout Galaxy*. Then again, I didn't realize Lux owned a car until last night, so maybe I'm missing something."

To be fair, I'd been missing a *lot* recently. And, considering I'd been drunk or sleep-deprived the last couple of nights, anything could've been easily overlooked in this entire mess. However, I'd been to Iris and Zane's apartments—something that made my stomach extra queasy now—and they'd complained about stuff being too far to hoof it sometimes. There was never an option to use a car, unless it was kept back at their secret base as a communal vehicle.

"Did you know of a car everyone had access to?"

Saint shrugged. "I remember a couple of cars, but I have no idea whose they were or where they came from. I don't recall any of them being *out*, and there were a lot of parts of the building that were off-limits for me."

He really was a prisoner. I felt my fingers twitch toward his, like the gremlins had taken full control and decided to all work together to get me to hold his hand. His *vampire hand*, I reminded myself. It was cold, dangerous, and could break every bone in my body at any given second.

Saint slowly shook his head. "Besides the car, this whole situation feels... odd. Why bite you and not immediately take you? Why *bite* you first? If you were drunk enough, which you must've been, he could've held off until you were at least in transit."

I bit my thumbnail, walking myself through the idea of clumsily escaping, getting home, and not even making it inside the house. The whole thing seemed fucking ridiculous. "Wait... I didn't get into the house on my own."

"Hm?"

"Saint, there are two people potentially working with

Severin, and one of those suspects brought me into the house."

His eyes widened. "You think he *let* you go?"

"That seems like the most obvious answer if I somehow walked away. Hell—Charlie could've gotten a ride for the both of us from them and had us dropped off outside. We were the only two there for a while."

"But why would Aaron let that happen? Isn't this because he's jealous that you and I were out together?"

"*True*," I said, pointing at his chest before turning it on myself. "But he's also pissed at my dad. He sent a whole bunch of vampires over there to stir shit up, so what are the odds that he had Charlie send me inside, thinking that I would immediately tell Dad I was a familiar? He'd be distracted. Then Severin and his groupies could have an easier time descending on the place. I was supposed to be a decoy, Saint."

"Shit," he hissed. "If that *is* the case, then we're back at square one. We have no idea where he's hiding."

I rested my arms on my head and chewed on my lip. "Iris and Zane?"

"No."

I frowned. "But I have a stake?"

"*No.*"

Saint took a step along the side of Mom's headstone, went for a couple more steps, turned on his heel and walked the same length back. Oh good. He was pacing. To avoid digging a trench around Mom, I stared down at the glittery stone slab and tried to conjure up that map in Dad's office—the one those goons tore down.

He'd pinned so many places that may or may not be

important that I wondered just how many of them were related to Severin. Because while Severin might've been a really good catch, I was fairly certain he wasn't the grand prize—not the vampire that killed Mom. I tried not to branch off to venture down that path since it tickled the back of my brain. I needed Severin. I had Saint. I had a vague recollection of data that could be connected to him. I could do this.

"Jules?"

Saint stopped mid-pace to find who'd said my name, and I whipped around at light-speed. My breath caught. "Aunt S —" I squeaked, quickly shoving that surprise down. "A-Aunt Syd? Wh-what are you doing here?"

I may be stupid. Like. Really stupid.

There she was, car keys in hand as she clutched the shoulder strap of her purse with a small bundle of flowers poking out. "I... was coming to visit Sophie. It looks like you beat me to it." Her keys jingled toward the single carnation resting under the headstone.

"O-oh, yeah." Cue nervous laugh as I swung my arms at my sides. I stole a glance toward Saint, who shifted his weight, not taking his eyes off of her. "Sorry, almost forgot where I was for a second."

She smirked and rustled the flowers free. "Who's your friend?" she asked, a bit of a quizzical twinkle in her eye that made the heat rush to my cheeks again.

"Saint," I blurted. "This is Saint. Saint, this is my aunt, Sydney."

He fidgeted with his hands after seeing both of hers were occupied. "Nice to meet you."

"Same to you," she said, a touch *too* cheerful for being in a cemetery. I shuffled back as she knelt to place her flowers next to mine. "Looks like someone was having a bit of a party, hm?"

The damn bottle. I smothered the lower half of my face with my hand. "Uh, yeah. Sorry. I'll be sure to clean up when I leave. I guess when I was out here the other night, I forgot to take it with me."

Holy shit, this was so awkward. I really wanted to take the bottle, grab Saint, and bolt. But what if Severin jumped out from behind a gravestone and started fucking things up? I couldn't just leave her here with everything else going on, could I? Well, unless *I* started freaking the fuck out because Severin decided to have some familiar torture time and have *me* attack her. But I really hoped Saint would step in to stop me if that happened.

Aunt Syd brushed off her pants as she stood. "It's fine, Jules. Though, I don't think your mom would approve of you downing a whole bottle in a night."

Probably not, especially considering all the problems this damn thing added to my life. I noted Saint shift again, and I felt terrible for keeping us here. He was likely antsy about tracking down Severin, but I couldn't exactly openly communicate my current dilemma.

Aunt Syd jingled her keys in front of us like she was trying to get the attention of a couple of babies learning sound and movement for the first time. "How about you two boys join me for a ride, and we can grab a bite to eat? My treat."

I almost threw my head back in despair. Aunt Syd, no, not *now.* I didn't need someone trying to needle at my sort-of-love-life in the middle of a crisis. "We'd love to, but we actually have to get going. Saint's shift starts soon."

"Oh, then let me drive you. It'll save you a walk, and we can chat for a bit, Jules."

Okay, she wasn't really getting the hint. "*Well*, I was, um, sort of hoping Saint and I could—you know—chat privately on the way."

Her mouth formed an 'o'. "Got it. Sorry. Silly me." Nervous smiles and chuckles all around until she followed up with: "Well, that's rather unfortunate."

Those words caught me off guard, my mind trying to make sense of *why* she'd say something like that before Saint hit the ground. I whirled around to the blur of pitch-black eyes and elongated canines pasted on a familiar face: Zane.

I shoved my arm into my jacket to grab the stake, my heart catching in my throat. "Aunt Syd, ru—" My vision doubled, my knees gave out, and a sickening sensation pulsed through me as Severin plunged his claws into my brain. Then everything went black.

16 MISCALCULATIONS

Voices skimmed the surface of my consciousness as I started to grasp at words like playground sand. I had it, but it slipped away just as quickly as I thought I could make something out of it. I always thought I'd react a little faster when it came to a situation like this, but my head felt muddled and groggy, like I'd been so deep in sleep that my brain couldn't comprehend the urgency of a blaring alarm.

"...house..."

"...Mason..."

"...now?"

Dad—they were talking about Dad. I scrambled to try to find a reason why that was important. Was I in the basement? Was Charlie talking to him? Where was I? Don't tell me I got drunk again. That didn't seem right. I couldn't be in the basement, though I struggled to comprehend the *why* of that thought until I managed to pierce the surface like a bobbing apple.

"What do we do with the vampire?"

A feminine voice. Stern tone. Familiar, yet wholly *unfamiliar* in a way I couldn't describe. I willed my body to move —to open my eyes—trying to speed up the process.

"Have Iris press him. If he refuses to tell us anything, we're just going to have to kill him. There's too much risk."

Iris? Another feminine voice? *Vampire?*

A surge of adrenaline shot through me as it clicked: Saint. They were talking about Saint. They were going to *kill* Saint—

My eyes flew open, head spinning as I shoved myself off a pinstriped duvet. I swung my legs over the bed, my brain sluggish to comprehend what kind of bizarre hideout I'd ended up in as I briefly noted the floral black-out curtains and powder-blue walls. Unfortunately, I wasn't quite ready to do any sort of stunts, let alone stand, which became super obvious when my socks hit the hardwood and I ate shit. My hip cried out as I bit down on my tongue.

"Jules! Oh my God—"

My heart hammered a bit harder as footfalls rushed around the end of the bed and someone grabbed my arm. I tried to shake them off and scoot away to push myself back to my feet. "Let me g—" I stopped the second I looked up.

Not to one person. But two. Two faces that looked similar, but one was about a decade younger. One I'd never thought I'd see again.

My throat was dry, clicking with my attempt to swallow before I managed a rasp. "Mom?"

I couldn't let myself believe it, even as her face crumbled from alarm to remorse. She squeezed my elbow and pulled me toward her, wrapping me in a hug. I was too stunned to speak. She was *here.* She was *alive.* The wrongness didn't register quiet yet, my brain chugging as it tried to piece together the obvious clues until she released me to cup my face. Her cold hands made my stomach drop.

"Hey, sweetheart," she whispered, her eyes faintly crinkling at the edges, even through her eternal snapshot of youth.

Aunt Syd exhaled. "Are you hurt?"

Even though the question was meant for me, Mom answered. "He's fine."

My aunt's hesitation gave me about a heartbeat to try to pull myself together before she said, "I'll give you two a moment." At least I heard her footsteps as she trailed to the other side of the room, letting me know that she was most definitely human. A door quietly thumped in its frame, and Mom's hands slid away.

My mouth worked. "You're... dead."

Her lips pressed together as she glanced down. "Yes, and no. It's complicated."

If that wasn't the fucking understatement of the year, I don't know what was. "H-how? Why?" Oh my God, Dad was on a rampage, hunting down every vampire he could when Mom was *right here.* "Dad thinks you're *dead.*"

She grabbed my hands, holding them tight. Normal-person strength kind of tight, not vampire hand-breaking strength tight. The whole action felt practiced and natural. *Seamless.* I teetered between the pain of knowing she'd been out of reach this entire time and the joy that she was finally in front of me, alive—alive-*ish.*

"I know this is a lot. But I'm going to try my best to fill in the blanks for you. I'd hoped to do it sooner, but..." Her shoulders fell. "Honey, I was sick. *Really* sick. Cancer."

The air left my lungs.

"My odds weren't great, so I... made a choice. It wasn't an easy one."

"Oh." That one syllable barely managed to make a sound, even in the room's silence.

She combed her fingers along the side of my hair, as if she was trying to get my stubborn bed-head to cooperate. But I was too fixated on her ghostly smile, like she was seeing me as the little boy she remembered.

"Dad—" she started, catching herself. "Sorry. *Mason* knows, Jules."

Wait, what? I thought the floor might disintegrate beneath me as I tried to rub those words into my brain.

"He tried to talk me out of it."

What the fuck was happening? He *what?* I opened my mouth, but she shook her head.

"Let me finish, okay?"

The anger was starting to resurface as I squeezed her hands, wanting nothing more than to throat-punch Dad for lying to me for *over ten fucking years*. But sure, that's cool, I'll wait. I clamped my mouth shut, turning into a corked bottle about to pop.

"I don't know how much you know—rather, how much Mason told you, but if I had to guess, I'd say he's told you nothing."

I clenched my teeth so hard I was sure they'd shatter. Time to brace myself for the other shoe to drop I guess.

"He and I come from two different lineages of witches."

Okay, the math checked out there. Lux wasn't lying, so kudos to her.

"Mason wanted to leave it behind. He didn't want any

part of this world anymore, and I had given it up too, aside from staying in touch with Sydney. We wanted a mundane life. With you."

My chest hurt from how badly I wanted to cry and scream with this new-found knowledge that I could've previously had the life I'd started to pursue, but the punches kept going because of course we weren't done yet.

"So, when I found out my odds of survival, and Sydney couldn't assist in the way that a well-versed witch could, she offered an alternative. One that Mason's former coven strongly disapproved of while mine considered it to be more of an... alternative lifestyle choice."

Ah yes, that old terminology equated with the argument against same-sex relationships that Dad probably used at least once in his life. I was starting to see his intolerance as a trend, which made me deeply uncomfortable that perhaps I'd been taught the vampiric equivalent of homophobia— vampire-phobia? Necrophobia? No, that was probably for something else. Anyway, the term didn't matter as much as the fact that my dad was possibly knowingly committing hate crimes, and I'd be foolishly helping him for parental acceptance points.

"He didn't want you growing up with a vampire for a mother, saying that it would dredge up too many questions and ruin the normal life he wanted for us."

Well, he's done a fucking terrible job doing that.

"He was convinced that I could pull through with the treatment. So we fought. I met with Sydney, and she linked me up with a respectable vampire who's an avid traveler. Mason still believes he can find and kill them like I'm under a curse he can break, but they could literally be anywhere right now. He wouldn't let me come home, so I moved in with Sydney. I begged her to continue keeping in touch with you as a proxy, and Mason made sure to cover his tracks for as long as he could about his quest to kill vampires so she wouldn't find out and report back to me. I eventually left with her when she had a custom home built up north, and I left Iris and Zane here to watch over you in the meantime."

My brain slammed on the breaks. "Iris and Zane? They're *your* vampires?" The screech of internet dial-up took over my brain as she nodded, allowing me to connect to a conclusion that I'd completely miscalculated when I'd been standing over her grave who-knows-how-long-ago. I ripped one of my hands free of hers and felt the bite at my neck. "Am I *your* familiar?"

She grimaced. "You were a bit too drunk when I found you at the cemetery the other night, so I thought it would be safest to take control and bring you back to the vacation rental. I didn't want you to hurt yourself, and you were so happy to see me that I realized I didn't want you to continue thinking I was dead. Unfortunately, when I stepped away to call Sydney to come get us, you managed to slip away, and my control with familiars isn't great. I don't tend to make them. Iris was the only one I had for a short while."

"Y... you..." My own mother fucking bit me. How was I supposed to react to that? I guess that also meant I was wrong about Severin, which meant that Dad was going after him purely because of the whole arch-nemesis-slash-mole debacle.

"I know, Jules. It's okay, we'll have time to catch up on everything later. Since your father broke the agreement to keep your life normal, I've already set some things in place to have you properly educated by your aunt when we head up to Canada."

I sputtered. "I-Wh—Wait, Canada?"

Her brows knit together like I was crazy for questioning her. "Yes, Jules. You're a witch. I should've pushed to have you raised as one the second Mason chose normalcy over having a happy family, no matter the cost. We're fixing that. Better late than never."

U-turn, fucking *U-turn*. While she had a point, there were a bunch of red flags popping up—mainly because this was a demand and not a question of whether or not I wanted to go. Both my parents were bat-shit insane, and they were playing tug-o-war with me. So much for a happy reunion when my anxiety was shooting through the fucking roof.

I scrambled to my feet, only for her to stand in one smooth motion. An immediate reminder that my mom could now break me in half. "W-what about Dad? Aren't you going to—"

"I will inform him of everything once we're home."

This was sounding more and more like a messy divorce with a kidnapping spin. Kidnapping—wait. Oh fuck. "Where's Saint?"

She put her hands on her hips. "The vampire Sydney brought back with you? The one that almost broke Zane's neck?"

Oh damn. I was super impressed until I remembered the trauma and how he was probably scared shitless that Severin might stroll in and lock him up again.

"Jules, please don't tell me he's your boyfriend."

This was like a repeat of Dad's question from last night, ultimately deciding Saint's fate in a matter of seconds. Saying 'no' would almost definitely damn him. So I told myself that the status of our relationship at that specific point in time didn't matter, though I'm pretty sure my heart sided with it anyway: "He is."

She threw up her hands. "What are you doing? Do you even know who he works for? He could be manipulating you."

"He's not! He was dragged into this mess by his asshole ex, and now he wants nothing to do with him."

"Who?" she demanded.

"W-who?"

"*Who* is his ex?"

I hesitated.

"*Jules*. Answer. Now."

"Severin?"

She soundlessly clapped her hands together, closing her eyes. "I need you to listen to me very carefully. You have two options: you break up with this vampire" —my stomach began working itself into knots— "or you inform him that the only way he's going to continue to date you is by formally accepting me as his surrogate maker. I will not tolerate another vampire potentially taking you away from me, understood?"

Her eyes narrowed, as if expecting an actual answer. Oh shit. She was helicopter parenting me at twenty-one. I think the worst part was that I knew how to talk to Dad. Sure, he had weapons and could be a buff scary dude, but he was *human*. Mom—Mom wasn't. And I wasn't exactly equipped with any up-to-date information on how to address her without feeling her wrath.

I decided to dip a toe into the water to test, praying I

wouldn't immediately regret it. "If I do this, will you get rid of the bite? Un-familiar me?"

Her body relaxed a bit, her head tilting to the side. "If you do this *and* you promise not to cause a fuss on the way home."

Yikes. She wasn't going to let me bargain my way out of this without getting as much as she possibly could in return.

"Okay," I said, though my stomach did an uneasy flip as she turned to head to the other side of the room. Boy, it was going to be a lot of fun to tell Saint that he was going to have to surrender his freedom or die. I also wasn't stupid enough to think that she was just going to let him *go* if I said we broke up. Not with the way she and Aunt Syd had been discussing what to do with him while I was still kind of out of it.

She opened the door, leading us into the hall, and started down the stairs. I had to hold onto the railing, wincing with every step, and praying that I wouldn't fall and slide all the way to the bottom. When I reached the landing, a smiling Iris waved at me from the kitchen peninsula and Zane was flopped on the couch, dead to the world. I tensed, awkwardly waving back like I hadn't been running from the two of them for the past day, and quickly shuffled after Mom.

At the back of the stairs, she put one hand on the golden handle and the other on her hip. "I need you to keep in mind that he's dangerous, Jules. His loyalty isn't with you, it's with his maker."

I wanted to argue if she was loyal to her nomadic vampire, but I didn't want to push it when Saint was on the other side of the door. So I swallowed those words in favor of, "I understand."

The door opened to another set of stairs, taking me down

to the basement. Another careful descent later, and I made it to the bottom. When I looked up, the door had been closed behind me. At least I'd get some privacy for this chat. Saint was seated in the center of the elongated room, his head bowed and arms pulled behind him around one of the metal beams. Everything else was industrial duct work and sterile white walls like a modern apartment unit.

I padded forward as fast as I could without slipping and falling on my ass. "Saint?"

His head jerked up, his face shifting from surprise to relief. "You're okay."

The way he looked at me made me want to run up and kiss him, but I slapped away that idea. I couldn't afford to make this weird when his life was in danger, and we were about to be forcibly moved to another country. Priority number one: make sure he's not injured.

"Are *you* okay?" I whispered, grabbing the pole as I checked his arms. My educated guess, based on the silver-threaded rope binding his hands, was that Aunt Syd had made sure he wasn't going to break loose on his own. That, and Mom, Iris, and Zane wouldn't be able to tie a proper knot because their arms would turn to jelly the second they touched that.

"They let me heal before they tied me up. Jules, your aunt—"

"I know, just—" I made a frustrated noise as I crouched down in front of him. "I have good news and bad news."

"Please don't say the bad news is that your aunt is working for Aaron."

"It's not."

His head lightly thumped against the pole. "Okay. Okay, I can handle the bad news then."

"Eh..." I grimaced. "Yeah, give me a sec, and we'll see about that."

"There's no way it can get worse, is there?"

"For me? You bet your ass it can."

He hung his head again, making my heart do some weird things that triggered a romantic need to hold his face in my hands. I refrained, telling myself it was probably easier to focus this way. "So my aunt is working with a *different* vampire. And that's the vampire who bit me."

Saint perked up at that. "Who?"

"Yeah, so this is both good and bad news: my *mom*."

I think I broke him. He stared at me blankly, like he was certain he misheard or that I was about to provide some sort of explanation. I went with the latter, hoping that he'd catch up if that wasn't the case.

"I guess she isn't dead, but Dad made me believe she was because of a bunch of political witch bullshit, which also means Lux wasn't lying about me being one. Long story short, she's a vampire, she's been living with my aunt in Canada, Iris and Zane are her minions, who have been looking after me on her behalf, and now she's gone a bit off the deep end."

"Your mom... turned you into a familiar..."

Oh boy, this was going well.

Saint squinted. "Why?"

"You, um, remember all of that... wanting a normal life stuff we talked about earlier?" He gave a painfully slow nod. "I guess my dad tried that. Mom got the big C and had herself turned so we could stay together, but Dad got pissy about it. So now he's gone on a vampire hunting bender, and Mom's mad because the whole reason why he pushed her out was to keep my life normal."

He blinked. "Your family is way more fucked up than I thought."

I held up my hands. "My thoughts exactly. Mom's kidnapping me to have Aunt Syd teach me how to be a witch."

Saint shifted in his chair. "Do you... want that?" A flicker of ache lingered there, like I was about to drop him after all my attempts to stop him from being killed.

"Fuck no," I spat. "Look, it's clear that I'm not going to get fucking normal, s-so—"

I did it. I pushed off my knees and kissed him, my hand cradling the back of his head. The gremlins sang like a choir of angels when Saint leaned in as far as he could, almost refusing to let me escape when I had to deliver the rest of the horrible news.

"I told her you were my boyfriend so she wouldn't kill you."

"Well, am I?"

My fingers trembled as they curled in his hair. "Seeing how I just discovered that my mom is a vampire and everything I've ever known is a lie, I think I'd be okay with a vampire boyfriend. If, um, you'd still be interested?"

Saint bit his lip, a smile tugging at the corner of his mouth. "I never stopped being interested."

17 ESCAPE PLAN

he upside to being alone with my once-again-boyfriend, Saint, in the basement, even though he was still tied to a pole, was that I could sit on his lap while we combed through the horrible details of our predicament.

"So," Saint said. "I can either do a ritual to pledge myself to your mom, or I can *die.*"

My cheekbone dug into the back of the chair from having slipped from Saint's shoulder. "Yep. And she's refusing to un-familiar me until I promise to willingly go with her to Canada."

"Assuming I go along with this, she'll take me too, which I don't think would be terrible until she finds a reason to separate us if one of us does something wrong. Kind of an Aaron play."

I cringed, trying to think of another way to force Mom's hand. This is going to sound terrible, but when I was there basking in my renewed relationship, I kind of wished my mom was dead again. Dad wasn't exactly blameless in this either, but Mom was my immediate issue. I'd deal with Dad and give him a piece of my mind about not giving me an unbiased vampire talk later.

"If I were to untie you," I wondered aloud, "I'm guessing the odds of us escaping are slim. I don't have my phone, my shoes, my stake, or my coat either."

"She'll probably kill me the moment I step foot from the basement. Zane also probably won't mind taking another swing at me."

"Yeah, I heard," I said, absently running my fingers through the tufts of Saint's hair along the back of his head. "I thought that was kind of hot."

He snorted. "I came out of it far worse than he did this time."

I shrugged, a smile pulling at the corner of my mouth. "Everything you do somehow ends up a million times cooler, even if you didn't technically win."

"You think I'm cool?"

I sat up resting my elbow on the chair back. "You *don't* think you're cool? You, an un-ashamed, pretty-boy bisexual with a sense of style who could easily have anybody he wants, are insanely cool, and it's absolutely wild to me that you're shocked by that. Did you think I wasn't going to text you?"

He coughed out a hint of a laugh. "Honestly, I thought you might get cold feet. Or say you had a boyfriend already. That'd be my luck."

I held my arm out to the basement. "Well, this is the luck you get when you're with me. So I guess you win some, you lose some." My hand dropped back onto my lap. "Do you know of another way to get rid of a familiar mark? I'm assuming no, but I thought I'd at least ask before I come up with something really stupid."

I couldn't stop myself from watching him worry his lips, making me wish we were back on his couch right now instead of being held captive in a basement.

"There is *one* other way that I know of..." Saint's look of discomfort meant that it wasn't a great way, quickly dashing my hopes. "It would require me to turn you. I don't think I'm comfortable with that, unless it's something you're sure you absolutely want. That, and your mom would also kill me in a heartbeat."

"Shit," I mumbled. "And that's the only other way?"

"I'm pretty sure."

I rubbed my bite mark, wincing with how it pulse under my touch.

Saint hummed. "The way familiars were once described to me by one of Aaron's vampires was that they... sort of have a wireless connection. The further you are from your vampire, the weaker it gets. The closer, the stronger. It determines exactly what your vampire can do. If your mom struggles with that, then she's going to struggle finding you the second you get a half-dozen or so blocks away."

"So... we can run." I can work with that. I was good at running away from my problems. If I put enough distance between us, I could guilt-trip Dad into dealing with her, and then the two of them could duke it out. "I think I have an idea. But I'm going to need to get my phone back for it to work. Which means I'm probably going to have to leave you again, and I really don't want to do that."

Saint kissed my jaw, and I turned into it, relishing one more taste of the win I had desperately needed.

"I'll be okay," he whispered. "What's the plan?"

———

I tried to close the basement door as quietly as possible, but Mom still appeared, jump-scaring me with the Saint Special.

"Well?" she asked, her arms already folded over her chest in girl-boss mode.

"It took some convincing, but he'll do it," I said. "He just... needs a bit of time. He's been on his own for a while, and Severin didn't exactly treat him well. The thought of pledging to someone else is a bit terrifying."

She huffed. "I know you're probably thinking I'm being too pushy about this, but it's for your safety."

"I-I know, Mom. This is just *super* sudden, and I'm trying to keep it together right now because my dead mom isn't dead, and my boyfriend is an abused vampire who's kind of freaking out, so—" I threw my hands out at my sides and let them drop. "Yeah. It's been a rough couple of days."

Mom's hard exterior crumbled as she pulled me into a hug, my traitorous heart warming with the action. If this had been before I'd even met Saint, there was a strong possibility I would've given the finger to Dad and relished the excitement of becoming a witch instead of trying to claw my way into the ranks of vampire hunters. But now I'd been thrust into a weird in-between space of not knowing right from wrong anymore.

The other problem was that I clearly had a totally different idea of Mom. She was supposed to be my guardian angel and champion to tell me I could reach for the stars. Someone like Aunt Syd, who probably relayed all my intimate conversations with her back to Mom. Considering her seemingly educated guess that I was with Saint and that she didn't bat an eye at for the same reason Dad would have, that would likely be a yes. Okay, so maybe Dad would've thrown a fit because he's a vampire hater, but he'd absolutely be really homophobic about it too.

Mom gave me a gentle pat on the back, signaling the hug was ending. "I do hope this boy is as good as you think he is, Jules. I don't want to see him break your heart." I melted a little as she pulled away, glad to finally have a bit of parental support when it came to my romantic endeavors.

I had to remind myself that she'd talked about killing him earlier and swallowed the tempting urge to point that out. So, I settled into the role of the obedient son. "Thanks, Mom."

Her eyes crinkled at the edges with her soft smile, almost making me reconsider my plan to break the hell out of here instead of being dragged away to live in the Canadian wilderness. "Are you hungry?"

Shit. There was a flaw in the plan. I'd been surviving off of various drinks, naps, and adrenaline for almost a day since my last actual meal had been with Saint at that pub. Weird how taking care of myself was quickly chucked out the window in favor of survival. I hadn't even realized my stomach was aching due to hunger because I assumed I'd probably gotten an ulcer from the stress.

Mom didn't give me much of a chance to argue anyway, leading me by the elbow to the kitchen high top stools, where Iris had claimed one of the two seats. She left me standing there awkwardly when she let me go and walked around the counter, heading straight for the bread box.

Was I about to abandon my boyfriend for a grilled cheese?

When she opened the cabinet and pulled out the skillet, I knew there was no way out. If I turned my nose up at this, she'd get suspicious. I briefly considered pulling a lie out of my ass to say that I'd grown out of the world's best grilled sandwich, but Aunt Syd had just witnessed me devour one the other night.

I hesitated, stealing a glance at Iris, whose chin rested on the heels of her palms, fingers curled to frame her face. The most cherubic vampire who I suddenly remembered knocked out Drew back at *Charm & Rit*. To protect me. To lure me back to meet Mom. To preemptively end my first relationship before it'd gotten any further than a date and leave me with a heaping dose of heartache.

"Sorry about earlier. I was getting Sydney to come pick us up, but I didn't realize you got yourself a boyfriend." Iris's eyebrows wiggled up and down with her teasing smile. "Zane isn't really his biggest fan, but I think he's cute."

I forced out a nervous laugh when Mom shot her a discouraging glare in the midst of quick-and-dirty cooking. This was going to be a lot to get used to. Iris being a vampire was even more unsettling than Zane, mainly because she just seemed so... I don't know—*social?* She was the one that liked to go party and got Zane and I into every exclusive area she could manage. That felt like a bit of a risk to me since the more normal people a vampire knew, the more likely they'd eventually question why their friend wasn't aging. Unless she managed to integrate me into the vampire party scene without me realizing it.

She patted the stool cushion. "Come on, take a seat."

Sorry, Saint. They've locked me in. He'd have to wait a little bit longer, despite how uneasy this whole thing was making me feel. I was just trying to hold myself together and pretend that I wasn't about to have a mental breakdown about my mom making me lunch like I was a little kid again. So I hoisted myself onto the stool.

"Are you excited to become an actual witch?" Iris asked, bouncing after her feet kicked the thin wood under the counter once with a dull *thud*. "Sorry—I just think that's super cool. I asked Sydney if she could teach me at first, but I guess I don't have magic in my blood. Plus, some witches can be a bit bitchy. Like the one that almost stabbed you."

I hoped the sizzle of the skillet covered the way I almost choked on my own saliva. I guess she *did* see Drew's knife. At least she'd known what she was getting herself into. "Um, I... don't know?"

Truthfully, I could only picture Lux patting my cheek and telling me that I had no other option but to submit to some unknown goddess. Since she and Drew were a part of the vampire-hating witches, I assumed that at least I wasn't walking into the exact same fate, fooled by the illusion of choice. But I didn't really want that—vampire-hating version or not.

Iris's arms fell to the counter. "What? Really? Think of all the cool things you'll be able to do, though!"

I jumped as a plate slid in front of me, already-cut sandwich ready with a side of chips, the cheese oozing onto the glazed ceramic.

"Give him time, Iris," Mom said. "Mason didn't prepare

him for this. He scrambled his brain and prepared him for killing vampires."

I'll give her that. But it didn't stop Iris from peppering me with other little questions and small talk about a future in which she'd be like a weird older sister figure. The upside was that it gave me time to eat and digest my surroundings as Mom wandered off to deal with a task in another part of the house. I hoped she was consulting with Aunt Syd because she was the only person I'd lost track of.

I knocked back some water and cleared my throat. "Is the only bathroom upstairs?"

"Oh, um, I think there's one off the primary bedroom down here, but I think Sophie's busy in there," Iris said. "So yeah, upstairs is your best bet."

Grilled cheese consumed. Check.

Excuse made. Check.

Now was the time. I slid from the stool and padded back to the stairs, dragging my eyes over Zane's still zonked-out form on the couch before I jogged up the steps. My tongue pressed to the roof of my mouth to stop my whimpering from Zane's earlier accidental man-handling, now that Iris spilled the beans that he was younger and less experienced with dialing in parts of his vampire strength.

Once I'd made it to the second floor, my palms felt mega sweaty. My shoes weren't anywhere to be seen downstairs, so they were likely in the bedroom I'd woken up in. I held my breath as I shuffled over to the door and pushed on the handle, doing my best to stop it from making a sound.

I only had to peer inside to see my shoes on the side of the bed. I'd passed right by them without noticing because I'd been too hyper-focused on Vampire Mom. Pushing the door open a bit further, I slid inside and shut it behind me, the loudest *click* ringing out when I realized I was standing across the room from Aunt Syd.

"Hi," I squeaked. "Just, um, looking for my shoes."

God, she looked like a parent from one of those old movies or TV shows where the teenager sneaked back into the house after climbing out a window. Arms crossed, legs crossed, lamp next to the armchair, and a single eyebrow raised in question.

"Do you care to explain what I saw outside?"

My heart was in my throat. "Wh-what did you see outside?" I already fucking knew what she'd seen because, spoilers, I'd found a pair of scissors in the basement and helped a certain vampire out of one of the windows to wait for me to get my phone and shoes. Risky? Sure. But at least he'd be able to *run* if things backfired. The worst thing that could happen to me is that I'd get extradited to the car and shipped up north. He'd, well, *die.* Now, whether or not he'd actually bolt is another story, and that was looking pretty bleak.

"Jules."

I sputtered, immediately folding. "Can we just leave him out of this, please?" I was screwed anyway. Mission failed.

She rubbed her forehead. "Don't you understand what sort of danger you're putting yourself in?"

"What? Because my boyfriend is a 'rival' vampire or something like that?"

"*No,* I'm not talking about your boyfriend—friend—whatever he is to you because I know that you'd lie to Sophie through your teeth if it kept the blood off your hands." Aunt Syd pushed herself out of the chair, starting for me as I stood there, unable to force myself to move. "I'm talking about going back to Mason, which I know is exactly what you're doing or else you wouldn't come up here for *this*."

She pulled my phone out of her pocket, holding it just far enough away that it would be a struggle to rip it from her hand. "I know Mason won't pick up a call from a number he doesn't recognize, and I also know that you can't go home because I went there to find you after Iris told me that's where you said you were going when you left her at the diner. I staked the place out until it was attacked and left to try to find you to stop you from walking into that mess. Unfortunately, Sophie gave me some poor directions."

Well, despite feeling like I'd been caught with my hand in the cookie jar, at least I knew Mom was shit at using her vampire-familiar radar, just like Saint and I had banked on. But now I had to feel like a bad son for spilling the beans about plotting to go tattle to Dad about Mom.

"Aunt Syd, I—"

"I understand he's your father, Jules, but please tell me you can see just how badly he's fucked up here."

"Trust me, I can, but..."

She remained still, watching me as I tried to formulate the best way to deliver the message that Mom isn't exactly the best parent either.

"I don't want to be a witch."

The blank mask of surprise that stared back at me didn't look that far off from Saint's lapse of understanding my mental gymnastics in the basement. I think I broke her too.

"What I mean is" —I shook my head— "Aunt Syd, I *begged* Dad to help me hunt vampires for years. He wanted me to have a normal life but then didn't actually give it to me.

And he didn't want me to go with you to see Mom and have my entire world turned upside down either. But Mom clearly has her own problems and expectations, and I... Fuck, I just want to be able to choose something—*one thing*—for myself."

My hands fell to my sides, smacking my jeans. "Dad almost ruined the idea of dating for me. Then I freaked out because after I got the courage to finally go for it, I found out my boyfriend was a vampire—all thanks to him noticing the bite that Mom left. He's literally the one thing I wanted in all of this, and my parents are too busy with their fucked up custody battle to realize that they're not letting me make my own choices. And I'm fucking miserable."

I choked back the lump in my throat, glancing away as I caught the briefest glimpse of pity. "Look," I said quietly, "I just want them to fight it out and let me figure out what I want. I don't want to be a witch. I don't want to go to Canada. I don't want to keep living in a house full of vampire hunters that end up actually being werewolves and witches who have a bunch of screws loose. I want to—I don't know—work a normal-ish job? Maybe get my own place or move in with a cute boy? Live for myself instead of trying to keep one or both of my parents from getting themselves killed?"

Aunt Syd's face softened before she pulled me into a hug. I had to refrain from feeling for my phone and making a mad dash for Saint. "Oh, Jules," she mumbled into my hair. I felt something slide into my back pocket—a speciously phone-shaped object that made my eyes widen. "You deserve that life. You deserve to make your own choices. I'd tell Sophie if she'd listen, but you're right. Your parents are a little too wrapped up in their battle over you, and I've always feared it'd get in the way of your happiness."

She stepped back, her hands moving to my shoulders. "Promise me you won't get yourself hurt, okay? And if Saint isn't who you thought he is, that you'll call me *immediately* so I can come find you."

I was on the verge of tears. Aunt Syd was literally the best. Of all my parental figures, she was doing the best job, which was a little depressing to think about too much. But I wasn't going to let her change her mind. I quickly slipped on my shoes and ran back to hug her again.

"Thank you, Aunt Syd."

"Don't thank me just yet. Let's sneak you outside first and hope I can distract Sophie."

18 ON THE RUN

When Aunt Syd helped me out onto the second-story window and onto the porch covering, I really did feel like a rebellious teenager. It only took me about half a decade to finally get a taste of it, but I was euphoric. I hoped she meant what she said about distracting Mom while I ran off with Saint, but I didn't waste any time sticking around to find out. Crawling to the lip of the roof, I saw Saint against the side of the house, his head snapping up and eyes widening when I swung my legs over the edge.

"Jules?" he hissed, quickly placing himself under me and motioning for me to jump.

When I slid off, I had to suppress a giggle as I fell into his arms. This was it—we were running away. Holy shit I was fleeing with my *boyfriend.* My heart pattered as the word echoed in my skull. I kept my arms wrapped around his neck, even as he set me down.

"The *roof?* Really?"

I finally pulled away, grabbing his hand. "It was Aunt Syd's idea. She found out about the plan, but I had some real-talk with her and now she's our distraction, so we need to go. *Now.*"

Thankfully, he didn't argue or ask any further details as we bolted for the sidewalk and hurried down the street. As long as we got as far away from the house as possible, we could figure out where we were, decide our next move to lure Dad over to Mom, and then call him to make him deal with this problem instead of hunting down Severin. Let's be real, he'd have plenty of time to deal with Severin later. And Severin wasn't the one who bit me, so hopefully he'd have his priorities in check here.

When we made it to one of the crosswalk lights, I slowed, feeling super winded and thankful for a brief pause. Saint, however, had other ideas. He took the lead, dragging me for another two blocks before I wheezed that I needed a break.

One of my hands went straight to my knee as I doubled over while the other remained firmly grasped in Saint's, like I'd vanish if he let go.

"Oh... my God..." I huffed and puffed, imagining how less hellish this would be if I went to the gym like all of these vampires around me, who clearly didn't need it because of their immortal physique and ungodly strength. At this point, I think they just want to show off. "I think... we need to make a turn... and keep walking until we figure out where we're at." I sucked down a deep breath, pushing myself upright again.

"You're sure?"

I almost wheezed with how easily he could ask that. My mind briefly drifted to the idea that perhaps Mom was onto something with the whole vampire deal, but then I quickly shoved that idea aside. How the hell did I go from vampire hunter wannabe to casually thinking about the perks of playing for the other team? Holy shit, my brain was scrambled.

Still panting, I nodded.

Saint checked over his shoulder as he pulled me around the corner, the two of us passing down a narrow, one-way street with cars lining each sidewalk. My breathing almost returned to normal by the time we were crossing another intersection to zig-zag diagonally away from the residential area and into the edge of downtown.

The good news: I was able to recognize some of the street signs and buildings. The bad news: we were *really* far from where I'd last tracked Dad.

I pulled my phone out, tapped his name in my recent contacts list, and pressed the glass to my ear. My pulse pounded against the receiver, and Saint glanced behind us as the first ring softly buzzed from the speaker.

Come on, Dad.

Second ring.

Pick up for your son, and ignore your hate boner for his boyfriend's ex.

The call cut.

I bit my tongue, holding back a million curses as I tried again. *Ring. Ring. Click.* "You selfish bastard," I muttered, cramming my phone back into my pocket as my tone turned high-pitched and mocking. "*No, Jules, I don't want you to hunt vampires. I want you to be normal, unlike me and my stupid deci-sions that got rid of your mom and turned her into a crazy vampire that wants to teach you witchcraft.* What the fuck kind of logic is that?"

When I turned to Saint for a laugh or possible answer, he let go of my hand and put his arm around me, briskly guiding me to his other side to sandwich me between him and the brick buildings. He took my other hand and picked up the pace, nearly sending me tripping on a crack in the concrete.

"Um, Saint?"

His reply was barely above a whisper. "We're being followed."

Every hair stood on end. Iris or Zane had caught up to us. Well, if Mom hadn't planned on killing Saint before, she was definitely going to now. I squeezed his hand so tight with sheer panic that I was glad he was a vampire who didn't seem to be bothered in the slightest by it. Of course, once I thought about him doing the same thing back to me, I quickly relaxed my grip. "Do you have any idea which one of them found us so quickly?"

"Huh?"

"Iris or Zane?" I said, trying to clarify my panicked question. "Which one saw us sneak out? Do you know?"

He hesitated and shook his head. "It's not a vampire."

I'm sorry, what? "Not a vampire? So, it's just a *person?* Wait—a vampire hunter?"

His nose scrunched up. "It smells terrible—trust me, it's *not* human."

I sniffed, coughing when I inhaled a bit too much street pollution. But I didn't manage to catch anything out of the ordinary—just the usual car exhaust with the occasional mix of light sewage or gasoline. "What does it smell like?" I swiped at my nose. "I don't smell it."

"Like body odor?"

"You *just* said it wasn't human, but you're going to tell me it smells like B.O.?"

He grimaced. "Maybe more like a gym?"

"Are you *sure* it's not Zane following us?"

Saint snapped his fingers, his eyes lighting up. "Wet dog. *That's* what it is."

That was the instant I could practically smell it—not because I was actually able to, but because I *had* smelled that horrid scent before. It was that pungent mix that had hit me when I'd been collecting phones for Dad.

"Oh, *fuck*. Do you know what a werewolf smells like?"

The alarm that took over Saint's features told me that was a huge *no*.

"Okay," I squeaked, recalling Adonis's tracked signal prowling around the map. The exact map I needed right now to solve a bunch of my problems. "How are we going to lose a werewolf without alerting the cops and causing a supernatural mess? We need to get back to your place and locate Dad because he's not picking up."

"Well," Saint said, avoiding eye contact by glancing down a side street, "I don't exactly know where we are."

My hand went to my head, hopefully slapping some sense into me for a change. I'm so stupid. I don't know why I expected him to know where we were at when he'd probably stuck to anything within a fifteen-minute walk of *The Crown Café*. Severin kept him on such a tight leash that he'd hadn't had the years of experience wandering around town like me, let alone dealing with werewolves either. And while Saint probably *could* beat the hell out of Adonis, I was really fucking worried that I might be wrong about that.

"Um... shit," I hissed, pulling out my phone again. I'd be lying if I said I wasn't really starting to panic, especially with how many tries it took me to unlock the thing with my sweaty hands. Tapping on Dad's name one more time, I prayed he'd pick up so I didn't have to come up with some improvised plan.

All at once, Saint's grasp on my hand tightened, we lurched to a stop, and the phone fell from my ear to the concrete as a figure darted through the parked cars between us and the other side of the street. Dread pulsed through veins as I froze, unable to make myself decide my next move.

"*Jules.*" Adonis threw his arms out at his side, a grin plastered on his face that could've matched Zane's if it didn't border on malicious. "Who's your friend? Boyfriend? New partner in crime?"

My brain was too busy screaming for me to hurry and grab the damn phone until Saint started to pull me behind him. What the hell was I doing? I needed to snap out of it and demand we make a run for it, but I also wasn't all that confident we—okay, mainly *I*—could outrun a werewolf.

"Can I help you?" Saint asked, the words so cold and sharp that I was reminded that he could absolutely bite back.

Adonis's eyes darkened, aside from a thin sheen of gold that made my arms break out in goosebumps. That manic smile remained as he stalked forward. "It's you, isn't it?"

Saint's head tilted, making me conjure up his most baffled expression. "What?"

Without another word, Adonis peeled back a panel of his jacket, showing off his stake and breaking just about every rule of engagement Dad had hammered into his crew when it came to confronting suspected vampires in public.

Honestly, my best guess for why he'd toss guidelines out the window was that he didn't give a shit anymore. He was ruthlessly tracking down prey, and I was unfortunately what he was hunting. That, and he likely believed that all our other housemates would gladly overlook a werewolf among them as a creature historically at odds with the undead. Or maybe that getting rid of a familiar that he believed was a spy would get him head-pats like a good boy. Either way, Adonis clearly had a one-track mind when it came to anything related to vampires, which meant there was no changing it with any sort of logical argument about—I don't know—telling him that he'd get punished for crying vampire in the middle of the street like an idiot or *killing his boss's son.*

"Don't act stupid, Dracula lite," Adonis spat. "You lured this twink out to be your familiar and help your good pal Severin. How easy was it to snag Mason's gay-ass son to rub it in his face and have him spill his guts about the whole operation? Did you enjoy seeing our place get ransacked while you sucked him like a juice box?"

My face felt *scalding.* I couldn't tell if it was from the way Adonis delivered all those lines with as much disdain as I imagined my dad having or if it was because I was getting really pissed that he'd painted that narrative so easily. I must've taken Saint by surprise with how quickly I moved to his side again, jabbing a finger at Adonis. "Fuck *you,* man. You have no fucking idea what I've done for all of you—"

"No, I think I do, daddy's boy." He ripped out his stake, spinning it around like a toy. "I'm sure you've really enjoyed throwing us all under the bus because Mason didn't give you everything you wanted, so you had to go find a vampire to validate your feel—" Adonis flinched and ducked with a wince.

Like a complete idiot, I stood there, completely immobile, watching him cover one ear as his stake-wielding hand shifted from skin to fur with wickedly sharp claws and back again. Saint let go of me and scooped the phone off the sidewalk. Honestly, thank God. Someone fucking had to, and I was too enraptured by Adonis's freakish glitching that I was far too slow to even consider that this was the lead up to him going into full werewolf mode.

When Saint grabbed my hand again and spun me around to run in the opposite direction, the two of us stopped short. At the entry to the skinniest alley with the chain link gate propped open, a figure was furiously motioning for us to hurry the fuck up, their eyes wide and blond hair disheveled, half-dripping from their hair clip.

Charlie didn't shout or draw attention to themself to try to light a fire under me because something else was in their mouth that I first assumed was a vape. I didn't get a chance to object and point Saint in another direction *away* from the potential danger because he dragged me toward them the second Adonis emitted a low, bone-chilling growl.

The gate clanged behind us. Saint pulled me along the wall, my jacket catching on the bricks. My heart worked faster as I glanced at Charlie, who kept close to my heels, though they were keeping an eye on the mouth of the alley. That's when I noticed the vape pen had a keyring on it. Well, that, and there wasn't any fog puffing out their lips because they still hadn't stopped to remove it.

It took me another second before it dawned on me: it was a fucking dog whistle.

No way they'd just *dog whistled* Adonis—

They finally popped it out of their mouth. "Take a right," they ordered.

Oh, hell no—That would take us closer to Mom and company. We needed to either keep going straight or make a left to juke Adonis. This screamed *trap* from a million miles away, especially since Charlie could very well be working for Severin.

I gritted my teeth, tugging on Saint's hand. He slowed, toning down his strength and speed enough for me to shove past a couple of garbage cans and dart left when I saw a six-foot wood fence blocking the intersection dead ahead.

"*Jules!*" Charlie shouted.

"What are you doing?" Saint whispered, barely audible above my pounding pulse and winded breathing.

"Trap," I gasped, throwing myself onto the next street and turning to sprint down the stretch of sidewalk with reckless abandon. If there was at least one thing I could try to do, it was attempt to keep Saint as far away from Severin as possible.

The sound of Charlie's heavy footfalls running after us made me push past the pain in my legs. A new spike of adrenaline gave me that much-needed boost that Saint easily kept stride with. I mentally mapped out where I'd seen Dad's little GPS dot last time and decided that was my best bet on getting out of this mess now if we couldn't get back to Saint's apartment without reigning hell down on us.

"God damnit, Jules! You're going the wrong way!"

Good. That meant we were getting further from Severin. Everything was going according to the new plan.

Until Adonis reappeared, glowing eyes and all, from the mouth of another alley to try to cut us off. I could only assume he'd followed down the one Charlie led us into and probably fucking launched himself over that fence with whatever werewolf powers he had to catch up so quickly.

My legs buckled as I came to a halt, Saint quickly becoming the only thing to keep me upright as he swapped from holding my hand to grabbing my upper arm. The flicker of headlights from the street gave me a second to think of how the hell I was going to manage this before the beams washed over me and my werewolf obstacle in a sharp turn toward the alley.

Adonis went flying between the buildings as the bumper of the car collided with his legs, his howl echoing as his body rolled along the pavement. Lux laid on her horn, her blue eyes lit with fury as she stuck her head out of the rolled-down window, completely unbothered by the fact that she was turning her ride into Adonis's new arch nemesis. "Get the fuck in the car, Jules!"

My jaw dropped.

It was probably a good thing that my mouth was already hanging open because Saint's next words were: "Get in."

"What the fuck do you mean—"

He lunged forward, grabbed Lux through the window as the door locks clicked, ripped open the door, and pulled her out of the car. I scrambled in a rush toward the other side of the vehicle as Charlie skidded to a stop behind me.

"Wait!"

Too late. I was already in the crystal-mobile, fumbling

with the seatbelt to the tune of Lux's outraged screams as she peeled herself off of the sidewalk. Saint threw the car into reverse, rolling us onto the street as the headlights passed over Adonis stumbling to his feet. Because of course this guy could shake off being ran over by a witch.

With the league of disgruntled hunters in the rearview mirror, I smacked the radio dial to shut off the K-pop tickling the speakers. "That was really fucking badass of you."

Saint chortled and wrestled my phone from his jacket pocket, the car swerving a bit as he held it out to me. I quickly took it and cringed at the scraped screen protector. I guess that was better than the screen, but holy hell I'd been playing with fire without realizing it. My sole lifeline to Dad could've been destroyed in an instant.

"You're going to have to navigate me," Saint said quietly, flipping on his blinker to avoid idling for too long at the red light ahead.

I swallowed. "Do we want to risk going back to your place with *three* vampire hunters chasing us? Two of them being supernatural creatures and the other being a huge question mark of possible allegiance to your ex?"

He stiffened. "Is that why you were running from h—"

"*Them*. Charlie. Yes." I sighed, sinking into the seat. "They might be working for Severin. That's why I didn't follow their instructions."

"All right... That's not great news."

"Nope." I pulled up the map app on my phone and zoomed out, re-imagining that series of lines and angles around the bar Dad had been camping out at earlier. The odds of him being there were slim, but it would at least be *something*. With enough pinch-zooming, I found that weird triangle slice and selected it as our destination.

I also made a note of the ATM icon a block down once I caught a glimpse of the little clock in the upper right corner of the screen. "It's already three. Fuck." I guess time flies when you're being kidnapped. "Keep going straight for a bit. We're going to make a left in a few blocks."

Saint's head bobbed. "I would suggest hunkering down in a parking garage when day hits, but I feel like that's a terrible idea if any of them come looking for the car."

"I'm thinking if we don't find Dad at the bar, we find a motel to crash in for a bit. Let's avoid dragging hunters near your place, and Mom will struggle to find me if she heads back to the the hunter house to try to find us."

"Sounds like a plan."

19 IN HIDING

We parked the car in an alley nearby, where I prayed it wouldn't get found or towed. As much as I wanted Saint to stay with it for multiple reasons—like avoiding facing my dad or keeping the car running for a quick getaway—I was honestly glad he insisted on coming with me. I really didn't want to do this alone, even if the odds were slim he'd still be chilling in this bar.

Saint took my hand again as we started down the alley, so I held onto it for as long as I could before we turned the corner. I wish I wasn't such a coward, but I wrestled it away the second the door came into view. If Dad miraculously was in here, I didn't want to watch his head implode at the sight of me canoodling with my boyfriend along with everything else going on. I grabbed the handle and the latch caught. The dim lights inside indicated what I'd feared: it was closed for the night.

"Well, he's not here. No one is." My hand dropped to my side as I took a step back.

Saint rocked back on his heels, glancing up and down the street. "Maybe try calling him again?"

"Yeah..." I pulled out my phone. "Let's head back to the car."

Saint led the way, and I jogged to tuck my hand into his again. I don't care if it's sappy, I was holding onto him for dear life as I pressed the receiver to my ear and hoped Dad would answer. Three rings in, the call cut, and I sighed. I was getting pretty fucking sick of being hung-up on when I had nothing but new information tucked into my distress signals.

My mood immediately soured as I crammed the device back into my pocket. Saint's face fell. "Nothing?"

"Fucking nothing."

He popped the door open for me, and my heart melted. I love how I'd been brainwashed into believing vampires were all inherently evil and this one was acting like true a gentleman. It left a bitter taste in my mouth as I climbed in. "Thanks, Saint."

He gently pushed the door shut and rounded the vehicle to drop into the driver's seat while I scrolled through motel after motel until I settled on the cheapest one nearby.

"There's an ATM around the corner." I said. "It's probably best to pay in cash and have a bit on hand until we sort this out."

Saint threw the car into drive and rolled us out of the alley as I tapped on my selection in the map app. I know hauling around a chunk of cash was basically begging me to get robbed on top of the rest of the shit I was dealing with. However, since we were entering the part of town that Dad deemed 'enemy territory', I didn't plan on casually handing over a card with my name printed on it to *anyone* on the off-chance they somehow made the connection between Dad and I. Even with dawn crawling closer, there could absolutely be a vampire or a familiar manning the desk of a shitty motel at this hour that might sound the alarm for Severin.

I quickly hopped out when the car shifted into park along the curb, the blue glow of the ATM beckoning me to quickly withdraw my emergency funds. I punched every one of those worn metal buttons on the sides of the screen. A shady five-hundred dollars later, I climbed back into the vehicle.

"Right at the light." I pointed ahead. Every subsequent direction eventually led us to a flickering neon sign posted above the double-door entrance.

Saint pulled into the small parking lot out front. The car's headlights shone against the chipped paint slathered onto the brick façade until the car shuddered when he pulled out the key and flipped off the beams

I sucked in a sharp breath as I jabbed the release on my seatbelt. "Maybe you should stay here," I said quickly, feeling guilty with the frown he shot me. "Because of the car. Someone should stay with it since it's out in the open."

Saint hesitated, but his shoulders fell. "Okay. I'll keep an eye out. Just... be quick, all right?"

I gave a little salute and scrambled out onto the pavement. So, Saint watching the car was half of my reasoning. The other half was that if, in fact, the front desk was manned by one of Severin's goons, I figured it was very likely they'd recognize Saint.

The door chimed as I jogged in and shuffled my shoes against the entryway's mat. When the clerk looked up from her phone, I gave what I hoped was a pleasant smile, but my reflection in the mirror along the wall looked pained.

I cleared my throat as I stepped up to the counter. "Do you have a room for today and into tomorrow? Two nights?" I pleaded that there was one available, really not wanting to risk driving Lux's car around any more tonight and possibly being spotted if it could be avoided. Plus there was the whole thing with the sun coming up that made us a bit pressed for time.

The woman pushed up her glasses and turned to the computer. "We should have one. Just for one guest?"

"Um." I held up two fingers, my face heating as I realized I was about to spend a whole day in a motel room with Saint. Just us and a bed after a reunion. No big deal. "Two, actually. They're in the car out front."

Good job, Jules. For once, I'd nailed that tonight. I didn't spill any identifying information, imply that I was meeting a hooker, or set myself up for possible disapproving looks for saying I was going to be chilling with my boyfriend.

The woman typed in a few things. "Looks like we have a few rooms available. Any preference on amenities?"

"Preferably something cheap? We're just passing through."

She nodded, hand falling to her mouse and clicked on something listed. "Eighty, plus tax—"

I pulled out a few bills and placed them on the counter, her brow arching in response. All right, I guess I wasn't getting out of making her think I was getting a room with a prostitute, especially with my next line: "Put it under the name James Smith, please."

"That'll be an extra fifty to hold onto for incidentals."

Well, fuck. I pulled out another bill and added it to the stack.

The clerk sighed, grabbed the cash, and rang it up. I drummed my fingers against the granite as she sorted through the change. When she handed over the small envelope with the keycards, along with instructions of where to park, and recited the checkout time I'd have to come reclaim my deposit, I thanked her and ducked out of the lobby. The chime followed me as I hurried back to the car.

"Are we good?" Saint asked as I pulled my door shut.

"Yep. The parking garage is behind the building, so we need to circle the block." I pointed to the roof of the car and twirled my finger. As the car backed up, I flipped open the keycard envelope and read off the numbers scrawled inside.

Room 452.

The sound of the blinker pulled my head up just in time to catch us turn into the garage. As much as I wanted him to park it next to the elevator, Saint found a far corner and slid Lux's vehicle between two other cars: one white and one silver. Easy to miss at first glance. We climbed out and trekked across the lot to the steel doors, where I pressed the button about ten times. It finally opened, taking us to the fourth floor, where it dumped us next to a walkway leading to the rows of doors and winding metal railings.

In the outdoor lights posted outside the elongated balcony, I couldn't help but notice just how pale Saint looked. Had his complexion always been that white? Was that rude to ask? Maybe it was just the shitty bulbs playing tricks on me.

I stopped us in front our room and passed Saint one of the keycards before popping the door open. Flipping on the light, I took in a single king bed, the foot of it jutting into the walkway between us and the vanity outside the bathroom. A thin beige blanket covered the mattress with two limp-looking pillows barely propped up against the headboard, all of it sitting opposite a thicker-bodied flat screen TV. My heartbeat quickened as Saint stepped inside behind me and the two of us wandered into our temporary living quarters.

He immediately moved to the window, pulling the thicker, light-blocking curtains over the wispy ones. The backs of his knees hit the bed and he dropped onto the worn duvet, where he immediately hunched over and scrubbed at his face.

"Um, are you okay?" I started toward him, my hand grazing the scratchy, yellowish blanket as I took a seat next to him. So maybe the paleness was unusual if he was acting exhausted.

He shook his head, and I felt a jolt of panic. "It's okay. I'll survive."

"Are you sure? Saint, I didn't want to bring it up earlier, but you're looking a bit like a ghost."

He grimaced, shielding his eyes from me. "I... think I'm in need of blood."

I froze, suddenly realizing that I hadn't seen him drink blood over the past couple of days because he *hadn't*. My hand went to my neck. What the fuck was I supposed to do here? Let him take a bite? I felt my neck disappear as my head lowered toward my chest. I'm sure some people had a bite-kink, but the idea felt super weird to me, especially since my *mom* had been the last person to bite me. Having Saint bite me after that made me gag a little.

He glanced over, his eyes widening when they landed on

my hand. "Jules, I'm not going to bite you. Trust me, that's the very *last* resort here."

"Okay, but if you *need* it—"

He shook his head. "I won't. That's a line I refuse to cross unless I'm on death's door. I swore off drinking from people unless there are no other options."

I pinned my hands between my knees and chewed on my lip. "But you need blood..." The soft glow of sunlight began to border the curtains. "You have some at your apartment, right?" The laptop was also at the apartment. Plus, if it was hitting daytime, I'd only have to deal with my housemates possibly seeing me. And if I took the car, I could be quick. Just zip back and forth in no time at all, rather than lugging around a laptop and blood juice boxes in the scariest walk of a lifetime. I stood up. "I can go get some and bring it back."

"I don't want to inconvenience you—"

I shook my head. "If Dad keeps refusing to pick up, I'm going to need to track him anyway. This is a win-win, aside from risking being seen with the car, right?"

Saint stiffened. "What if someone *does* see you and follows you? I won't be able to help."

"I got this. Trust me." I held out my hand for the keys, and Saint stared down at it. He chewed on his lip for a moment before his shoulders fell and two sets of keys appeared, falling into my palm. I'd just become a blood delivery driver. Well, that was a thing I'd never thought I'd end up willingly doing.

My heart fluttered as I did something new I'd always wanted to do: I leaned forward and kissed Saint—a brief action that made my head spin with the idea that this could become the norm. Like a quick kiss before work. A quick kiss before bed. A quick kiss before an 'I love you'.

Saint grabbed my arm. His eyes locked with mine, boring into my soul with that pleading gleam. "*Please* be careful, Jules."

"I will. It's daylight, right? I can manage it."

Doubt crept into his features, but his grip loosened, letting me slip away to venture out into the bright light of day. I glanced back, watching him get up and rub his arms as he moved to another, darker part of the room to avoid the sun when I stepped out. With a nod, I pulled the door open and shimmied through to the balcony walkway, like I was hiding something extremely illegal in my motel room that I didn't want anyone to see.

I headed back to the elevator, mashed the button several more times, and sped-walked across the garage to the shady far corner to liberate the car for my mission. My hand shook as I turned the key in the ignition. I slowly rolled out onto the street and tensed when other cars and people came into view. I just needed none of them to be Adonis, Lux, Charlie, or Rory. Just four out of hundreds of people I'd pass. Oh, and no cops. Because that would be a nightmare to get caught with blood in a stolen vehicle.

I started down the street and navigated every light until I conjured up the best way to conceal the car while I ducked inside Saint's apartment. There was a small parking lot off the alley of *The Crown Café* I prayed would have free space. I slow-rolled down the alley and whipped the car into the first spot I saw. Perfect. All according to plan. I hopped out of the car and kept my head down as I fumbled with Saint's keys to find the one for his apartment on my way inside.

Wincing, I hurried up the stairs and slotted the key into the lock. It was fucking weird to walk into his place by myself. This was basically a free opportunity to snoop, but as much as I itched to, I decided it was in my best interest not to waste any time. I kicked the door shut and bolted for the fridge, popping it open to find a pitcher of filtered water, a half-dozen eggs, oat milk, and some other food staples that seemed rather surprising.

I guess vampires still indulged in human food, even though they relied on blood? Either that or Saint had left a bunch of empty containers in there to make it look normal just in case the landlord stopped by. But, I mean, Saint had tried food when we went out. Sure, that might've been for show, but I liked to at least imagine he enjoyed it. I nudged the egg carton, and my lips pressed into a thin line. Yep. Empty. This might as well be a showroom refrigerator.

The one thing out of place was the cardboard casing with soda cans sitting at the bottom, so I pulled one out. My fingers squished against a bag, and I shivered. Found it. I set the can to the side and spun around the kitchen, looking for a container to put it in. All the cabinets I opened were empty or held a single pot and pan until I reached one at the far end. Saint owned an insulated lunch tote. Thinking back on it now, it was probably to smuggle the blood in to begin with, so it made sense it was there.

I unzipped it and tossed one of the baggies in, my whole body rippling with a discomforting chill. I sealed it and hung the strap off my shoulder as I replaced the soda can and closed up the fridge. After I scooped up the laptop and yoinked the drive from under the couch, I quickly detoured into Saint's room for his laptop case. My tunnel vision kicked in to avoid any distractions as I tossed the devices into the bag and hurried out of the apartment.

Now I just had to make it back without incident. I heaved out an exhale once I locked up and started downstairs. When I pushed the door open, the light of day searing into my vision, I winced and covered my eyes.

"Jules?"

I jumped, my head whipping toward the source of my name.

Allie waved, walking toward me with a toothy smile. "I didn't expect to see you over here at this time of day. What brings you out?" She glanced at my bags.

"Uh—um." I forced out a nervous laugh. Holy shit, Jules, think of *something*. Literally anything. "Saint is—uh—taking some classes and he forgot some things. He asked me to come pick them up."

"Oh. I didn't know he was enrolled in some courses." Allie grabbed the strap of her purse. "Did you two hit it off with your coffee order? The poor guy seemed a bit solemn until a few days ago, so maybe I have you to thank for giving him a bit of friendship." She beamed.

"Y-yeah," I said, rubbing the back of my neck.

"Well, I was just heading out. My shift ran a bit over with all the building water nonsense I've been helping the owner deal with. Tell Saint I said hi, would you?"

"S-sure." I don't know what came over me, but when she turned and held up her hand to say goodbye, my mouth opened. "Wait—"

She stopped, her head cocking to the side.

"Um, you, uh—you wouldn't happen to have any openings for the night shift right now, would you?"

Allie blinked in surprise. "Are you asking for a friend?"

I swallowed and tugged on one of the nylon straps hanging off of my shoulder. "No, actually. I'm... sort of looking for a change of pace."

The way her eyes lit up gave me hope. "Really? Look, Jules, it probably isn't going to pay you as much as you get doing security—"

"No, I know. But I think I'd like it, and I would rather do a job I enjoy instead of a job I'm paid well-ish for." And could hang out with my boyfriend, who seemed like the only person in my life that wasn't actively trying to ruin it—aside from Aunt Syd, but she'd eventually have to leave for Canada.

She practically *bounced* with giddiness. "Okay, well, I'll talk to my boss and put in a good word for you. I can't exactly make any promises, but if you toss in an application, I'll make sure it's seen."

My lips curled into a smile, unable to hold back my excitement. "Thank you, Allie."

20 RED-HANDED

I sank into the driver's seat with relief once I was finally alone in the car, carrying a laptop bag and a cooler of blood. Now I just had to do the easy part: make it back to the motel without getting tailed. I plugged in a slightly different route from the one I took to get to the café and made the trip back with the radio off and my pulse pounding in my ears. Some cars had vanished from the previously-taken parking spots in the garage when I rolled inside, but at least one of the two white-silver car camouflage duo was in the far corner.

So I parked, got out, and tossed both bag straps over my shoulder on the way to the elevator. I had to shield my eyes from the sun as I tapped the button and yawned. My heart fluttered at the brief recollection that there was only one bed in the room, making me think I might be able to at least cuddle with Saint as I got some shut-eye. Well, until I got the image stuck in my head of him enjoying his blood bag like a kid with a juice pouch. I cringed, a chill working through me that I quickly shook out.

The elevator chimed, I stepped inside, and the sudden pounding of shoes on cement made me whip around just in time for someone to grab fistful of my shirt collar. Everything after that was a blur as my back hit the side of the elevator car to the sound of panting and the manic pressing of buttons.

"What the *fuck*," Charlie said between heaved breaths, "do you think you're doing?"

Oh, *shit.* What was Charlie doing here? They didn't follow me back, did they?

I tried to jerk to the side to rip free, but they pinned me with an arm. "Oh, no you don't. You have a *lot* of explaining to do."

"*Me?*" I spat, trying to fight off the urge to vomit with how quickly my adrenaline had kicked back in. "What about *you?*" I jabbed a finger against their shoulder while I tried to wiggle my other arm between us to pry myself free. "How long were you following us?"

The elevator dinged again. They grabbed my arm and hauled me out, dragging me across the walkway to the stairs. It clicked then, much later than I hoped. When I'd searched for Dad's location and checked to see who was on the move, I'd completely forgotten that I'd found Charlie's little dot posted up in a motel. I didn't realize it was *this* motel.

"*I* was doing Mason a favor by making sure Adonis didn't kill you," they ground out, taking me down the steps and pressing a keycard to the first door on the right.

A strong lie to start on. Honestly, it was kind of weird for them to try to lure me into a false sense of security before

Severin would likely jump out from behind the shower curtain and eat my face, but it was certainly a move.

They shoved me inside, the light flicking on before the door slammed shut. When Charlie flipped the deadbolt and put the chain on, I knew I was fucked unless I managed to knock them out. But then their face fell, all frustration and anger dissolving into what I could easily have mistaken for concern. "A *vampire*, Jules? Really?"

I sputtered. "What do you mean? *You're* the one hanging around a vampire." Deflecting all the way, baby.

They're brows knit together. "Excuse me? Lux said—"

"Oh, don't act surprised when you're the mole."

They hesitated, and I could already feel my suspicion coming back to bite me with those words. "What? I'm not. But I was starting to believe that *you* were after Adonis's crazy ramblings and then tonight's incident of Lux screaming about a vampire ripping her out of her car right in front of me."

Oh.

Wait. That could still be a lie, Jules. Don't be a dumbass. I shook my head. "Then where were you trying to lead me when we were running from Adonis? You can't tell me that *wasn't* toward Sever—"

"*Severin?* You think that *I* would work for Severin?" They jabbed their thumb against their chest. "Believe it or not, I was trying to get you—and I guess your damn vampire—to a twenty-four-seven diner that might've either been able to mask our scents or let us at least use it as a public shield for a bit. So if *anyone* is going to be interrogated here, it's *you* for betraying Mason like this."

Okay—they had to be telling the truth, right? There's no way they'd guilt-trip me like this if they were just going to kill me to send Dad a message. "W-wait—" I held up my hands. "Look, I'm not the mole either."

"Then why were you—"

"I've been running around with a vampire because I got bit the night you found me on the porch!" It all came out in a rush, like I'd opened the floodgates to release all of the slow-building pressure with all the secrecy and stress. "I got drunk, got bit, couldn't remember anything, and I thought if I could figure out who my vampire was and kill them, then Dad might actually let me join the hunt and treat me with some respect." I felt my chest rise and fall as the bags slipped down my shoulder and grazed the bed. "Like how he treats *you*."

Charlie's frustration faded with the downward curve of their lips. "Jules..."

Well. I'd finally done it. I'd let my jealousy show. My arms dropped to my sides with a sigh and I turned my head, unable to look them in the eye. "And the cute guy I started seeing turned out to be a vampire, who I told to leave me alone, and then he *didn't*."

That beat of pity dissipated, their eyes hardening from my light mention of Saint.

"But he saved me from Lux, who wanted to make me a coven witch, who saved me from Adonis, the scary buff were-wolf—ugh—" I put my head in my hands for a brief moment in an effort to compose myself. "Look, it's all really compli-cated, and I can't go into all the details because I need to talk to Dad about it. Just... trust me when I say I've got so many other problems that I wouldn't have even found the time to play spy for some shitbag vampire, okay?"

Their mouth pressed into a thin line, but I could see them softening at the edges with doubt. "And what's in the bags?"

I glanced down. "Laptop with the backup tracker to find Dad because he fucking sucks and won't pick up my calls to explain that Severin *didn't* bite me like I originally thought."

They waited as I fidgeted with the other strap.

I cleared my throat. "And some blood for my vampire boyfriend because he's been self-conscious about drinking in front of me and refuses to bite me. I think that's the least I can do when he's continued to save my ass multiple times because he actually cares about my well-being and doesn't hang up on me repeatedly."

They paused. "So he doesn't feed on people directly?"

I shook my head.

"Did *he* bite you?"

"Charlie, do you really think he'd bite me and then tell me he refuses to bite me?"

"Fine, okay." They held up their hands in surrender. "So, then that means mole has to be Rory..."

I snapped to attention. "We have to let Dad know it's him, and I *really* need to talk to him—preferably in person."

"I actually just got off the phone with him. We're meeting in about an hour."

A twinge of hurt rippled through me again. I know it's because he was trying to get Charlie to try to take him back to Severin's new hideout, but it still stung that he didn't even bother calling me back yet. "Great." I couldn't keep the bitterness out of my voice.

They started toward me, dropping onto the edge of the bed and patting the spot next to them. "Do you feel like Mason is replacing you with me?"

I continued to stand, awkwardly rubbing my arms because I knew I probably sounded like an idiot to them for implying it.

"It's okay if you do," they said quietly—that familiar, chill, collected Charlie returning to replace the one that'd cornered me in the elevator. "But you should know that, even if you haven't really noticed it, Mason holds us to different standards. Sure, he might be proud of me in some ways, but it's more like an apprenticeship sort of pride instead of the pride that comes with raising a kid."

I scoffed, shaking my head. "I think he'd trade us in a heartbeat if he could. You're some stoic, strong, level-headed person that meets all of his expectations—"

"For a *job*, Jules."

"And he respects your identity, which is more than I can say for how he's behaved with me."

"I honestly think it's easier for certain individuals to tolerate or accept others when it doesn't feel like a reflection of themselves. Some parents struggle to separate their identity from that of their children, so I think if our positions were swapped, he would still behave the same toward a co-worker and his kid." They moved their hands to their knees and stared down at the bulky heat-and-AC unit under the window. "I kind of hoped that when I left you two to talk the other night that he'd give you a chance. I actually talked to him a bit afterward about having you shadow me because I didn't think it was fair to treat you any differently when you've been trying to prove you can handle it."

I laughed. Charlie jolted in surprise as I grabbed a chunk of my hair. "It turns out that I *can't*, so that doesn't fucking matter anymore."

"Getting bit doesn't mean—"

"I'm not talking about feeling like I can't do it because I got bit. I'm talking about how my dad taught me vampires equal evil, and it turns out not all of them are." I let go of my hair to jiggle the soft cooler. "*Some* of them were turned against their will and abused for years or some of them had to choose between death and undeath. None of it's black and white, despite Dad brainwashing me into thinking there was only one way to handle it all." I rocked against the wall, wincing as my back hit that corner framing the window.

Charlie chewed on their lip. "You're sure that this vampire isn't just trying to win you over to hurt you later?"

With everything that had already happened and knowing him as a person, I could say the next part with more confidence than I had in my own housemates after the last few days: "If he was going to, I'm pretty sure he's had plenty of opportunities by now."

Plus, Saint had been held prisoner in a vacation rental basement by my mom, which was a stellar introduction to my family that somehow didn't send him running. No one in their right mind who wanted to do me harm would decide the risk was worth the reward at this point.

They scrubbed the side of their face. "I... just don't want to see you get hurt."

"Why? Because I'm Mason's kid?"

"Because I've always sort of thought of you like the little brother I never had."

Holy shit the emotional damage I received the second they threw that card down. It was like being slapped through every instance where they'd been subtly nice to me. *Subtly* because that was their way of doing things and I was a dumbass who hadn't noticed until now.

Charlie could've just dumped me in the living room after I'd chugged that pink moscato in the graveyard, but they'd hauled me down to the basement so Dad and everyone else wouldn't have witnessed that low point. They didn't *have* to offer to let me shadow them either, but they'd done it anyway, even if Dad likely shut that shit down before everything had blown up with the mole. And here I'd been painting them as a rival or nemesis.

"Dad contacted you to try to see if he could send you out and follow you to track down Severin." I tugged on my hoodie sleeves to cover my hands. "So I should probably go with you to help prove you're not the mole and Rory is."

"Ah." They clicked their tongue. "It makes sense why he sounded tired and a bit disappointed now." They pushed themself up. "Where is he?"

Huh? "Dad?"

"No, your vampire. Which room did you stash him in? I'm not letting you leave unless we go together, and I get to make sure he's not going to rip anyone's throat out."

My grip tightened on the bag straps, every part of me revolting against the idea of bringing a hunter straight to Saint when he was probably at his weakest. "You have to promise not to hurt him."

"As long as he doesn't pose a threat to *you*, specifically while we're in the same space, I won't hurt him. If I see signs of manipulation, I'm going to call it out and act accordingly."

I hesitated. Well, I guess this was the best I was probably going to get, and Saint was probably getting a bit worried about where I was by now. "Fine. Just—just please give him a chance."

Charlie started for the door and flipped the deadbolt. I supposed that was the only answer I'd get. After they pulled the chain away and swung the door open, I led the way up a set of stairs and back to the room. I unlocked it and shimmied inside, Charlie thankfully following suit.

Saint's head popped up from where he was sitting on the floor at the end of the bed, and he began to push himself to his feet as I hurried over. I swung the soft cooler around my body just as Saint did the same to me, the room spinning with the motion.

"*Leave*," Saint commanded once I realized he'd put himself between me and Charlie.

"Saint, wait," I grabbed his arm, half using it to quickly stand at his side. "They're not with Severin. We talked. It's okay."

His eyes nervously flicked between us as Charlie waited at the door, seeming to observe how I was going to handle a vampire before deciding whether or not to intervene. I unzipped the cooler and handed it to him, hating how his hands trembled, almost like someone with low blood sugar— though I guess it was low *blood* in his case. He watched Charlie as he gripped it, clearly feeling uncomfortable about drinking in front of someone he didn't know or trust. Considering he hadn't even done it in front of me, I probably should have anticipated something like that happening.

I dumped the laptop bag on the bed and grabbed the chair in the corner, dragging it over to the nook where the closet and sink sat outside the toilet and shower room. Fortunately, there was a curtain, so I jogged back, turned Saint toward the vanity—his anxious reflection in the mirror making my stomach knot—and guided him to sit in the chair.

"I'll be on the other side of the curtain. Drink, and I'll deal with them." I didn't give him a chance to argue before pulling it and spinning around to face Charlie. "Happy? Can he drink in peace now that you've met him while we're not running for our lives from a werewolf that we used to live with?"

They started forward, rubbing their arms. "Do you trust he'll be fine here while we go talk to Mason?"

I jumped at the sound of choking behind me. "Y-yes," I said quickly, half-turning to project my voice through the dividing fabric. "Charlie's meeting Dad in a bit, and since he's not picking up my calls, I'm going with them."

The curtain slid back a bit, Saint's body filling the empty gap. He shot Charlie an uncertain glance before focusing on me again. "If something happens, I can't exactly *leave* to help you."

"I shouldn't need help, unless Charlie decides to betray me, right?" I shot them a hesitant smile, knowing that they very well could do that, much like everyone else in my life.

They shook their head, wisps of loose blond hair from their clip swaying. "I won't tell Mason about this either." Charlie pointed to the laptop bag. "You sure you want to leave that *here?*" They didn't have to ask the follow-up question: *with a vampire?* I already heard it in my head.

"I'd rather leave it where it's protected than in an empty room. Plus, if something does happen to go horribly wrong while we're out, then Saint can track us down when it gets dark." My voice dropped to a mutter. "Not that I can honestly picture Rory managing to somehow murder us all, but you never know at this point." I jingled Lux's keys in my pocket.

"We'll take our new ride and be back before you know it, okay?"

Saint stepped forward and paused, like he was about to hug or kiss me until he locked onto Charlie again. So I wrapped my arms around him.

"Please be careful," he whispered.

"I'll be back for a nap in about an hour. Don't worry." I moved to give him another quick goodbye kiss before redirecting to his cheek. I don't think I'd enjoy the taste of blood lingering in my mouth on the drive over. "Drink up and rest."

With that, Charlie and I left. The moment the door clicked behind me, they shot me a glance. "What does Severin have to do with him?"

I twirled my finger around, the keys jingling in my grip as we started toward the garage. "Remember the whole part I mentioned about being turned and abused?"

They blew out a long breath. "Okay, so he's not planning on going back anytime soon..."

"He's not going back *ever*—not if I have anything to say about it. If I get the chance to kill one vampire and Saint isn't able to do it himself, I'd want my one and only kill to be Severin."

Charlie half-shrugged, a smirk tugging at the corner of their mouth. "Maybe we can make that happen. Maybe you're cut out for hunting after all."

A small spark of pride welled up inside me, even though I'd all but given up on the idea. I honestly think I was just glad that Charlie had seen my potential for something I'd previously wanted to do. I tried not to let it get to me as I headed for the car tucked into that far parking space, instead allowing myself to imagine my possible new future on the other side of all this—one where I'd be bite-free and no longer dealing with the stress of Mom and Dad fighting like a couple of kids unable to share their favorite toy.

Charlie's nose scrunched up when we climbed into the car. "Ugh. I hate lavender."

I chortled, started the engine, and let them navigate me to Dad.

21 CONFESSIONS

"Do you know why I joined Mason's crew?"

Charlie's question caught me off guard at the first traffic light. I squeezed the steering wheel a little tighter, unsure how to respond. Honestly, I felt like kind of an asshole for not bothering to ask, but, at the same time, vampire hunting tended to come with a lot of trauma and some people would rather not bring it up.

I opted for the easy way out: shaking my head.

"When I was seventeen, I had a friend who was obsessed with vampires."

I chortled, stealing a glance to find the faintest smile tugging at their lips. The light changed to green and I pressed the gas. "Did they read a lot of fantasy books or something?"

"Maybe a bit," Charlie said with a chuckle. "But I think she really was in love with the idea of living as a teenager forever. Looking back, it sounds like hell to consider, but she was pretty, popular, and worried about what she'd do beyond high school. Normally someone like her wouldn't have been seen with someone like me, whose fashion sense is still fairly non-existent, but we'd been friends since we were kids living on the same street. We continued to bond over our love of supernatural and paranormal romance because it was something that was real but *not*. God, I wish it weren't real sometimes now..."

"Tell me about it," I muttered, rolling to a stop at the next light as that little voice in the back of my mind already zipped straight to the end of this story. She was likely dead. That catalyst Charlie needed, just like how Dad had snapped. But I truly *wanted* to hear myself proven wrong. "What happened to her?"

They hummed through their exhale, shifting in the passenger's seat. "She started sneaking around and seeing a guy that was taking night classes at our community college. The first time I met him, I felt the wrongness radiating off of him. But I don't think it was so much because he was a vampire as much as he was just a *creep*. She was eighteen, so everything was technically legal, but it gave me the ick.

"He didn't like me. I was pretty quick to put my foot down in a lot of situations that my friend wouldn't, so we... started to grow apart. I was too straight-laced and could see through this guy's bullshit, but she tried her best to do things alone with me for a while. Then that stopped. We stopped talking. She started ignoring me. He was definitely building a narrative where he was her savior.

"I didn't hear from her the summer after graduation. Not until about a week before I was going to start classes at the same damn community college. She showed up on my back patio in the middle of the night. My parents were dead asleep upstairs." Charlie's head slowly shook back and forth, their eyes closed as if they were there again. "Her shirt was *covered* in blood. I remember her covering my mouth and telling me not to scream or call the cops. She'd flinched at the sound of a dog barking on the other side of the street and asked if she could come in. Looking back, she'd probably been under the impression that she couldn't break in, or maybe that's what he'd told her—I don't know."

I could feel my brows knitting together. Covered in blood? *Asking* to come inside? "She was—"

"She was turned. She'd managed to escape and said that she'd been beaten within an inch of her life, but that bastard wouldn't let her die. He just forced her to drink so she'd heal and locked her in a room. But the girl I knew who wanted immortality was gone. That haunted look in her eyes hurt to see. She asked me to kill her, and when I didn't, she broke off one of the legs of our dining chairs and jammed it through her chest."

Oh my God.

I couldn't even begin to imagine what I would've done after that. Who the fuck would believe me? Who would've believed *Charlie?* "Wh-what did you do?"

They shrugged. "They said it was self-inflicted because of drugs. I told myself it was the truth because it was easier to handle, but I knew that was a lie, deep down. I dropped out of college after the first semester and joined the National Guard because I couldn't help but think about running into that piece of shit and not being able to know how to fight. I tracked him down once I felt confident enough and then I killed him. I made a promise never to let another person fall victim to a manipulative vampire like him if I had the chance to stop it."

I wiggled against my seatbelt, suddenly feeling very restricted.

"I couldn't help but think of her back in your motel room. He had her jumpiness and fear, even if he was seemingly ready to take me on. You called him Saint, right?"

I swallowed and nodded.

"And Severin turned him against his will?"

"Yeah," I said quietly.

"If you want to kill Severin, I'll help you do it. I know you said it'd only be if Saint couldn't do it himself, but if you don't think he can..."

When they trailed off, my grip tightened on the steering wheel. I wanted to believe Saint *could*. After all, he'd escaped by clobbering Severin until he surrendered. Then again, Saint hadn't killed him, and he'd had a relationship with Severin that probably gave him some hesitation. And Severin had likely underestimated Saint the first time he rebelled, so the odds of Severin crushing Saint the second he saw that spark again seemed rather high. While it didn't seem fair to deny him that right to beat the shit out of his abuser, I also couldn't help but worry that Saint might die in the event of a second round.

"I'll... consider it."

"Just let me know." Charlie propped their elbow up against the window. "I honestly didn't think any *good* kind of vampires like Saint existed because their souls got crushed by the ones who treated the world like their own personal playground. I'm glad you proved me wrong, but I regret not being able to stop my friend from giving up and using her immortality for joy and protection instead of pain."

That last bit cut me deeper than I care to admit. I sank

further into the driver's seat as I considered what could've happened to Saint—or honestly, any other non-murdery-vampire—if they'd ended up in the crosshairs of Dad's crew over the years. How many *good* ones did we, the supposed heroes, kill? I understood that Adonis and Lux already had some biases, but Charlie had been in the same boat as me: assuming a visible vampire was an evil vampire because that's what we'd been taught. There was a stark difference between hunting vampires and hunting *monsters*—Dad just refused to acknowledge that there was one.

I let myself marinate in that horrible truth while auto-piloting with Charlie's instructions until we ended up in a shitty, pothole-ridden back parking lot with lines so faded that I had to guess where a spot was based on the other cars. We climbed out, and I pressed the lock button on the key fob as I took in the hulking building behind the car.

Corrugated shutters covered the arched brink openings where I normally would've anticipated old-looking windows to be. Washed out painted letters peeked out under a rusted sign that touted: 'STORAGE'.

Oh, good. Storage units. Nothing screamed suspicious quite like meeting in a thirty-dollar-a-month locker with vampire hunting equipment. Charlie and I were halfway to one of the white doors with a series of distressed number stickers for the units inside when it popped open.

The way my dad's eyes lit up when he saw me felt like a slap in the face. But it helped a little when that look shuffled through surprise, confusion, and then *terror* as he locked onto Charlie. They grabbed the door as I jogged to catch up.

"Jules?" Dad sputtered. "What are you—"

"We ran into each other and talked," I said, trying my best

not to emphasize the point about talking because, oh boy, we'd have *way* fewer issues right now if Dad had just picked up his damn phone over the hours I've wasted with attempted calls. "It's not them."

He hesitated but stepped aside, letting us join him in the wide corridor with garage-like shutters on either side. It stretched to the opposite side of the building, broken up by a couple of gaps that must've been additional halls, before it dead-ended to a padlocked door at the far side. Dad motioned for us to follow, thankfully not asking any more questions just yet as he turned and led us to a stairwell.

Part of me itched to grab his arm and spill the beans right then and there in front of Charlie—consequences be damned —because my hip was going to try to kill me during the climb. I gritted my teeth and death-gripped the railing after lagging behind, having to gesture for Charlie to go on ahead when they'd glanced back. There was no way I was going to swap places and have them sandwich me between them and Dad as I hobbled up the stairs. I wasn't going to embarrass myself further if I had any say in it, especially in front of Charlie.

One sweaty, shaky ascent later, Dad popped the lock off a unit with a regular door at the end of another intersection. He snapped on an emergency lantern that looked like it was meant for camping. A warm light fell over the thin desk, a stack of storage totes along the entire back side of the unit, the black acoustic panels lining the walls, and a blue plastic bag from a Swedish furniture store. My stomach bunched up when I saw a stake or two mixed in with tools to build the desk alongside another bulky black bag.

I pulled the door most of the way closed behind us, a

small part of me absolutely fearing being locked in, even though the lock was in Dad's hand. Plus, I'd seen the keypad outside the main door, so there's no way anyone besides a unit owner could be up here, right? Cue internal nervous laughter.

"Jules, I thought I told you to stay put—" Dad started through gritted teeth.

"Mason," Charlie snapped, folding their arms over their chest. "Focus. He's here, and that's not going to change right this second, so let's get to the point."

I wanted to clap. Holy hell, I'd wasted so much time thinking of Charlie as my nemesis when I could've recognized them for being a champion in my corner. "Charlie isn't the mole."

Dad's mouth worked like a fish, horrified that I'd blatantly come out and said it in front of them. "Charlie, could you step out for a—"

"*No*," I said firmly. "Not yet. I've already explained to them what's going on, so let's not dance around the point."

"He's right, Mason. If you're looking for your mole, it's not Adonis or Lux because they've had other motives as a werewolf and a witch, and it's not Jules because he told me that his vampire isn't Severin. And I'm inclined to believe him."

Dad's jaw dropped. "Wait, what?" He shook his head. "Jules, I thought you said—"

I threw my hands out at my sides, preparing to lie my ass off for a little while longer by omitting Saint. "After you were trying to find Severin yesterday and came up empty, I decided I was done with waiting and tried to track him down myself. Things stopped adding up, and I figured out who it really was. But you'd know all of this already if you'd actually pick up your damn phone and *try* to be a decent parent for once instead of continuing to ignore and fucking *lie to me*."

The way Charlie stared at me with their eyebrows nearly reaching their hairline, I think I might've caught them by surprise. They cleared their throat. "We came to the conclusion it's Rory. But I think that maybe you two also need to work some things out, so I'll just..." They jabbed their thumb toward the door and shimmied past me, stumbling into the hall. Footsteps echoed, growing quieter for the next few seconds until they stopped somewhere far enough that the foam panels would likely drown out any more words I decided to hurl at Dad.

Dad's hand ran over his mouth, scratching against the stubble shadowing the lower half of his face. "You know who your vampire is? And it's not Severin?"

What the actual fuck? I scoffed. "Not even a sorry, huh?"

"Jules—"

"It's *Mom*."

He blanched. That's when I knew I was about to successfully drag his ass. Well, that, and the fact that I'd rendered him speechless, which gave me an easy win. I'd basically paralyzed my opponent and was about to kick the shit out of him while he was down.

"And it was really funny to hear her side of the story while I was in shock about discovering that she's been alive—well, not *really* alive, but you fucking get it—for *years*. Aunt Syd has been checking up on me for her because you couldn't stand the idea of your son having a vampire for a mom because you'd rather her be dead instead of a *monster*. Because I'm learning that all vampires are monsters in your eyes, which isn't reality, and that's also a fucking tough pill to swallow. How much hate have you fed me, Dad? Are we fucking serious?"

My hands found my head as my eyes darted around the room, locks of hair pulled taught to keep me anchored with how quickly I felt like I was unraveling. "Like, holy shit. You've been so hell-bent on keeping me from falling into this mess that I was drawn to it to help you—because everything I've done has been to help *you*. You could've let me go visit Aunt Syd in Canada, but you *knew* that Mom was up there, right? You couldn't afford to let it slip that Mom was still very much not six-feet-under, so you just covered up lies with more lies.

"And I'm sure you thought you could keep this whole hunting thing from Aunt Syd and Mom, but they fucking knew what you were doing. You know the kicker in all of this? If you hadn't denied my request to join you as a hunter, I wouldn't have been bitten by Mom in the first place—*I still wouldn't know.*"

My arms fell back to my sides as I stared him down. "I spent my whole life trying to be someone I wasn't for you when our whole relationship is built on a bond of blood and lies."

He started to shake his head, his eyes glossing over. "I am *so* sorry, Jules." My traitorous heart squeezed with how long I'd wanted to hear those words. "I wanted you to have something I couldn't have, and—"

"Yeah, well, Mom wants me to learn how to be a witch," I said, bitterness lacing my tone. "So if you want to at least try to fix *this*," —I motioned between us and to my bite— "then *you* need to *talk* with her. Both of you need to figure your shit out and give me time to figure out what *I* want for a change because I'm not here to endure a custody battle. I'm an adult. No more lies and no more bites—no more shit to try to manipulate me into doing what either of you think is *best* for me." I turned, grabbing the edge of the door.

"Oh, and one more thing." I spared one last look at Dad, the cool metal digging into my palm. "Find a new assistant. I quit."

I shoved my way into the hall, the bright, white walls blinding me as I forced out a long breath. Charlie's footfalls started up again as I glanced over to find them heading toward me. "He's all yours to chat with now. I need some air. I'll be outside if you need a ride when you're done."

Their nod was all I needed before I started for the stairs. As much as I was trying to ride the high of almost completely freeing myself from both my parents' tyranny, I wasn't about to abandon Charlie. Not when they'd somehow made it to one of the top slots in my family circle next to Aunt Syd, despite not even being related to me by blood.

I hobbled my way down the steps, taking my time as I breathed the air of a free man. Being unemployed honestly felt refreshing in a sick, twisted way. I wasn't obligated to clean the whole house while everyone was out hunting. I wouldn't have to get everyone coffee or meal prep for them ever again. No more avoiding my social life and lying about my occupation.

A smile crept onto my face when I hit the last landing before the bottom, the hallway already tunneling out before me. I didn't even get to tell Saint that I talked to Allie about getting a job at the café. I could apply *today*. I could kickstart my new life working with nice people who made coffee and tea and served pastries. And, best of all, I could see Saint every night.

I winced on the last step, the pain puncturing that high I was riding. Rocking back against the edge of the railing, I pulled out my phone and tapped through it to find Saint, opening our text thread. The messages that greeted me might as well have been from an eternity ago—an era before we knew about the other's secrets.

> Hey, I talked to Dad and told him to deal with it. I also quit my job.

I pushed on the edges of my rubber phone case and peered past the scraped screen protector as I waited for his reply. The vibration of the phone sent a pulse of warmth through me.

> Really? You quit? Are you sure you want that?

> I'm sure. I ran into Allie earlier when I was at your place... I might've asked her about the night shift? :)

I started my walk across the grungy linoleum tiles, making my way toward the door. The screen lit up as the phone shook with a call, and I pressed it to my ear. "Hey," I said, unable to suppress my grin.

"You're sure you want to work at the café?" Saint asked. "I don't want you to feel like it's your only option or—"

"I'm sure. I really want a change of pace. And I honestly really want to work with someone I know if I'm going to try something new—if that's okay, that is."

Saint's quiet chuckle made my cheeks hurt. "Of course that's okay," he said. "It's okay as long as it's what you want and not what you think I want."

I pushed through the door, the sunlight slapping me in the face compared to the brightness of the storage facility. "It's what I want. I'm excited to finally be done with this mess. I'll just be glad when this bite's gone and—"

The second the door slammed behind me, I jolted as I caught a shadow in my periphery where it'd been perfectly concealed by the outward swing. The scrape of shoes on pavement turned into an afterthought as something dark pulled over my head, the phone was knocked out of my hand, and the breath ripped from my lungs with a swift punch. I gasped, my pulse pounding in my ears as I heard my phone clatter against the pavement with Saint repeating my name through the speaker. When his voice cut with a crunch of metal and glass, my stomach lurched. Plastic dug into my wrists as my arms were wrestled behind my back.

"Keep trying the door code and get this one to the car."

My blood went cold. I knew that voice.

Rory.

22 EXES & OHS

elieve it or not, when Dad first sat down with Rory about joining this entire vigilante squad, I had been *excited*. Stupid of me, I know. But at the time, I was doing all the heavy administrative lifting on my own, and Rory seemed... on my level, I guess? I wasn't really friends with any of the people I lived with, and I hoped that Rory might be able to fill that void. Mainly because Lux was too snooty, Adonis was too jock-y, and Charlie was too intimidatingly perfect. And, well, I was being a jealous bitch with the attention Dad was showering them with.

Rory radiated research nerd and video game geek energy, which resonated with me. Until I put myself out there to make a new buddy by asking what he did in his free time and got hit with a blank stare, followed by: "Um. Research?"

I'd given a nervous, awkward laugh. "Yeah, but what do you do to relax?"

"Research." That slow blink should've told me he was lying by omission. Or maybe he wasn't, and research was quite literally his life, aside from his fucking betrayal. After that, he rarely interacted with me unless he absolutely had to, as if I was beneath him. Like he wasn't also an admin assistant.

So I decided just to be happy that he was taking research, reports, and monotonous data off my plate. Because surely that meant I was another step closer to stepping out of the house and onto the street to slay vampires.

But, uh... yeah. Clearly some things had gone horribly wrong because he'd gotten the promotion, I was officially unemployed, and now the fucker was kidnapping me.

I struggled as hard as I could against the grip of what had to be a couple of very meaty dudes dragging me through a nook of a parking lot crammed between buildings. I wish I could've screamed, but my head was spinning with the lack of oxygen from the punch and the panic locking me in a chokehold. Whatever noise managed to make it out was panting and wheezing.

My entire body tensed at the sound of a deep, unsettling *pop* that I immediately associated with a car door or—God, please no—a trunk. Just as I was finally able to suck in a decent breath, I was tipped back, my legs flailing as someone grabbed them. I kicked as wildly as I could, my heart going a million miles a minute. Gasping, I tried to force out a scream, but it came out as a yelp as I hit the scratchy carpeting of what was, unfortunately, most definitely the trunk.

It slammed shut, and I pressed my cheek against the interior, dragging my face along the inside of the black bag over my head. Every part of me snapped into survival mode as the engine revved to life.

Get out, get out, get out—

Each second was too fast and too slow, contradicting all of my progress as the bag's cinching tickled my nose. The car lurched backward and I rolled forward, face-planting into the carpet. I gritted my teeth and wriggled the rest of the way out of the bag, thoughts racing as I tried to take stock of what I had at my disposal. I slid again, scrambling for purchase as the vehicle shifted into drive.

My wrists throbbed as I tried to pull them apart to steady myself in the rock back-and-forth. At this rate, I wouldn't have a chance to keep steady long enough to do anything, let alone escape. With that in mind, I started to fucking panic.

I nudged the toe of my sneaker against the far end of the trunk, my sole firmly pressing against that wall. When I jerked my leg back, my heel smacked against the pultruding tire enclosure before I drove my kick home against the back of one of the tail lights. The tiniest *smack* sounded in the whole four-to-six-inch range of motion I had. I tried to hit it a few more times as the car bounced, my foot colliding with light, the top of the trunk, the curve of the enclosure, and several other places that weren't the intended target.

My shoulder rubbed against the carpeting as I struggled, wishing my hands were free so I could look for a safety latch or the tail light wires. Fuck the rule Dad made about avoiding getting the cops involved. If I was being kidnapped by a gang of familiars, I was going to do what I had to, especially since I was dead set on tossing this life in the trash in favor of a wholesome happily-ever-after where I could live my cozy coffee shop dreams with my vampire boyfriend.

I kicked again, gritting my teeth as I replayed the way Saint had urgently called my name through my phone before hearing that horrible crunch of my lifeline being absolutely obliterated. Was he pacing the motel room right now trying to call me again? Or was he frantically searching through the laptop to find my location? I wasn't even in the tracking system anyway because I was always at home, but I couldn't assume that he would know that. If he could note down Charlie and Dad's locations on the map, that would be *something*. Too bad the trail would be cold by the time night fell.

I thumped my head against the carpet and cursed myself for not giving Saint Charlie's number. He could've at least alerted them to this. I kicked again, throwing as much force into it as I could, my heart pumping so hard I felt like it might burst. Maybe ripping into Dad was a mistake. What were the odds that he'd feel like this was a well-deserved lesson and leave me out to dry after giving him an ultimatum? God, what were the odds that *Mom* would absolutely strangle me if she somehow managed to properly tap into her familiar-locating abilities to find me?

I kicked again, again, again, *again*.

Every hit slid or bounced, not giving me any solid feeling as to whether or not it was working. Despair was starting to claw its way in with each heavy, panicked breath. I should've counted turns, stops, and seconds, but instead I started mentally preparing for whatever hell Rory had sentenced me to. I swallowed down the bile climbing up my throat at the thought of standing face-to-face with Severin—a vampire I'd only ever known by name and from stories told by my room-mates-slash-coworkers and my boyfriend.

What the fuck would he do with me? I'd thought that he had turned me into a familiar, but maybe he'd rather kill me instead. It'd be so easy for him to do that and claim he still had me alive to taunt Dad for a bit. Then Dad would have a dead family member for *real* this time.

I kicked again, my leg feeling like jelly and my body shaking as that terror set in. I could be riding to my death. I might not ever see Saint again. I was going to die to a vampire.

All because my parents had fucked up my life, and I'd been too absorbed in trying to gain their approval instead of finding happiness. And now I was going to lose the little I'd managed to find.

I kicked harder, blinking away the tears building in my eyes. I was either going to kick this fucking tail light out in the nick of time and escape or I was going to die. In either scenario, I refused to cry in front of my enemies. I wasn't going to let them the satisfaction of feeding off of my relief or fear, no matter the outcome.

My body bounced as the car made a slow turn, the sound of gravel crunching under the tires telling me the fight was over. We were no longer on a paved road that the cops would notice a busted tail light. The car rocked as it stopped, and I held my breath to try to hear over my pulse. A screech and clatter sounded from somewhere beyond the confines of the vehicle, lingering for about a minute before the car rolled forward again, moving from the pop of gravel to something smooth. The second time it stopped, I heard the gear shift. The screech sounded once more, and doors opened. We were parked.

I'd lost. Deep breaths. Pull yourself together, Jules.

All that anxiety and dread had built up to that moment, piquing as the trunk opened, and I flinched away from the shadowy figure that grabbed my arm. I quickly found the source of the screeching as I was hauled from the trunk, catching the last gasp of light trickling into the building as the garage door reached the edge of the concrete.

Any face I saw that wasn't Rory's immediately stopped mattering when the trunk slammed shut behind me, echoing through the garage. If I was able to perform one last act of defiance without a stake—Aunt Syd had refused to give that back to me—I was going to spit on Rory for being a traitorous bastard and for using me as fodder.

I didn't see his reddish mop of hair as I was dragged through the door leading out of the garage, my shoes scraping against the concrete as I tried to slow my captors down. Every sound bounced off the walls ten-fold as we stepped into the cavernous warehouse. All the small windowpanes had been painted or papered over, leaving candles and camping lanterns as the sole sources of light, likely only for the sake of the familiars.

My eyes darted back and forth at the people stepping aside and staring me down as we passed by a grated stairway. When my eyes followed it up to the second-floor catwalks, I bit down on my tongue to try to avoid a panic response upon seeing figures move from metal folding chairs to lean against the railing. They were prepping for a show. And I was about to be thrown on stage.

I tore my gaze back to the center of the warehouse floor, where a few more people made way, save one individual who cocked his head. I'm honestly not quite sure how I originally imagined Severin. Maybe something along the lines of an out-of-style, stuck-in-the-past kind of guy who still dressed up like he did four or five decades ago. Or maybe a corpo-pire, never seen without a business suit. But I truly don't think I ever would've guessed he looked like he'd just rolled out of bed and pulled on a hoodie.

I shit you not, his blond hair stuck up at odd angles, and said hoodie had a table top role playing game logo on it. For a second, I thought that Severin hadn't even shown up yet. But when one of the familiar goons kicked the back of my knee, and I hit the floor in front of this unassuming vampire, I realized that this was him. This was the guy I'd been told about. A guy that looked like a generic college student that played board games. You know, he had enough vampires around that I could picture a mandatory game night.

"He didn't see how to get here, did he?" Severin—probably?—asked with a slight jerk of his chin toward me.

"No," said Goon Number One. "He was in the trunk."

"And you're sure you weren't followed?"

"Positive," Goon Number Two answered.

When Probably-Severin's eyes flicked down, I held my breath, as if I was waiting to get the shit slapped out of me. His resting bitch face softened a bit, taking me by surprise. "You must be Mason's kid, aren't you? Rory wouldn't have bothered sending you otherwise."

Should I even answer? Saying yes might get my head lopped off and saying no would *definitely* result in that sort of reaction. I tried to swallow the lump in my throat, hearing a dry *click* instead.

When I didn't say anything right away, he crouched in front of me. His arms rested on his bowed legs, one forefinger running along the length of his thumb as his eyes bore into mine. "You're either being very brave or you're scared shitless right now, but you're doing your best to prove to Mason you're worthy of hunting with him, hm?"

I froze. The first thought that shot into my brain was: how the fuck did he guess that? But then I remembered the statue of the saint on the mantel. The camera Rory placed. Severin had likely heard my argument with Dad before this entire nightmare was set in motion, even if it might not have had the best angle to necessarily *see* us.

He hummed. "Jules? Was that what he called you?" Every word chipped away at my shield with the delivery. His calm tone and smooth cadence lulled me into forgetting we were surrounded by an entire warehouse of vampires and familiars. There was no way that I could be wrong about him after all of this, right?

Almost immediately, alarm bells went off in the back of my mind as I recalled everything Saint had gone through with him. There's no fucking way he'd lie to me about that. Was *this* how Severin ensnared him? By putting on a specially-crafted disarming front? Because it was sure as hell working. I wished he looked and talked a little more like a dick so I could feel warranted hatred for the guy.

I hesitated, fearing that he might lose his patience if I didn't produce *something* for him to work with. "Y-yes," I said quietly. "Jules." Oh, God, what else did he know about though? Did he know about Saint? Was he going to break my neck because I slipped up and confirmed my name?

A small smile tugged at the corners of his mouth. "It suits you. I'm sorry we couldn't meet under different circumstances, but I think it's time Mason and I talk. And, unfortunately, you seem to be the best way to facilitate that without him killing me and my own."

So I was going to be a bargaining chip? Was that all? It was probably more likely that I was being used as bait. I tried not to squirm under his gaze until one of his lackeys moved, then I jolted. I couldn't help it, my nerves were shot in a den of vampires.

Severin's eyes narrowed to slits, his mouth forming a thin line as he shot his underling a glare. He pushed himself back to his feet. "Keep an eye out for the others," he ordered, grabbing my arm and hauling me up. "Inform me when Rory returns."

I stumbled as he squeezed my bicep and guided me toward the steps. Matching his pace proved to be a feat in itself with my hands still bound behind me and my hip still making my life hell. My eyes watered by the time we reached the catwalk, where he pushed open a door next to a painted-over interior window, judging by the lack of light creeping around the edges.

The former office had been turned into a spartan shelter room, complete with a cot, a couple of metal folding chairs, and a peeling leather couch. He shoved me into a chair and stepped back to flip the lock on the door. Would this be where he'd rip into me about Saint?

I flinched as he brushed past and angled the other chair to face me before taking a seat. Without any preamble, he grabbed the collar of my jacket and peeled it back. I barely had time to react, and once he saw the mark, I couldn't undo it. But that didn't stop me from breaking out into a sweat.

For a split-second, his eyes widened, then he clicked his tongue. "Rory suspected as much... Who's your vampire?"

"I-I don't know." I'm glad it was the first thing that came out of my mouth to keep it a private family problem because telling Severin that my mom bit me would open up a whole arsenal for him to use against Dad. I wasn't going to stoop to Rory's level of assholery.

"*Jules*," he said, my name turning into a warning.

"R-really, I don't know. I promise. I-I—" I grimaced, heat spreading along the back of my neck with the embarrassment that I was about to tell *Severin*, of all people, about what happened the night that kicked off this entire mess. "Um..." I shook my head. "After I fought with Da—Mason, um, I got a little drunk. I don't remember much. It sounds fucking stupid, but—"

He patted the jacket back into place. "If you're lying, you should know that your vampire isn't going to turn you."

Huh? My mouth worked, trying to comprehend what he was talking about.

"You don't have to try to protect them, but if you sought out a vampire to stick it to your father, you should know that they're going to keep you as a familiar for as long as possible. You're more useful to them that way. That's all there is to it."

I'll admit, I was a bit shell-shocked by this truth bomb he'd just dropped on me, though it didn't exactly apply to my situation. I knew it absolutely was how he went about familiars though, considering everything Saint had told me.

"I'm afraid that they're just going to string you along like Mason." He shrugged. "That's just what most of us do."

"Oh," I said quietly, giving him just enough to keep yapping so I could dodge putting my foot in my mouth. The less I spoke the better.

He sighed and ran his fingers through his hair, poorly attempting to fix his bedhead. "You don't really want another *boss* to answer to, do you? From what I've heard, you seem smart and capable—you shouldn't have to try to continue to prove yourself to someone like Mason. Does he even know about you being a familiar?"

Oh boy, how did I want to spin this? Would saying no get me more pity points? I only had a split second to mull it over, so I kept with the half-truths: "He... thinks it's you." Considering everything going on, mainly Dad's renewed hatred of Severin, I figured that would be a safe bet. "You, um, you *are* Severin, right?" Also, might as well check.

He blinked, seemingly surprised. "I guess that shouldn't come as a shock since he's always looking for a reason to pick a fight with me. Naturally, he couldn't help but come up with the narrative that I'd turn you into a familiar to do my bidding." He rolled his eyes. "And yes, I am Severin. I'm sure he's told you a million horrible things about me."

Not quite, but I faked it and shrank a little further into my seat. I still didn't know what the fuck he was planning on doing with me because there had to be *more* to it. He was being too fucking nice, and that made me mega uncomfortable.

"I'm not going to hurt you, Jules."

As genuine as he *sounded*, I seriously doubted that.

"All you have to do is stay put, behave, and after Mason and I come to an agreement, you'll be free." He hesitated. "Unless you don't want to leave with Mason? I can understand if you don't since he's been rather... neglectful."

Why was he starting to sound like a therapist? I squirmed in my seat, unable to refrain from showing discomfort any longer.

"It must be lonely and frustrating dedicating all your time to the one person you thought you can always count on, just for him to push you aside again and again. Going against that takes courage, even if you're discovering it's more of the same. But if you want a change for the better, I can help. I can release you from Mason and your vampire if you'd like."

I knitted my brows together in feigned confusion to keep them from shooting to my hairline. No way—was he seriously offering me vampirism? Holy shit. How pissed would Rory be if he found out about this? A part of me started to panic as I thought about how Saint said Severin turned him without warning. I had to make this a firm *no* because that needed to be off the table as long as I was trapped here. Then I just had to hope Severin would stick to my request. After all, he just met me. This wasn't like Saint's situation. I should be fine. Hopefully.

"H-how?"

He stood and grabbed the back of my chair, leaning in as I pressed myself against the metal to put as much distance between us as physically possible. "I said your vampire wouldn't turn you, but if you want to be freed from being a familiar, that's the only way out."

Oh, good. He was telling his familiars that there were no take-backsies. Cool. Awesome. I shook my head. "N-no, thanks."

Severin drew back, frowning with disappointment. "Is that not what you wanted?"

Shit. "I... I don't know."

"You're afraid."

I opened my mouth and closed it again, looking away. I wasn't just afraid, I was petrified of the idea. It was one thing to know my life might be nearly over and make that sort of decision, much like what Mom did, and another to agree to it simply because I could. If I ever decided that being a vampire

—gross blood-drinking and all—was what I wanted to commit to, I'd rather it be done by Saint. Not by Severin. Especially not by Severin in his weird, creepy vampire warehouse while I was zip-tied.

"It's okay to be afraid, Jules. It's a big decision. That's only natural." He stepped back, letting go of my chair. "If you change your mind, let me know."

Severin started for the door, my ears perking at the flip of the lock before he left, pulling it shut behind him. I released the biggest exhale when I was finally alone, my entire body trembling as I tried to cope with the reality that I was stuck in a building of vampires with no way to escape.

Fuck.

23 BLOOD FOR BLOOD

After Severin left, I counted the number of *clangs* that rang out on his way down the steps. Maybe he'd been so used to putting on a show in front of humans that he did everything in his power not to be dead silent, unlike Saint. When the noise settled, I'd gotten to thirty, meaning it was probably around a thirty-or-so-foot drop if I bashed open the window.

Shaking like a leaf, I forced myself out of the chair, doing my best not to eat shit on my way to the couch. My knee dipped into the cushion as I tried to peer through the thin gaps and streaks of paint. Even if there was a way for me to push it open, what were the odds of something being at the bottom to cushion my fall? I doubted there'd be a dumpster full of soft trash, considering this place likely hadn't been occupied until recently. This was a backup shelter, and backup shelters didn't exactly have many signs of life—or *unlife*—before they're occupied.

I tried to avoid thinking about what kind of garbage a

bunch of vampires might generate, along with the logistics involved in that as I tried to focus on what information I could gather instead. My nose pressed to the window as I squinted to take in the building next door. The glint of sun in its obscured panes didn't exactly offer much, besides the fact that it was nearing noon. But it was another warehouse. Which I guess told me that it was a warehouse district—a place I was wholly unfamiliar with.

The last time I'd been in an area of town like this was when Dad still had a car. He used to slow-roll a few neighborhoods with abandoned buildings and shopping hubs with blacked-out storefronts. I remembered him navigating me through an area like this when he was teaching me how to drive, but I'd been so focused on the rules of the road that I wasn't really paying much attention to the structures. After Dad took that vehicle to a single job and got in a vampire-related collision, I was thankful we lived somewhere walkable. But I didn't exactly see myself being able to walk out of this one without getting lost, let alone outrunning a pack of vampires before sundown at this rate.

I worried my lip and slowly sank into the couch cushions. Every possible idea I tried to conjure up immediately slipped into nothing. I didn't have a phone. I pissed off my dad. My mom was a vampire with terrible familiar radar functionality. My boyfriend was *also* a vampire, who was currently stuck in a motel room and was probably the only one that knew I was missing...

I thumped my head against the back of the couch and squeezed my eyes shut. There had to be *something* I could do, right? I think I mulled over that question for what had to be the next two or three hours as I shifted in my position on the couch. A couple of times I swapped from pacing the room to see what was available for me to utilize—spoiler: nothing—and sitting, anxiously awaiting Severin's return to learn my fate.

My wrists felt raw and irritated, burning at every movement until it was the only thing I could focus on. The sheer discomfort and pain of feeling trapped made me reconsider every choice I'd made up to this point. If I'd rebelled against Dad and somehow became a vampire hunter, would that mean I would've never met Saint? *Worse*—would I have *killed* him? What about Mom?

I shook my head, hating the distress that came with those thoughts. Even if I'd ran away from this mess earlier, who's to say that Rory wouldn't still have targeted me to use as bait? This entire situation didn't discriminate against the choices I'd made. Dad made an enemy. An enemy who would've attacked the house, despite whether or not I'd been spared from being locked in the basement. An enemy who would've continued to spy on him through Rory for as long as possible. An enemy who would've exploited any possible weak spots along the way, including using *me*.

Jolting, I sat up straight, my body going on full-alert as I heard the groan of the garage door. My heart pounded in my chest as I readjusted to peer out the window, as if I'd be able to somehow see the vehicle or people pouring inside when all the action was happening around the corner, out of sight. Voices echoed from the base of the warehouse, and I scrambled to my feet, catching myself before I pitched forward on my way to find a gap in the painted window for a look.

"What took you so long?" The sound of Severin's normal tone through the glass made me wish there was a way to turn up the volume or pop on subtitles. I had to strain to make sure I didn't miss anything over my heavy breathing as I told myself to calm the fuck down for five minutes.

Good God, Rory was even harder to hear. I knew it was him from the small sliver I could make out, catching on his reddish hair. My brain did its best to fill in the gaps from how quietly he spoke. "He had backup, and they managed to lose us."

"On foot? You managed to lose Mason when you had a car and he was *on foot?*"

Rory's head moved—I think it was a shake to indicate a no, but he said something else about the car that I couldn't catch.

Severin's hand moved to his face, the railing from the staircase obscuring part of it, but I think he was pinching his nose. "Time. Plates. Make. Model."

Wait—did Dad and Charlie get away in a car? I swayed, feeling the weight of Lux's car keys still heavy in my pocket, my heart plummeting as I realized Saint's house key was attached to them. Fuck me. Okay, focus, so they must've managed to call a rideshare and escape, right? Something like that? It seemed risky, but if they were dealing with people instead of vampires, it was way safer to run so the police didn't get involved.

"What do you *mean you don't know—*"

I jumped back, Severin snapping straight to a roar. The backs of my knees hit the metal folding chair, sending it skidding back before I smacked down onto it. My heart raced as I considered just how bad that could've gone if I'd fell over it and gave myself about fifteen other bruises. Then again, another part of my brain was telling me that I was probably going to die if Dad continued to evade Severin.

Deep breaths, Jules.

Easier said than done, especially with the small black specks floating around the edges of my vision. The sour tang in the back of my throat wasn't helping matters either. My body tensed up at the sound of voices reverberating off of corrugated metal.

"You told me you could bring me Mason," Severin half-growled in his irate shout. "You *promised* that this would be over *tonight*. And I'm holding you to that because I've had enough of this bastard trying to control *my* city."

"It will," Rory said, a little louder with a bit of an edge to it this time. "I got you Mason's son, didn't I? That's all the bait needed to get him wherever you want him."

"With preparations, yes. He'll bring the rest of those damn hunters."

Rory's voice lowered again, and I quickly pushed myself up, my legs shaking as I pressed my ear to the window.

"—one left."

Severin guffawed and turned, pacing toward the other end of the warehouse before pausing and making his way back. "Only one? And where are the others, hm? Dead? Because I don't trust that—"

"They're—"

Another vampire seized Rory by the collar. "Don't fucking speak out of turn, familiar."

"Because," Severin started again, getting so close to Rory's face that he tried to lean back to put distance between them. "I don't trust that whoever came to rescue Mason and his little follower isn't going to miraculously show up to fight with him if we set up a meeting. Even *with* his son, another hunter can still try something stupid. And when we lose what leverage we have, everything crumbles."

Silence took over as everyone's eyes fixed on Rory, waiting for his response to their leader's flawless logic. No wonder Severin had managed to survive for so long. He was fucking paranoid, even with Rory being right if he was trying to communicate that only Charlie remained to support Dad.

Rory's explanation came out in a near-whisper, so I wasn't able to get any of it, but it made Severin pull back. More uneasy silence, though the other vampire still held onto Rory's shirt as if Severin might tell him to take him away to the dungeon. Or, I mean, whatever the equivalent to a dungeon they had in this warehouse. It might just be a room like solitary confinement, which wasn't all that far off from what I was dealing with at the moment.

Severin nodded, and the vampire let go. Rory said something else, and Severin folded his arms over his chest, the two of them having the most intense stare-down possible before Severin turned his head away from where I could see his face. I heard him say *something*, but I wasn't able to pull out any words that made sense.

I could figure a bit of it out though when Rory started for the steps. My blood went hot. He was coming up here. This son of a bitch was going to come gloat that he'd won and I'd lost in a million ways since I'd last seen Rory's fucking stupid face. I quickly circumvented the chair and stood in front of the couch, putting as much distance between me and the door as possible.

Hiding along the wall next to the door so I could kick him in the balls and make a run for it was a close second decision, but the whole warehouse full of vampires dissuaded me from making that rash choice. I really fucking wanted to do that though. If anything, it would give me that taste of revenge before I died a horrible death. At least I would die knowing that I'd fought back.

The door opened, and Rory stepped inside, shutting it behind him before he leaned against it for the briefest second. "It's been a while, hasn't it?"

"Shut the fuck up with the small talk," I ground out, "and tell me why you're doing this."

He held up his hands, taking a few steps forward. Just enough so we were in normal talking distance, but not so close that I had to stare up at him with my height disadvantage. I would've imagined him going for the latter to assert dominance, but it was possible he was being subtly respectful to me out of habit. "You're honestly fodder in this. I don't have anything against you, Jules. Take this as one familiar to another."

I scoffed. "You're trying to kill my *dad*—"

He motioned to me. "Like you haven't had enough of him. You can't tell me you didn't choose to serve a vampire to escape him."

"I *didn't*."

Rory rolled his eyes and shook his head. "Say whatever you want, but I chose to follow Severin because I know that he's the one who will shape my future. Mason, Charlie—even Lux and Adonis—they're all afraid of what it means to be immortal. They just want to kill what they can't understand because they've decided it's destructive and abhorrent—"

I couldn't help it, I laughed. "You think Severin's going to turn you, don't you?" Oh my God, I was *so* ready to shit-stir. "He just told me that familiars don't get turned."

His eyes narrowed. "Familiars like *you* don't get turned."

"Like *me?* What the fuck does that even—"

"You really think that you can cut it as a familiar if you can't even prove to Mason that you can be a hunter?"

Oof. Okay, 'nothing personal' my ass. "Why did you even bother being a hunter for my dad then? If it's really not that personal, why not just leave that position for me?"

"Severin told me to," he said simply. "So I did what I had to. And once Mason is dead, I'll get what I was promised."

My brows shot up. "You think Severin's going to turn you after he kills my dad? You're serious?" Rory nodded matter-of-factly. "Dude, did you not fucking hear what I just said Severin told me? He literally uses familiars until they're no longer useful."

He sighed. "Most vampires do unless you make a deal. This is my deal. And when Mason's dead, you can bargain with Severin to let you go so you can try to make it as long as you can with your vampire. Everyone wins." Then he *shrugged.*

My jaw hung open. Rory was absolutely delusional. Dread pooled in my stomach as I realized how little he cared about the fact that I was about to lose my dad. Had my dad sort of been a piece of shit? Hell yes, but that didn't mean I stopped loving him. I wanted to give him a chance to make it up to me, assuming he actually cared enough not to abandon me here because of everything I'd said. Nothing in this situation was fair. I didn't want any of this to happen. But I didn't have any control.

I clenched my teeth, a fresh wave of anger pulsing

through me as my hands curled into fists, wrists straining against the zip-tie.

Rory took another step forward, his eyes boring into mine. "You can make this easier on everyone here if you tell me everything you know about where Mason and Charlie have been hiding out."

Every detail about the motel had been suffocated by blinding rage as I stared at Rory. Rory, the dumbass computer wiz, who'd wormed his way into our house as a familiar and pulled the rug out from under all of us. He'd barely spoken to me over the couple of years I'd lived with him, and now he was asking me to fucking roll over on the one person I'd known my whole life.

I took a step toward him, closing the gap as I snapped my head back. It happened so fast, I only heard the *crack* and Rory's scream before I realized I'd actually done it. Specks of blood warmed my face as Rory stumbled and covered his nose, red splotches dotting the floor.

"You *fucker*," he snapped, ripping his hand away from his face and punching me in the side of the head.

Everything blanked for a second until I collided with the ground, my ear on fire and the world spinning. Rory was already grabbing the collar of my jacket and climbing on top of me, fist recoiling for round two. My legs flailed as I tried to kick free, unable to do much else with how sluggish my mind was working.

The door burst open, and Rory paused, looking between me and Severin with shock and horror. Then he scrambled to his feet. "He—"

In one instant, Rory was standing, beginning to plead his case. The next, I was flinching at a horrible crunching sound before Rory fell to the floor, his eyes wide and lifeless as I stared into them in the stretch of space between us.

Dead. Just like that.

"*This,*" Severin said evenly as he stepped over Rory like a piece of trash, "is what happens to familiars that stop being useful."

My stomach heaved as the soles of my shoes found purchase against the shitty office carpet. I scrambled to sit upright, pushing my back against the wall. If I fucking threw up in front of Severin, he'd immediately pounce on that weakness. It didn't matter that I was seeing double and just witnessed someone fucking die, I had to keep it together.

Severin and his ghostly after-image pointed to Rory as two other vampires appeared. "Get rid of that. Make sure the others see. No one is an exception, not even the teacher's pet."

Bile coated my tongue. If Rory was his favorite familiar, then holy shit was Saint right. When I saw Rory's leg finally disappear from my tunnel vision, I tried using the wall to stand, my knees buckling with the concoction of ebbing adrenaline and panic. Severin hadn't fucking moved, despite his goons hauling away Rory's body.

I stared down at the floor, holding still the best I could manage with my possibly concussed state. Severin crouched into view, just out of the corner of my eye. I jumped. I was teetering on the edge of breaking into hysterics with the knowledge that this guy would've absolutely killed me if Rory hadn't fought back.

"You understand now, don't you?"

I tried to suppress the urge to cry, though my throat was closing up anyway.

Severin's thumb ran across my cheek, and I jerked away, the back of my head hitting the wall so hard I winced. The pad of his thumb was smeared with light streaks of Rory's blood before he rubbed it between his fingers.

"You struck first. I know he didn't get that bloody nose on his own."

I tensed, fearing the worst as my stomach worked itself into knots.

"He should've shown more restraint."

I almost laughed—the *oh my God, I'm going to fucking die* unhinged, helpless sort of laugh—with how violently I started to shake. It didn't come out, but it sure would if one more terrible thing happened in the next five minutes.

Something lit Severin's gaze, my mind unable to comprehend what it could possibly be with how much I was internally fighting. "You have so much more potential than a familiar."

I had no idea what he meant by that until he bared his teeth and his eyes went black.

24 HIGH STAKES

When Severin grabbed my neck and pinned it to the wall, I half-gasped, half-choked, and tried to squirm in vain. His fangs sank into his wrist—at least, I *think* it was his wrist from the blurred halo of a second image starting to finally fall back into place overtop of him. His mouth came away bloody, and I shuddered.

"Mason doesn't see your value like I do. To him, you're still a child in need of protection, even while you're taking steps to free yourself. I'm giving you that freedom. It'll hurt, but you'll thank me for it later."

I turned away as his wrist lifted to my face. He seized my jaw and held it in place as he squeezed my cheeks to force my mouth open. The lukewarm syrupy consistency made me gag, followed by incessant coughing with the sugary taste that followed. It was like drinking still-cooling caramel. Normally, that would've been a pleasant surprise, but at that moment, I thought of that damned spiked caramel apple hot chocolate that'd started this mess.

As hard as I tried to keep from ingesting it, Severin snapped my mouth shut when his wrist moved away, keeping me from spitting it onto the carpet. I didn't fucking want this. I didn't want Severin's blood anywhere near me. I didn't want to suffer the same fate Saint had all those years ago with the fear that Severin might continue the cycle and kill Saint in front of me to teach me a lesson.

"Don't be afraid, Jules," Severin crooned, gently running a knuckle down the skin along my throat until I slipped up. I coughed and sputtered when he let go, knowing I just consumed fucking vampire blood and there was no way to undo that without a lot of time I didn't exactly have. "Let's see how Mason really feels about you when he learns you're a vampire."

White-hot pain took over as Severin's face vanished from view. I might as well have been a baby animal with how my body went limp, fangs latched onto my neck and quickly siphoning as much blood as possible. I was too stunned to scream. My thoughts were everywhere and nowhere. The edges of my vision pulsed black and red.

I was sure my mind was playing tricks on me between the punch to the head and the lack of blood when I swore I'd heard the garage door. But no one was coming to save me. Severin's fangs pressed deeper, and my eyes burned as I let out a whimper. It wasn't until the garage door sounded a second time that I heard something else I wasn't so sure was fake: a scream.

Severin's head lifted, that pain slipping from knife-like to a sharp sting. I crumpled, every breath a struggle as Severin moved to one knee. The brightest flash of light consumed the doorway, followed by echoed shouts sounding from downstairs. I did my best to look up without collapsing to the carpet.

There you are, Jules.

What the fuck?

A split-second later, a blur of a figure burst into the room and plowed into Severin, knocking him prone against the blood-dotted carpet.

"You—"

Like a knight clad in black street clothes, Saint held his arm against Severin's throat. "I'm going to finally fucking kill you, Aaron."

Severin did his best to chuckle, but it sounded more like a wheeze. "Jealousy doesn't look good on you. This one's just—"

"My *boyfriend*, you piece of shit."

I swayed, catching the surprise in Severin's eyes as a new message clawed into my brain: *I'll be there in a moment. Stay awake, please.*

"Hey, asshole," I said, the words slurred. "You were right about my vampire not planning on turning me. She's my mom."

The confusion took over his face right before Saint punched him. I didn't care. It felt good to see that, despite my head being pretty fuzzy and overall not being able to fully comprehend what was happening. Someone grabbed me by the arm and lifted me up, cutting me free of the zip-tie before I collapsed into them.

"Saint—" Their arm swung, and I held tight to Charlie as they pulled me from the room and onto the outer rim of the catwalk. A few more screams sounded in the chaos erupting all around us, but I could only focus on Charlie as they ran their hand along where my bite—well, *bites* were.

I could've sworn I heard the *whoosh* of a sudden fire and smelled something burning as they cupped my face.

"How much did he take?"

I might as well have been drunk when I held up a series of fingers, as if that'd indicate something substantial. Or maybe I was attempting to tell them how many minutes Severin had been sucking me dry. Honestly, I couldn't tell you.

Nothing really registered until Charlie jolted. A hard *thump* vibrated the grate of the catwalk, which I first believed was just my body doing a fun new thing from blood loss. Their head whipped toward the direction of the office door, where Saint had Severin pinned against the railing. Severin's hand had paled with his tight grip on Saint's wrist as he tried to push a wooden stake closer to his heart.

My initial question of where the hell Saint managed to get that was answered with a glimpse of the inside of Charlie's jacket, right where theirs should've been. I think if I'd been fully functional at that point, I either would've been proud that Charlie viewed Saint as trustworthy enough to hand over their stake to him or absolutely horrified that they'd just given him one of the few weapons that could kill him if Severin decided enough was enough.

I decided on the latter when Severin slammed Saint against that office window, the dull *thud* of the glass shaking me to my core. If all the blood hadn't already been drained from my face, it would've with the way Severin knocked the stake from Saint's grasp. Charlie scrambled to grab it, but it bounced and rolled through the horizontal gaps in the railing.

"*Shit—*" they hissed as they reached for it just as the stake plummeted to the concrete below.

Seeing Severin move in a flash, black eyes streaking through the dim building, enough adrenaline pushed through my veins to get me to my feet. The world swayed as Saint punched Severin in the jaw, and I thought I was falling over before I realized that Severin had grabbed a chunk of Saint's jacket to try to save himself from falling backward.

Backward down the *stairs*.

I gasped as Saint pitched forward, the two of them heading straight down to the scene of utter chaos I hadn't gotten the best look at before. Mom one-punched a vampire goon, knocking them out cold, and turned to bare her teeth at a familiar. Dad swung around a *fucking flamethrower*—I guess that explained the burning smell—to keep a few more vampires back, surprisingly not chasing them down with it to roast them like campfire marshmallows.

Zane hurled another Severin supporter across the warehouse, their body rolling along the floor like he was playing a round of bowling, though his back was to one of the rooms below. Iris darted out from behind the door Zane was guarding, paper take-out bag at her side, and skidded to a stop, her eyes wide as she took in Saint and Severin heaped in the center of the room before they started trying to kill each other again.

Grabbing onto the railing, I hurried past Charlie, who started to pull themself up. "Jules—"

My brain barely comprehended their call for me to stop as I fumbled the first step. Arms screaming, I held onto the railing for dear life as I found my footing again and tried to take them as quickly as possible. My heart raced as Severin wrapped his hands around Saint's neck.

Charlie's footfalls on the grated steps sounded behind me, and I picked up speed, letting that rush carry me to the bottom. I didn't think. I threw my body against Severin as hard as I could, falling over Saint as I tackled him to the floor.

When I quickly started pushing myself up to get away, I locked eyes with Severin. I couldn't see his pupils when the whole of his eye matched that pure black, but it was clear that he realized I wasn't Saint the second his mouth unhinged like a wild animal.

Yep. He was still fucking dead set on finishing the job. I loosed a gasp as something yanked me back by my shirt collar.

"Oh, no you fucking don't, you bastard." Saint.

I stumbled behind Saint just in time to witness Severin's leg get stomped as he was getting up. A sickening *crack*, and my stomach lurched. This time, silence didn't follow like Rory. Instead, a screaming howl tore from Severin's throat. The entire warehouse seemed to stutter to a stop, aside from the scrape of shoes against concrete as I glanced behind us, near the stairs.

"Saint," Charlie called, tossing the stake in the split-second he glanced over to them too.

Severin, panting as that inky blackness of his eyes darted around, somehow had the fucking audacity to say, "Don't do this, pet."

Just calling him *pet*, of all things, made me wish I could lunge forward and choke him if it weren't for the fact I'd immediately fall on my face. Fortunately, Charlie grabbed my arm, helping me to stay upright.

It happened so fast, I barely even registered Saint's swing.

Watching a vampire die instead of a normal human being made me feel like I'd stepped into a fantasy world. Shock took over his features before they slipped into a mask of peace. When Severin fell back to the warehouse floor, only his clothes remained. Dust spilled from the holes in the fabric, spreading along the floor like ash. Saint held the stake out to Charlie, who took it in the midst of the stunned silence that fell over the room.

Well, minus the flamethrower until the vampire that Dad had previously been fighting off decided to take several steps back. Then the *whoosh* stopped.

Saint pulled me from Charlie's grasp as Mom hurried over. She was immediately grabbing at me. "Jules, baby, are you okay?"

I don't know if I nodded or said something, but after that, things fell in and out. I remember seeing Zane and Iris putting themselves between me and Severin's brood on the way to an unmarked white van that looked like the perfect kidnapping vehicle. Aunt Syd helped me into the back with Saint, saying that I looked pale and how they needed to hurry. Then the rest piled in with something shouted as a final warning to the survivors. The ride to *wherever* was in pitch black. And my final memory was settling into Saint's arms, his cooling touch enveloping me as I slipped out of consciousness.

———

When I woke up, I was back in the vacation rental bedroom

where I'd reunited with Mom, but this time, Saint was holding my hand.

"Hey, Jules," he said quietly, brushing a lock of my hair from my forehead.

My throat clicked, relief washing over me. I was fucking alive. Severin was dead. It was over. "I can't believe he called you *pet*," I rasped. "What a dumbass."

Saint sputtered, breaking into an uncontrollable laugh.

It hurt to smile, every movement leaving a trace of ache before that jolt of panic hit me: did I actually make it? "W-wait, did you—did you have to turn me?"

Saint shook his head, his smile receding as he put his hand on my head. "No. Your mom keeps quite a bit of blood on-hand, and your aunt knew quite a bit about how to treat you. You're still very much alive and not undead. Just like you wanted."

My vision glossed over before I could tell myself to pull it together. Tears spilled out over the bridge of my nose and down to my pillow. Saint couldn't wipe them away quick enough, so he stopped trying as he climbed into bed next to me. I sobbed into his shirt, the stress of the past day finally taking its toll as the suffocating scent of the trunk, the image of Rory's lifeless eyes, and the sugary taste of vampire blood flooded my senses.

"You're safe now." Saint kissed the top of my head and ran a hand along the back of my shirt. "Let it out."

I wanted my room. My clothes. My dimmed lights. I wanted this hug to never end and the world around us to pause for an eternity, all so I could finally catch my breath.

The gentle motion of Saint running his fingers along my

spine soothed me as I surfaced from that pit of despair. I'd be lying if I said I'd eventually climb out of it, but after staying in fight-or-flight for so long, my body refused to fully relax. I was waiting for something to pop out from the closet or from under the bed to ruin the moment.

"How?" I finally asked, my voice sounding impossibly quiet to my own ears.

"Hm?"

"How did you find me?"

"I tried to find you on the laptop. I found Charlie's number instead since you weren't on there. I told them that I thought something happened to you, and they saw a car leave. I... don't really know how they got away, but I think your aunt had something to do with it. They got me at the motel and I met your dad, which was... *interesting.*"

"Fuck."

Saint's chuckle rumbled through me. "He wasn't exactly thrilled, but he was able to put things aside for the time being, thanks to Charlie and your aunt. They smuggled me in the trunk to come back here. Your mom still isn't over the escape, but she said that was a later issue, which is probably a *now* issue."

"Great." I rolled my eyes and sniffed.

"Aunt Syd had a van parked out back, so we all geared up, piled in, and drove around where we thought Aaron might be. Your mom was able to locate you when we got close, so we knew you had to be in one of two buildings. They also agreed to let me kill Aaron, along with your mom's stipulation that your dad didn't kill *every* vampire in the building. I think we all made a lot of deals. Iris got your dad's stolen documents and computer hardware back for him, your dad got to use his new vampire hunting toy from the storage unit, everyone else got a punch or two in, and I got to finally put an end to our nightmare."

I held onto him tighter and squeezed my eyes shut. "Thank you. I didn't think anyone was coming for me."

"Everyone here did everything in their power to save you, Jules," he whispered. "Your dad seems really remorseful. And your mom doesn't want to show it, but I think she regrets giving you that ultimatum. I think your aunt might've talked some sense into her after we left."

"I hope so," I choked out. "I feel guilty and fucking ungrateful."

"Don't." He moved, sliding out of bed and tugging on my arm. "Come on."

I crawled out after him, his hand taking mine once I found my footing. I still felt a little wobbly as we made our slow descent down the steps.

Despite Saint entering the living room first, all eyes snapped to me. Iris, Zane, Aunt Syd, Mom, and Dad. Mom got up from the couch, abandoning her vampire children for her birth one, and wrapped her arms around me. I held tight to Saint's hand, refusing to let go like I might lose him. Aunt Syd made a jab of her thumb behind her with a pointed look at Iris and Zane. They peeled themselves off the couch and skittered away to another room, Iris giving me a quick, hopeful wave and Zane looking back with a kicked puppy expression.

"I was so scared—"

"*Sophie*," came my aunt's annoyed tone.

"I'm sorry, Jules." That was clearly the response Aunt Syd

was looking for, judging by her frustrated sigh. She pulled away and cupped my face. "We can fix this, I promise Saint is safe. I'm not going to hurt him—"

"That wasn't the point, Soph."

I pushed Mom's hands down one by one. "Un-familiar me. Please." My voice sounded tired and raspy, mainly because I was too exhausted to rip into her at that moment.

She hesitated, and I shook my head. "Mom, if you want me in your life, I'm giving you the same stipulations as Dad: fix your issues and give me space. I know you just saved my ass, and I'm incredibly grateful—" I started to choke on the words, glad that Saint was there, giving my hand a squeeze to get through the rest of it.

"But," I said, swallowing the lump in my throat. "All I could think about was whether or not I was being a selfish brat while I was stuck in that warehouse and if I'd even been able to avoid the situation in the first place. I *couldn't*. I couldn't because so many of my major life choices were made for me. Maybe I would've ended up there at some point anyway because Severin was my boyfriend's ex, but I was kidnapped because of Dad. I was going to be turned because of Mom's bite. I was told you two agreed that I was supposed to have a normal life. One of you broke that promise, and the other is trying to force me into a life I don't want. I want to stay here. No more vampire hunting. No more family secrets. No more life-altering decisions I don't get a say in."

Mom's mouth quivered. "I just got you back—"

"I know," I said quietly. "But I need to set boundaries. I love you, but I need you both not to smother me or neglect who I am."

She hugged me again. "I love you *so much*."

The guilt resurfaced, even as she released me and took a couple of steps back. Like that sort of physical distance—a type of imaginary bubble—would solve all our problems.

"Mom."

"Yes?"

"The bite." No fucking way was she getting away with that.

She feigned embarrassment, tucking her hair behind her ear before she moved forward and tugged my shirt collar back. If she bit me, I didn't really feel it—not like Severin's fangs piercing my flesh. There was a hint of pressure, and then I felt like I could breathe again. I instinctively touched the spot when she drew back. No more bruise-like sensation.

"Thank you."

Dad shoved his hands in his pockets and stopped next to her. "I... I am sorry, Jules. I fucked up."

My brows shot up. The fact that he'd said it just like that was a shock to my system, but I was honestly glad to hear him owning up to it.

He glanced down and rubbed the back of his neck. "I haven't exactly been supportive of... certain aspects of your life." Way to hint at Saint, cool. I'll take it, I guess. "And I should've listened to what you wanted. I also... should've considered how not having your mother around might harm you. Even if I still believe that indulging in the company of vampires isn't exactly the best—"

"And I think that's enough for now," Aunt Syd said, pushing past them both. "You've been through plenty over the past few days, so we'll revisit this later. Go put on your shoes."

I hesitated, but Saint tugged on my arm, and I followed

him toward the entry as the jingle of keys trailed behind us. Saint grabbed my jacket off the hook, and I pulled it on, surprised to find my own key collection missing when I crammed my hand into the pocket. I slipped on my shoes, and Saint opened the door as Aunt Syd told everyone she'd be right back.

The crisp air of night pushed into my lungs while Aunt Syd trailed behind us to the rental car—a much more normal sight than the van. "Um," I said. "Where'd the keys go?"

Saint patted his pocket, signaling he'd retrieved his own. "I gave Lux's car keys to Charlie. They're doing a dead-drop with them before calling it a night."

"Oh," I said, trying to push the disappointment from my response. It kind of sucked that they hadn't been there when I woke up, but I guess they had enough on their plate.

We climbed into the car, where Saint and I buckled in and held hands in the backseat. I wasn't even sure where we were going until the café came into view. I almost cried again as she pulled up to the curb. When I unbuckled, I finally let go of Saint and leaned over the center console, giving her an awkward hug that she gladly reciprocated.

"Thank you, Aunt Syd."

"Of course. I love you, Jules."

Don't cry, damnit. "I love you too."

I managed to make it onto the sidewalk and wave before Saint guided me into the building, the car firmly planted on the curb until we were inside. The walk up felt so practiced by now that the pain I had was a complete afterthought—that, or whatever drugs Aunt Syd had given me were doing their job.

Saint unlocked the door, and his soft voice strung together

the most beautiful two words I'd ever heard: "Welcome home."

"Really?" I choked.

"Really."

Jolting at the sudden sound of heavy footfalls sprinting up the stairs, I whipped around. Charlie jogged toward us, breathing heavily like they'd ran the entire way here. I blinked, speechless with how many questions were cycling through my mind, but when I stole a glance at Saint, he shrugged and feigned innocence. Did he tell them we were here? Did he seriously give Charlie, a *vampire hunter*, his address?

"Sorry," they said. "Lux was really suspicious of her car, so I couldn't slip away without being caught. I had to witness her examine it for twenty minutes from my hiding spot." They dug through a plastic grocery bag and held out a slim box. "It's one of the cheaper ones, but I figure it's better than nothing for now."

I took it, hesitantly examining the packaging until I realized it was a phone. "You didn't have—"

They held up a hand. "I wanted to. I... also would like it if we shared the same family-tracker app group I set up on my own phone. Just in case. Saint, um, already has it." Their lips pressed together as they rubbed one of their arms.

I looked up from the box. Was Charlie—the stoic, cool, calm, and collected *Charlie*—seriously getting flustered because they were trying to join a little family group? I gave them a quick hug. "Thank you."

"They're free to come in for a bit to help set it up," Saint said. "I can grab some food from downstairs, and Allie might give me a bigger discount since I had to explain that I'm missing work because you were in a bit of an accident."

I loosed a breathy laugh, glancing back at them. "Want to hang out for a bit?"

They blew their hair from their face. "I'd like that."

25 NEW NORMAL

I t's been about three months since Mom's fake death anniversary and my brush with undeath. To be honest, it feels like another lifetime ago.

A week after everything happened, I finally had enough energy to go home and deal with the official move. Returning to my old room was bittersweet—the closing of one act and opening of a brand new one. I tried to sort things into boxes based on whether or not it would merge well with Saint's things—or, rather, *lack* of things. Dad nervously stood in the doorway a couple of times to ask if I needed anything, including once when all that was left was the bed, three boxes, and a nightstand.

It was also pretty weird to use the bathroom I'd discovered my bite in, especially when the guy I saw in the mirror didn't have that fear in his eyes. Instead, I looked *healthier* in a way. No dark circles or paleness, outside of the lack-of-sun bit. I was someone else. Someone who knew what he wanted and had a fresh start in front of him. Finally, something for *me*. Not someone else.

I did one last walkthrough of the house at the end of that week, looking for anything that I'd left in some random room and ending up having to catch my breath when I glanced down the upper hall. Doors had been opened wide with the scent of lemon cleaning solution overtaking whatever had been left behind. I'll admit, I ducked into Adonis's old room, and I was surprised that it didn't smell like dirty socks and wet dog. That odor must've been crammed away in the boxes Dad had begrudgingly packed before doing a storage unit drop for him.

Shame. I kind of wished I could've burned it.

The only room left untouched, other than Dad's, was Charlie's. Fairy lights ran along the ceiling, casting the muted and forest greens in a gentle light, almost like fireflies hovered above me. That's how I learned they were staying—something I hoped they weren't doing for the sake of me or Dad. But they told me later that this was *home*. They had every intention of sticking around to fight off any more vampires like Severin and the one who'd killed their friend. Plus, they wanted to stay close to their little brother.

It didn't sink in that they were talking about me until they ruffled my hair—an action I normally would've slapped away if I wasn't mega emotional from all of the shit I'd recently been through. After that, I gave both Charlie and Dad hugs, catching Dad a bit off-guard, and was on my way.

I said my goodbyes to Mom and Aunt Syd a week later when they needed to head back up to Canada. I wish that hadn't been so fucking hard, but all of that lost time felt like a knife to the heart. She told me I was free to visit any time, and

Aunt Syd eluded to finding a more permanent residence down here. Even though my parents were still struggling to have a conversation that didn't end in a shouting match, at least they were doing their best to compromise when it came to me.

Things will get better with time. At least, that's what I've been telling myself while trying to ease into a new normal. One thing that hasn't changed in all this: my nightly walk to *The Crown Café*. Though, that's a much shorter trek now.

Just like last night.

Charlie, Iris, and Zane huddled around their table in the corner of the café—their new official hang-out spot before sunrise most days. Iris tapped at her phone as I replaced the empty tray of cookies in the case, all pastel colors with white designs to look like ornaments fit for a Christmas tree.

Zane knocked back the rest of his cup, and Charlie got up with a stretch.

"Don't work too hard," Zane called, a wry smirk on his face as he crammed the lid on and aimed for the trashcan a few yards away, tossing it like a basketball player. It *swished* into the bag with a crinkle, and he fist-pumped.

I laughed. "I think we're almost done. Enjoy the walk home."

Iris quickly sprinted for the counter, reached over with her arms thrown wide for a quick hug, which I indulged with a pat on her back. "We'll see you at Christmas! I can't wait for you to open what I got you." She half-danced with the giddy energy of a small child.

"Looking forward to it," I said, pasting on a smile for her sake. I was honestly over the whole holiday season by now since it'd started the day after Halloween, but I wasn't about to take that away from her. It was probably because I'd made enough peppermint drinks to last a lifetime. That, and listening to the same fifteen songs on repeat for the past fifty-ish days was starting to drive me mad.

Charlie waved a hand as they half-corralled Zane toward the door. "Tell Saint we said bye! See you for Christmas!"

I grinned, waving back. "Will do!"

The door chimed as they all hurried outside, passing by the large window with *The Crown Café* vinyl logo reversed on my side. It was weird to think that the three of them hadn't really interacted a couple of months ago, and now they were almost always attached to each other. Now they ended their nights with a drink from the café after doing who-knows-what on behalf of one or both of my parents.

Honestly, it was nice just to enjoy the company of my friends at the end of my shift without the mess of vampire hunting or whatever other dangerous things they fought. Maybe a combination of all sorts of crazies running wild at night? Wasn't my problem. And I was very much okay with that.

I rocked back on my heels and stretched, eyeing the register monitor's clock as it counted down the minutes until I could sign off. Large paper snowflakes twirled from strings connected to plastic hooks on the ceiling—a job Allie insisted I help her with, despite Saint's offering that he take my place for fear of me breaking my neck.

Behind you.

I felt a hand graze my back as Saint slid past me to one of the other machines, where he replaced the missing carafe.

"Did you finish restocking the pastries?" he asked, wiping his hands on his apron.

I nodded. "All organized and ready for the morning crowd in about an hour. Imagine getting up at five." I gagged.

Saint chortled and gave me a quick kiss on the cheek. My heart fluttered, leaving me with an undoubtedly goofy smile until the holiday music flooded the speakers.

God damnit. I love Allie, but I'm going to kill her. I bit down on my tongue as Saint's laugh cut through the noise on his way to the sink.

Wipe down the counter. I'll get the tables, and we can get out of here.

I wasn't going to argue with a possible escape. Allie emerged from the back office with a cheery smile as I jogged over to the sink.

"Happy holidays!"

"Happy holidays," I said in unison with Saint, his joy masking my pain. I've been telling myself that this year will be different, but I honestly feared my parents trying to gain custody of certain holidays with me or just—well—*fighting*.

We were a whole two days out from Christmas, and they were still bickering in a text thread about the schedule. Part of me wanted nothing more than to shut off my phone and stay at home with Saint before our break was over and we'd be back to dealing with some more weird late-night customers passing through during holiday travel days.

Allie shook a tin of goodies and popped it open in offering as Saint started into the dining area and I dropped my soapy rag on the counter. "Caramel?"

I swallowed down the urge to vomit and waved a hand. "No thanks." I could barely look at it, let alone *think* of tasting it. "I had way too many caramel-based shots before Halloween."

She clicked her tongue. "Ugh, I ran into the same problem with jelly shots a few years ago. I couldn't eat gelatin for *months*. Saint—you want one?"

"I'm good. Thanks anyway, Al."

"*Fine*." Allie snapped the tin closed and set it down. "I wanted to remind you two that I'll be off starting tomorrow, which means we won't see each other for a week." She fished two small envelopes out of her pocket, both about the size of credit cards, and offered one to me. "Happy holidays, Jules."

I took it and flipped it over while she strode over to Saint, finding my name jotted onto the front in cute, rounded letters with a little snowflake next to it. The brain gremlins took over, telling me to push my thumb under the flap and tear it open, so I did. Inside, a little blue card peeked from the top, and I tugged it free to find a thank you note, complete with a gift card inside.

A small holiday bonus.

Sure, it wasn't much, but it was the thought that caught me by surprise. Her scrawled message about being glad I applied so she could work with a new friend really plucked at every heart string. I quickly folded it all back into the envelope when she turned around.

"Thank you, Allie."

She beamed. "Thank *you* for being such a great person to work with. This is the smoothest night shift team I've ever dealt with, so you deserve it. Both of you do. I hope you guys have a wonderful holiday break."

God, that recognition smacked me harder than ever. With Saint's echoed thanks, I tried to brush it all off as I tucked the card into my pants pocket.

We chatted a bit more as Saint and I finished wiping down

the counters, then the three of us welcomed in the next shift as we shedded our aprons for our coats in the break room. Allie waved us goodbye as we stepped outside, leaving Saint and I to walk the short distance to the stairs.

I'll never get tired of the door opening to our place. The soft glow of my LEDs tucked into makeshift crown moulding welcomed us inside. Video game posters and blackout curtains covered the once-bare walls and drab windows. All of it framed the TV, couch, and coffee table, the latter a new home to Charlie's gift of a couple of succulents that were managing to thrive between me moving them in and out of the window before Saint and I would call it a night.

Rest in peace to smiley face plant. He will be missed.

I hung up my coat in the entry, kicked off my shoes, and made a beeline for the kitchen to gather a blood bag and heat up some leftover honey chicken and rice from the Chinese place down the street.

The hum of the microwave faded to the background as Saint finished his juice box. "How are you feeling?"

I turned my head, catching him pop open the trash can and drop the bag into the bin. "About Christmas? Like it's going to be a disaster."

He shook his head. "About the familiar bite."

"Oh." My hand immediately went to that spot on my neck that'd both looked and felt horribly bruised months ago. "You know. I honestly keep forgetting about it."

"It doesn't feel weird?" he asked, leaning forward against the kitchen peninsula, his head tilted. "Me being in your head isn't *strange*?"

I moved to lean against the counter, staring him in the eyes. "No," I said, a smirk slipping onto my face. "It feels nice to have you there. Plus, you're way better at this than my last vampire." I mean, seriously, it hadn't even felt tender the day he did it, which was a pleasant surprise.

He chuckled and kissed me on the cheek. "Jules, if you ever don't want it—"

"I know. I know I can ask." I took his hand and squeezed it. "But I think I like being a familiar when I'm yours."

The microwave beeped, and I jumped up to grab my dinner. By the time I collected my bowl, Saint was already popping on the TV and booting up my game console, that peppy startup tune flowing through the room. I dropped down on the couch as he collected two controllers and put one next to me for later.

I scooted closer to him, the steaming food warming my face while Saint's little character roamed around the screen, picking weeds in his flower garden. Our familiar routine that I wouldn't trade for the world.

ACKNOWLEDGMENTS

I originally contemplated querying this book to some agents but decided against it. While I was writing this story, I realized that I would rather send this book out into the world on my own terms. I'm a mess. Jules is a mess. This entire book is a mess. But it's a mess in the best way. I'm not sure a publisher would appreciate that, and they'd probably ask me to tone it down for a younger audience. However, I wrote this in my thirties while still struggling with the underlying parental acceptance issues that Saint had.

So I guess I should take a moment to thank myself since I rarely do. Thank you, Cara, for making it this far in life. You almost gave up a few times, but you didn't. I'm proud of you for that. And I'm excited to see what you will become in the future. You are your own person. Never forget that.

As for the people that helped me along the way, I have to start with Freddie. Thank you for being my (and this book's) biggest supporter over the past several months. I've been so happy to find someone who matches my brand of weird and fascinating with blends of cyberpunk and fantasy. You helped keep this book going, and I'm thrilled to see what we both continue to come up with in the coming years.

A big thank you to my beta readers, Taff and Elpida. Your feedback was invaluable, and I can't express how grateful I am to get such positive notes and thoughts to help me smooth out the story.

Thank you to everyone who helped in promoting this book alongside me, whether through assisting with the cover reveal or otherwise. It means so much to have found your support.

Finally, I haven't forgotten about you, the reader of this book. Your support means the world to me as someone who used to dream about others reading and enjoying my work. I hope to thank you again in the future with whatever piece I publish next.

MORE BY CARA NOX

For an up-to-date list of all of Cara Nox's books visit their website:

caranox.com/books

ABOUT THE AUTHOR

Cara Nox is an urban and science fantasy writer, combining their love of magically-inclined chaotic idiots and modern/futuristic tech. They also love mysteries, thrillers, and anything that draws inspiration from stars. Cara works as a web developer by day, holds BA in Japanese Language and Literature they occasionally use to read video game announcements, and resides in Ohio with their younger sister and two black cats.

For more information on all of their books, visit **caranox.com**.

To find some of their newest works-in-progress, bonus content, serialized stories, where they're at on social media, how to get deals on their current and upcoming works, and where to preview the first few chapters of their other books, visit **caranox.com/links**.